Praise for

"I am in such ——————————————— r-
prises. I kept —————————————————— 's
writing gift s ——————————————————— t-
rending, and joyful story of love."

—Laurie Alice Eakes,
author of *Choices of the Heart*

"Fresh and heartfelt, this is a novel to savor. Peopled with memorable characters and ordinary circumstances turned extraordinary, *A Home for My Heart* is an enduring story filled to the brim with history, romance, and spiritual truths. Highly recommended!"

—Laura Frantz,
author of *The Colonel's Lady* and
Love's Reckoning

"With the warmth and wonder of hearth and home, Anne Mateer weaves a rich historical tale of abiding love, family, and faith in difficult times. Reminiscent of the graceful style of LaVyrle Spencer, *A Home for My Heart* will find a home in yours long after the last page."

—Julie Lessman,
award-winning author of the
DAUGHTERS OF BOSTON and the
WINDS OF CHANGE series

"An engaging love story full of tender twists and turns that keep you reading, with characters who swiftly become friends."

—Tamera Alexander,
USA Today bestselling author of
A Lasting Impression and
To Whisper Her Name

A HOME *for* MY HEART

Books by Anne Mateer

Wings of a Dream
At Every Turn
A Home for My Heart

A HOME for MY HEART

Anne Mateer

BETHANYHOUSE
a division of Baker Publishing Group
Minneapolis, Minnesota

© 2013 by D'Ann Mateer

Published by Bethany House Publishers
11400 Hampshire Avenue South
Bloomington, Minnesota 55438
www.bethanyhouse.com

Bethany House Publishers is a division of
Baker Publishing Group, Grand Rapids, Michigan

Printed in the United States of America

Library of Congress Cataloging-in-Publication Data
Mateer, Anne.
    A home for my heart / Anne Mateer.
        pages cm
    Summary: "It is the early 1900s when an unexpected opportunity arises at the orphanage where Sadie works; will she have to choose between marrying her beau and a job she loves?"—Provided by publisher.
    ISBN 978-0-7642-1064-8 (pbk.)
    1. Single women—Fiction. 2. Orphanages—Fiction. I. Title.
PS3613.A824H66 2013
813'.6—dc23   2013016856

Scripture quotations are from the King James Version of the Bible.

This is a work of fiction. Names, characters, incidents, and dialogues are products of the author's imagination and are not to be construed as real. Any resemblance to actual events or persons, living or dead, is entirely coincidental.

Cover design by Dan Thornberg, Design Source Creative Services

13 14 15 16 17 18 19   7 6 5 4 3 2 1

To Elizabeth, Aaron, and Nathan

My greatest joy is watching you walk in the truth.
(3 John 1:4 paraphrase)

Chapter 1

I barreled through the large kitchen of the orphanage, skirts billowing out from my ankles. "Where's Cynthia?" I called. "We have to go over her recitation again."

Mrs. Fore's gray head turned toward me, but she never quit stirring whatever bubbled in the pot on top of the steel Wehrle range. The pungent aroma of onions and garlic mingling with the smell of meat stopped me.

"Stew?" I moved in for a closer whiff.

A giggle caught my attention. I swooped eight-year-old Cynthia into my arms. "Got you! Now it's time to say your poem."

Her head shook, but her eyes laughed. I smacked a kiss on her cheek and set her on the floor. "After supper. No excuses." I tapped her freckled nose with my finger.

She turned to help the other girls gather tin plates, cups, and utensils to set on the dining table. Overhead, footsteps thumped. Other children's voices drifted from various parts of the large house.

The yeasty smell of two fresh-baked loaves of bread resting on the counter curled beneath my nose and caused my stomach to rumble. I pressed a hand to my middle. Hunger pangs still brought memories to the surface. I glanced out the window, past my pot of drooping daffodils, looking for a distraction. Brown grass covered the backyard, and gray clouds skittered across the late-afternoon sky, obscuring any light from the sun. I shivered, then rubbed my hands up and down my arms.

From the corner of my eye, I spied a horse dancing to a stop at the corner of the house. My heart skipped a beat as I smoothed my skirt and licked moisture into my lips. I glanced back at Mrs. Fore. Her wrinkles rearranged themselves into a smile.

I flung open the door. Frigid air sent the little girls shrieking and huddling together. Then Blaine Wellsmith filled the doorway, a red knitted scarf half obscuring his face, a wooden crate perched on his arms. He strode inside, kicking the door shut with his heel.

He placed the box on the kitchen worktable before unwinding the scarf. His grin flashed in my direction, warming me through in spite of the sudden chill. A sprinkle of dirt littered Mrs. Fore's pristine floor when he removed his gloves.

"Cold out there." He peeled off his coat and draped it on the back of a chair before straddling the seat. "I'm ready for spring, but looks like we'll have more snow by morning."

Mrs. Fore set a cup of hot coffee on the table. Blaine cradled the warmth between his hands.

"The children will be happy about that, I imagine." I joined him at the table, my eyes feasting on his strong features. Dark hair combed back from a high forehead. Dark brows hovering low over eyes black as midnight. Not a lean face, but not one with extra flesh, either. And though some might not deem him handsome in the usual sense, I'd recognized the beauty inside him when we were but children.

"The kids haven't mangled the sleds I made for them, have they?" He sipped the steaming blackness.

I shook my head, making note to have the boys locate the sleds before morning.

Mrs. Fore shooed giggling girls into the dining room and wiped her hands on her apron. Then she pulled the crate closer to her and sorted the produce—food Blaine had generously donated from his cellar to the Raystown Home for Orphan and Friendless Children, in spite of his need to sell the extra in order to save enough money to buy farmland of his own.

Our own.

"Sadie's got her posies in a bad way, Blaine." Mrs. Fore set the empty crate beside the back door. "You'll have to see to them if they'll be fit to go in the ground come summer."

One of his eyebrows rose in my direction. "Have you been neglecting your flowers?"

I flinched. Blaine had coaxed the daffodils to life in the middle of winter. He'd stood stiff and uncomfortable in his only suit, his large hands cradling the oblong clay pot as gingerly as if it were made of crystal when he arrived on Christmas Day. *"A bit of color,"* he said, *"to cheer you until spring."* I rewarded him with the press of my lips to his wind-chapped cheek—and a red knitted scarf. The devotion that had shone from his eyes in that moment made the flowers more precious than if they'd been fashioned of real gold.

But just days into March in the new year of 1910, the buttery yellow flowers had paled to the color of chicken stock.

The leaves had curled. The petals sagged. I couldn't seem to make them thrive the way Blaine did. My gaze grabbed the table as my fingers skimmed across the smooth wooden surface. I bit my lip. They were only flowers, yet they'd been his gift to me. It was my job to keep them alive.

Blaine crossed the room and lifted the pot from the windowsill. "I can take them home with me and . . ."

I hopped up as quick as if I'd sat on a pin. "No, I'll take care of them." I snatched the container from him and mashed one finger into the soil. It seemed soft enough. The flowers just missed the sun.

Bustling toward the parlor, I listened for Blaine's heavy steps to follow through the short hall. They did, along with his chuckle. My lips pressed into a firm line. I would find a way to make these flowers grow. I would.

I set the plant in a side window, praying for a break in the clouds. Any sunlight would be better than the solid mass of gray. I primped the sagging leaves to no avail.

Blaine stood close behind me. "Let it alone, Sadie. Light and water, that's all they need. Simple things."

I relaxed, then turned to him with a genuine smile on my face. "Like the children. A little love and a little discipline. The simple things."

"And don't forget food to fill their bellies."

"Thanks to you." I let my fingers brush his.

"I'd bring more if I could. When I own a farm instead of working someone else's land, I will." He winked.

Heat radiated from my cheeks. Would my daffodils think they had found the sun? I ducked my head, seeking a less intimate subject. "Any word from Carter lately?"

Blaine's broad chest heaved with a sigh. "No. I wish those 'simple things' worked with my little brother."

Shyness fled as I covered Blaine's hand with mine and peered into his worried eyes. "I wouldn't be too concerned. He's still a boy."

He shook his head. "Sixteen is nearer a man than a boy. I wish I knew what he was thinking sometimes."

"Remember, you had a much longer time with your mother than he did."

"I know. But when I think of that man—" His fingers curled into fists.

Many years ago, Blaine had taken Carter and run from his stepfather, Carter's father. After wandering about on their own, they'd arrived at the doorstep of the Raystown Home, cold and hungry. Carter a little tyke of three; Blaine a gangly boy of eleven. Both had stolen my ten-year-old heart.

I stroked his hand flat again. "Let's not think of that man now."

Blaine's tension eased. He slipped his fingers between mine. "Sounds good to me. I only want to think about us."

My face blazed again, and a fist seemed to close around my heart, squeezing all the breath from my body. I wasn't sure when our friendship had turned into love, but it had. No one knew my heart like Blaine did.

He brought my hand to his lips. "Walk me out?"

The tightness in my chest released. "Of course."

My hand clasped in his, we returned to the kitchen and bundled up against the Pennsylvania winter. Outside, the cold stole our voices until we rounded the corner of the house, out of the stabbing ferocity of the wind.

He pulled me close. I buried my nose in his wool coat, drinking in the smell of woodsmoke and pine. One glove-clad finger lifted my chin. "You'd better get back inside before you freeze."

I nodded, teeth clamped to keep them from chattering. His arms still circled their warmth around me. I couldn't make myself pull away.

"Don't fret over your flowers. I'll plant you rows and rows of them when we have our own—" His gaze traveled to my lips. I swallowed hard, my hands stealing around his neck as his face lowered toward mine. Just as I could taste his breath, the creak of the back door cut through the frigid bluster.

"Sadie? There's someone here to see you." Mrs. Fore let the back door bang shut again.

I pressed my forehead into Blaine's chest and groaned. I couldn't wait for the day when we'd enjoy kisses uninterrupted.

A pale-haired woman pulled a woolen shawl closer around her hunched shoulders as she stood in the foyer. Her tongue wet her lips as her eyes darted from the door to the staircase to my face, faster than a hummingbird in a flower garden.

"I'm Miss Sillsby," I said. "The matron's assistant. How may I help you?"

Before she could speak, a waif of a girl appeared from behind her skirts. I noted her threadbare clothing before my gaze fell on the little face. Perfect—except for eyes that focused on her nose instead of straight in front of her.

My mouth filled with the remembered taste of cod liver oil, and my hand covered my curdling stomach. No tonic would cure this girl's ill. Nor would sunshine and good food. An awkward silence filled the space between us.

The woman huffed and set a fist on her hip. "I'm told you take in kids what we can't feed."

My hand fell away from my stomach as her words dissolved the old memories. Another mother in search of help for her child. I glanced at the closed office door and chewed my bottom lip. My job didn't include admitting children. That responsibility fell to Hazel Brighton, matron of the Raystown Home. But she'd gone to deliver a child to a foster home and wouldn't arrive back until late that evening.

"I'm so sorry, but our matron, Miss Brighton, is not available today. If you could return in the morning, I—"

"I'm here now. I can't come back later. Can you take her or not?"

I studied the mother's face, trying to discern her character, her motives. She seemed much older than my twenty-three years, yet something about the pull of skin around her eyes made me question that first impression. Maybe her life hadn't been longer, only harder. My heart pinched. I remembered other eyes older than their years, eyes that had peered darkly into mine, then turned away and let me go.

With a deep breath, I straightened to my full height and tried my best to mimic Hazel's quiet authority. "We do consider cases where there is great need, but as I said, I am not the one—"

The woman's scrutiny raked up and down the length of me, as if I were a beggar and she the queen. "I was told this was a place of Christian charity," she spat. "I guess they told me wrong." She snatched her little girl's hand and turned toward the door.

"Wait!"

The woman stiffened and stopped.

My gaze snuck down to the child. She looked as cold as winter snow, with her almost-translucent skin and puffs of nearly white hair standing out over her ears and forehead. I cupped her jaw in my palm as she stared up at me, unblinking. What did she see out of eyes that wandered toward each other instead of in my direction? My arms itched to pull the girl close, whisper assurances in her ear. I knew from experience she could find healing in this place, for both body and soul.

One small doubt niggled. Hazel had expressed concern over money in recent months. But this child needed us. I knew it deep inside. Hazel had placed out one child today. This little girl could take his spot at our table. And there were plenty of beds available in the girls' room.

Hazel wouldn't want me to turn her away.

"Please, Mrs.—?"

"Ashworth." She hitched her shawl higher over one shoulder.

"Mrs. Ashworth. I think we can work something out." I motioned them into the office and switched on the electric wall sconces. Mrs. Ashworth squinted into the bright room as the light illuminated the dinginess of her shawl, her dress. How long since they'd seen a washtub?

She sat, but her little girl remained standing, no touch passing between them. The woman's focus zigzagged, never settling on anything.

In Hazel's seat behind the desk, I folded my hands, remembering words I'd heard Hazel say so many times, praying I was doing right. "We do consider cases where parents need a bit of time to find work and catch up on their bills in order to provide for their children. When we consider these cases of short-term care, we generally ask for a pledge of support to the Home to help cover the cost of caring for the child."

Mrs. Ashworth's face hardened. One fringed end of her shawl fluttered to the floor. "If I had money to care for her, I wouldn't be here, would I?"

The sullenness of her tone grated on me. I sucked in a breath and bit my tongue until I could make my voice a perfect imitation of Hazel's—all kindness and compassion. "I understand. But we've found that often there is a family member or a friend who can step in and give a small amount to help with the child's keep. We're not asking for the full cost of caring for her. Just a bit to help offset expenses. I'm sure you realize that we exist solely on freewill donations."

Mrs. Ashworth snorted and grabbed up the end of her shawl that trailed on the floor. "If I had anyone else to appeal to, be assured I'd have gone there first."

"As I said, it is not a requirement, but we always ask."

Mrs. Ashworth hesitated, then leaned forward, a work-worn hand clutching the edge of the desk. "You'll take my Lily Beth, then?"

I pulled a large ledger book from the top of the cabinet between the front windows and opened it to a blank page. "After you answer a few questions, I believe we can take your daughter into a temporary situation with us."

I'd make sure we helped this girl, this Lily Beth.

In spite of her mother.

Or perhaps because of her.

Chapter 2

As soon as I'd handed Lily Beth into Mrs. Fore's care and closed the front door behind Mrs. Ashworth, I wrote *questionable* in the space reserved for comments on the mother's habits. After a moment's consideration, I added *(quite)* before shutting the volume. The space designated to record the name of the father read *not known*. If Mrs. Ashworth returned for her child after the stipulated three-month period, I'd repent of my uncharitable thoughts about her. But I doubted that would happen. I'd seen her type before. They seldom returned.

As I transcribed the details of the arrangement into our admittance registry book, my mind raced with other possibilities. Like getting Lily Beth's eyes fixed. Feeding her a good meal. Introducing her to Jesus. Finding her a stable home. I knew she needed those things, for I'd needed them at her age, as well.

Shoving aside memories best kept packed away, I joined the others already in the dining room. Eleven boys squirmed with life while conversation teemed among the half-dozen girls.

Mrs. Fore looked frazzled. I patted her shoulder and sent her back to the kitchen with my whispered thanks.

Then I noticed Miranda Jennings, the housemaid, in my usual seat. She leaned across the table to help Timmy wipe a dribble of broth from his chin. She saw me watching. Her body tensed. She pulled back from Timmy and lumbered to her feet as her expression turned hard and cold.

"Thank you, Miranda." I sat as she lifted her bowl and plate from in front of me. I expected her to leave. But she didn't.

She alighted on the empty seat at the head of the table. The one reserved for the matron. For Hazel.

I could have taken that place, but I hadn't. I didn't dare presume, even in Hazel's absence. And yet Miranda did. Miranda, the middle-aged woman who scrubbed our floors, our clothing, our windows.

Mrs. Fore set a bowl of stew in front of me, but my eyes remained on Miranda, steam gathering in my chest until I feared it would burst into the room. Her steely gaze pivoted to mine. My eyebrows rose. She looked away. I couldn't chastise her in front of the children. In fact, it wasn't my place to confront her at all, even if I wanted to.

I needed a distraction.

Beside me, Lily Beth's spoon clattered against the side of her bowl. I rested my arm around the back of her chair, my ire subsiding. This child needed my attention now. I hoped my presence would soothe the pain I knew she felt, in spite of her outward lack of emotion. Her mother hadn't even told her good-bye.

Stew languished in her bowl, but I noticed crumbs littering

her plate. I reached for a slice of bread and spread it with a generous amount of butter. Her mouth gaped when I set it before her. Then it disappeared down her slim throat in almost one bite. I smiled and fixed her another as she slurped at her stew. Content, I turned my attention to the other children.

"Are you ready to recite for me, Cynthia?"

The girl's corkscrew curls shook with a fury as tears welled in her hazel eyes.

Janet stuck her arm in the air and waved her hand as if she were still in the classroom. "And me. I need help with my math homework."

My stomach flopped. I'd much rather try to coax stubborn words out of Cynthia's mouth than try to make sense of arithmetic.

Spoons clanging against the bottoms of empty bowls signaled the end of mealtime. I dismissed the children from the table, and Miranda began clearing dishes, her demeanor returned to its usual dreariness.

Lily Beth tugged at my sleeve.

"Yes, love bug?"

Her left eye seemed to find mine, but her right eye wandered off somewhere else. My heart squeezed.

"Do I have to go home now?"

I hugged her to my side. "No, sweetheart. You're going to stay here for a while. A little later, we'll tuck you under warm quilts in a bedroom upstairs with the other girls. You'll like that, won't you?"

She hesitated only a moment before she nodded, her white hair dancing around her delicate face. A perfect face marred only by eyes that refused to sit straight.

After our evening prayers, the children—including Lily Beth—quieted without protest. I breathed the usual relief of another day finished. And a good day, at that. Joseph placed with a family in Centre County, and Lily Beth enveloped in our safe and loving environment. Exactly the kinds of things we existed to do.

I stopped in my bedroom to pick up a book. A downstairs door closed with a solid thud. Had Miranda left—or had Hazel returned? Best to check, and to lock up if Miranda had gone for the day. I hurried downstairs, keeping to my toes in hopes of not waking those who already slumbered.

In the foyer, Hazel unwound a snow-crusted wool scarf from her head and hung it on the hall tree. Wisps of brown hair frizzed out about her head as she pulled gloves from slim fingers before shrugging out of her overcoat. "It's starting to snow."

"Did you get Joseph situated?"

"What?" Hazel seemed as startled as if I'd asked after the health of Mr. Granville's dead cat. "Oh, Joseph. Yes, he's fine." Her cold fingers curled around my hand, and her eyes shone with excitement. "But, oh, Sadie. I have so much more to tell you."

She pulled me into the parlor, to the worn velvet sofa opposite the coal stove. I'd never seen calm, unflustered Hazel quite so . . . alive. Her right hand held my left one. Then she laid her left hand atop mine. A milky white pearl winked bright in the dim light. My head jerked up. Our eyes met and held.

"Professor Stapleton?" Her long-time beau had driven her

and Joseph over the mountain in his new automobile, but I hadn't thought it anything unusual. I pressed my hand to my chest as tears sprang into my eyes. Years of proposals, of refusals. "And you finally said yes."

Hazel nodded, her face as bright as the first star on a moonless night.

I shrieked in delight, then covered my mouth as we both dissolved into girlish giggles. Laughing. Crying. Hugging. Finally, we calmed. I turned serious and studied her face. "You're sure this time?"

Hazel twisted the new ring on her finger. "Ten years ago, God called me to be a missionary to needy children. I've gladly done as He asked. Now I believe He's asked me to take a different path. To become administrator of a different home. My own." A blush stole across her heart-shaped face.

"I'm so happy for you." And I was, though my throat felt strangely tight. Hazel deserved a husband. Children. She'd been preparing to serve on the mission field in South America when one of her professors at the Brethren college in town approached her. Would she consider being a home missionary? A missionary to children? To orphaned and friendless children? She'd answered yes all those years ago, forgone the pleasure of a life of her own for a decade. She deserved this happiness now. As did faithful Professor Stapleton.

"When?" I managed to squeak out the question that both fascinated and terrified me.

"The end of April, though we won't take our wedding trip until after the college term is over for the summer." Hazel blew out a long breath as she rested her head on the back of the sofa. Then it popped back up again. "You'll be my bridesmaid, won't you? There's no one else I'd want to stand up with me."

"Oh, Hazel!" I hugged her again. "Of course I will!"

But even as I spoke, my mind whirled. The calendar had turned to March. The end of April would come quickly. A few short weeks for Hazel to plan a wedding and a life outside the orphanage. A few short weeks for the rest of us to transition to a new matron.

My stomach churned faster than Henry's eight-year-old legs running downhill. I swallowed down the rising fear. "Do you have any idea . . . who . . . ?"

Hazel's eyes danced in time to the chuckle deep in her throat. She clutched both of my hands and leaned in close to my face. "That's my other news, dear Sadie. I want *you* to be the new matron."

Breath seemed to disappear from my body. I didn't know where to find it again.

"You're pleased, aren't you?"

I wasn't sure my heart was still beating.

"I told John I couldn't put his ring on my finger until I had things resolved here, so we stopped at Mr. Riley's on our way back into town and told him the news. He telephoned all the board members. Once they agreed to extend you the offer, I knew what your answer would be, so I took the ring!"

Mr. Riley. The president of the Raystown Home's board of trustees and a longtime friend of my foster family, the Ramseys.

Hazel's exuberance gave way to her usual seriousness. "I couldn't think of anyone I'd trust more than you."

I pulled in a long breath, trying to calm the squirm in my

middle as the past tore through my mind. A child drawn out of dire circumstances, like Moses from the basket in the river. Mama Ramsey had always told me it meant my life had purpose. Great purpose. Until this moment, I'd never actually believed that.

Few knew the dark words hidden in the 1892 admittance ledger, though some still remembered that I'd resided at the Home until the Ramseys took me into their family six years later, after my body had grown strong and well. Since then, I'd worked hard to erase the shame that followed me like a shadow. Would achieving the position of matron eradicate it forever?

Yes, yes, yes, said the silent scream in my head. I wanted this. Needed this. Was made for this. My heart swelled with unexpected joy, though ecstasy and fear danced cheek-to-cheek.

"Oh, Hazel. I'm honored. I'm . . . thrilled beyond belief. Of course I will step into your place as matron."

Hazel leaned forward and kissed my cheek. "I knew I could count on you, Sadie."

Then the yellow daffodils winked against the dark window. I drew a quick breath. The board of trustees would not employ a married woman.

"When I own my own land," Blaine had said the year he'd turned sixteen. *"Then I will ask you to be my wife."*

Since then he'd worked other men's farms, scrimping and saving toward purchasing his own. And still we waited. Would this be my way to contribute?

As matron, Hazel's salary was substantially higher than mine. I'd get a raise on top of the continued opportunity to work in and for the place I loved. I could help Blaine save toward our land. By the time we amassed the amount needed, I felt sure I'd have accomplished enough to follow Hazel's example and set up a home of my own.

A perfect situation. The answer to so many years of prayers.

Hazel yawned, covering her wide mouth with her palm. "I'll call Mr. Riley in the morning and let him know you've agreed. We have so much to do, starting tomorrow. Morning will come far too early—for both of us."

I nodded. But I wouldn't be sleeping tonight. How could I, when the unspoken dreams of my heart had suddenly come true?

Chapter 3

I waved to the children through the front office window as they made tracks through the new dusting of snow the next morning. Ten-year-old Janet held Lily Beth's tiny hand, promising to deliver the little girl to the right classroom. Contentment pushed out a sigh.

I turned from my view of the empty street and surveyed our office. An enormous old desk placed toward the back wall, two straight-backed chairs angled in front of it. A small round table off to one side. A tall cabinet between the two windows that looked out over the street, and a fireplace now fitted with a coal heater along the opposite wall.

Cozy yet professional, a room that would soon become my primary domain.

"I met our new girl this morning." Something about the tightness around Hazel's lips worried me.

I gripped the back of one of the chairs. "Lily Beth."

Hazel rubbed a finger above her eyebrow. "I guess with all the excitement last night, you forgot to tell me."

I cringed. "Sorry. I know I overstepped my bounds, but you weren't here and her mother—" I shook my head.

With a half smile on her lips, Hazel flipped open the admit-tance ledger and read over my notes on Lily Beth Ashworth. "I can't exactly scold you, seeing as how you'll be doing this kind of thing on your own very soon. But I had hoped to gain a little ground after placing Joseph out."

"Gain ground?"

"You know we exist on freewill offerings. That presents problems on occasion."

My heart thumped as I swiped my tongue over dry lips. "What kind of problems?"

"Money problems. We anticipate generous donations of food, such as Blaine and others give. We can even expect clothing, though we never know if the gift will fit our needs. Holidays are rarely a problem. But cash for bills and other expenses sometimes runs short. Like now. We've been low on funding for the past few months. Or high on expenses. Or both."

This was nothing new. Mama Ramsey often lamented when donations to the Home lagged. She seemed to take it as a personal affront, though her only connection to the orphan-age was in a voluntary capacity. Hazel, of course, had more reason for concern. As did I. "How many times have I heard you say, 'The Lord will provide for His work'?"

"I know. And I still believe that." Hazel twisted the ring on her finger. "But I also see what it says in my ledger. One less mouth to feed, one less body to clothe always gives us a little space."

I stiffened. "Lily Beth won't eat enough to make a differ-ence. She can have my portion if need be."

Hazel's bowlike lips lifted in a smile. "I know. It's just—"

27

She waved her hand. "Never mind. We'll—you'll get through this crunch, just like we have all the others." She pushed back from the desk and stood. "I'd best telephone Mr. Riley and tell him you've agreed to the post. We'd like to finalize things as soon as possible."

As Hazel's footsteps faded away, I leaned back in my chair and considered her revelation. But I couldn't make myself adopt her dire outlook on the situation. The finances would right themselves, as they always had before, because the Lord wouldn't let these children suffer on account of something as trifling as money.

"Miss Sadie!" Janet threw her arms around my waist and buried her head in my shirt after school that afternoon. I stroked the thick braid that dangled down her back. She lifted her face. "You'll help me with my math, won't you?"

I tweaked her nose. "Of course, you silly goose. Have I ever left you alone with your numbers?" But I breathed relief that soon I would no longer be the one helping with arithmetic homework. That would be one of my assistant's duties.

"Say, Miss Sadie . . ." Twelve-year-old George sauntered in my direction, reaching for a slice of buttered bread on his way.

Mrs. Fore slapped his hand. "Not until you've hung up your coat and hat. Then you'll sit at the table like the civilized hooligan you are." She winked as she poured milk into tin cups.

George whipped off his hat, then peeled off his coat and hung both on a peg near the back door. Then he renewed his quest. "Miss Sadie, do you have any good books I could read? Teacher says we have to read one and write up a paper saying what we think of it." He looked me straight in the eye. Another few months and he'd tower over me. I swallowed past the lump in my throat and prayed again for a family to take him in, love him, guide him, maybe even school him in a trade.

"If we can't find a book that suits your fancy on the shelves here, I'll take you to the library in town on Saturday."

"Aw, Saturday? We've got a baseball game scheduled then."

I pushed up on my toes just a tiny bit, needing to be bigger than he was for a little while longer. "After your chores, of course."

His whole body sagged as his chin dropped toward his chest. "Yes, ma'am." Then he looked up with a grin. "Can I have—"

I held up one hand.

His nose scrunched as if he'd smelled a skunk. "*May* I have my bread and butter now?"

I looked at Mrs. Fore. She nodded.

"Take your food to the table, please," I commanded those still lingering.

The back door opened again. A gangly youth loped inside.

"Carter!" I threw my arms around Blaine's younger brother, then pulled back and looked up into his face. Carter didn't have Blaine's stature, but then the boys had different fathers, so I guessed that accounted for their opposite builds. And coloring. Carter's hair and eyes were as light as Blaine's were dark. "You've grown since I last saw you. And that was just a few weeks ago!"

Carter's infectious grin appeared. The brothers were as different as peas and corn in personality, too. Blaine's serious nature didn't always appreciate Carter's love of fun and laughter, especially when it landed the boy in trouble.

Carter slid the coat from his narrow shoulders as I led him to the table. "Is everyone feeling better at the Comstocks?"

He shrugged. "Mrs. Comstock still coughs a good bit. But we should make it back to church on Sunday."

"Wonderful! I'm so glad things are working out well for you there." It was his third foster home in the dozen years since he and Blaine had arrived on the Home's doorstep.

Cynthia sidled closer to Carter, her eyes wide under his disarming grin, the one I felt sure sent the girls at the high school into a swoon. I studied the floor to hide my smile. But when I realized Mrs. Fore's huff and bustle to prepare supper, I sobered.

Pulling at Carter's arm, I lowered my voice. "Won't the Comstocks expect you at home for chores and such before supper?"

Carter shrugged. "I could eat here instead."

I thought of Hazel's words this morning about mouths to feed. She wouldn't be pleased to have another for supper. And Mrs. Fore didn't take kindly to unannounced guests at mealtime, either. After Lily Beth last night . . .

I lowered my voice. "We've already tried Mrs. Fore's patience this week. We'll see if we can work out another time."

He crushed his cloth cap between his hands and looked at the floor. Looping my arm around his, I led him to the door. "When we see you at church Sunday, I promise we'll plan a visit."

Carter's quick grin fell into a frown. Grabbing his coat, he bounded out the door and into the frigid air without a glance back.

"Miss Sa-die!"

Janet's crowing called me to the parlor. I left off slicing bread for supper and scurried through the narrow hall. Miranda and I nearly collided.

"Sorry," she mumbled, pressing her back against the wall, mouth twisted into a scowl.

The shock of such a look held me in place.

Had she and Mrs. Fore quarreled? I couldn't imagine it. Maybe one of the children had upset her. I certainly hoped not. In spite of the fact that she and I had never moved past tolerating each other, Miranda worked hard to keep the house in order. We couldn't function as well as we did without her work. Maybe she needed something good to think about. Like Hazel's engagement.

"It's nice about Hazel and the professor, isn't it?"

Hazel had announced her engagement, though she'd kept my appointment a secret for now, since I didn't intend to tell Blaine until everything was official.

Miranda's head jerked back and her eyes narrowed, regarding me as if I were a boy with muddy shoes come to tread across her freshly mopped floor. "And what will happen to all of us, I wonder, now that she's off to play house?"

My jaw clenched. Then I softened. It had to be hard for a woman almost forty years old and never married to hear of Hazel's good fortune. I kept my voice quiet, as I did with upset children. "She'll be happy, and we'll all be fine."

"Some of us will," she muttered as she turned her face away.

My spine went rigid. When I took over as matron, Miranda would answer to me. Best to let her see now that I couldn't be bullied. Yet Mama Ramsey's voice rang through my head. *"You'll catch more flies with honey than with vinegar."*

I took a deep breath before pasting on a smile, determined to keep my comments as vague as possible. "I can't imagine much will change after Hazel leaves."

"Miss Sa-die!" Janet's shrill impatience.

My skirt swooshed past Miranda as I dashed into the parlor. She probably fretted as much about keeping her job as she did her lack of a husband. And who could blame her? This was about as good a place as she'd ever find with her sixth-grade education. Once I held the position of matron, I'd reassure her that I intended to keep her on. In spite of her occasional surliness, it would be easier to retain her. Hiring my own replacement would be challenge enough. No need to add a maid-of-all-work opening to that list.

Chapter 4

Janet twisted her mouth and studied the problem on her page. Then she scribbled a number beneath the two already written.

"There. Is that right?"

I hid one hand in the fold of my skirt and counted on my fingers. One, two, three, four. And yes, she'd written a four.

"Perfect. All done now?" My shoulders ached from the tension of an entire page of addition problems. Why wouldn't numbers come as easily to me as they did to others?

Janet arranged the completed work in her book while I turned to Cynthia. Copper curls framed her pale face. Big hazel eyes stared at me, looking like the marbles the boys hoarded their pennies to buy.

She shook her head. "Not with them here."

I sighed. "You have to practice in front of people, Cynthia."

"Not today. Please?"

I rubbed my eyes. Janet's math had been taxing enough. Perhaps this could wait. "All right. But you can't put this off forever."

She threw her arms around my neck. "I love you, Miss Sadie," she whispered in my ear.

I patted her back. "I love you, too, sweet pea."

When I gathered all the children for evening devotions, Lily Beth crawled into my lap before George handed me the big Bible from the stand in the parlor. I turned to Philippians 4:13, for Cynthia's sake—and my own. "'I can do all things through Christ which strengtheneth me.'" I emphasized the *all* and then prayed aloud that we would have faith to believe.

I lifted Lily Beth and followed everyone upstairs, noting that the girl weighed little more than a bucket full of water. I prayed that a few weeks of Mrs. Fore's cooking would fatten her up. I pushed the silky white hair away from her face and gazed down into her off-kilter eyes. One of my first orders of business would be to talk with Dr. Lawson about fixing them. I had to know if it was even a possibility or I'd feel I had failed the child. And I refused to fail these little ones.

Fifteen minutes later, flannel-gowned girls scrambled into six of the dozen single beds pushed up against the long walls of the oversized room. Most of them were waiting for circumstances to change so their parents could care for them once more. Only two—Cynthia and her older sister, Nancy—were waiting for foster or adoptive homes. And they wouldn't wait long. Girls never did.

Perfect girls, that is.

The thought pricked as I pulled the covers around Lily Beth's thin shoulders. I turned to Cynthia and peeled the covers down from her face to kiss her forehead.

"You'll pray, Miss Sadie?" Janet asked from the next bed, eyes wide above her upturned nose.

I sat on the edge of Janet's bed, then reached across and stroked her hair and let my eyes drift shut. I never knew what it was to pray until I arrived at the Home. Here I'd learned to talk to God, to tell Him my fears, to trust that He heard me. When Mama Ramsey took me to her house, she knelt by my bed night after night and taught me more about Jesus. That He loved me enough to die for my sins and make me clean and new.

I'd wanted to be clean and new, not stinky and dirty like the place that haunted my little-girl dreams. I conjured up the scent of Mama Ramsey's milk-and-honey-fragranced hair. The ache of grief gripped my chest as I closed my eyes. "Dear Jesus, Giver and Sustainer of life, bless these dear ones as they sleep. Cover them with Your love as with a warm blanket, and fill them with peace as with a hot meal. May we all be thankful for Your bountiful blessings. May we ever strive to be Your obedient servants. Amen."

The rustle of squirming bodies on bedsheets rose and then hushed. I shut off the overhead bulb, plunging the room into darkness.

Down the hall, around the corner, I reached the circus that was the boys' room. Voices bounced off walls, punctuated by thuds and creaks and cracks. I shook my head even as a longing pressed against my heart, a longing for each of them to know the love of God through a real home. So few willingly took a boy. At least, few who weren't looking for free labor. We worked hard to keep our boys out of homes where they would be little more than slaves. Thankfully, our board of trustees agreed.

Standing in the doorway, hands fisted on my hips, I waited for them to notice. One by one the boys stilled and silence descended. I raised my eyebrows and peered at each impish face, fighting the temptation to laugh as eleven boys scrambled into beds, diving beneath quilts and covering up their heads.

Walking between the two rows of bed frames, I brushed back sweat-damp hair, pushed errant shoes out of my path, tweaked a scabbed-over nose. Then I knelt and prayed as I had with the girls. After I shut the door behind me, whispers whined into the silence. I flung the door wide, bringing with it the light of the hallway. I put on my stern look. Or what I hoped was my stern look.

"Shhhh." I put one finger over my lips, knowing that they could discern my gesture. I pulled the door toward me and tiptoed away, stopping only for a moment to put an ear to the girls' door.

Quiet.

Tomorrow I would sign my name to a contract and accept these children as my responsibility. Suddenly I couldn't wait to tell Blaine my news. He of all people would understand what this job meant to me. It was the same as his pursuit of a piece of paper with his name on it that declared that a strip of earth belonged to him.

Both of our dreams would come true. First one, then the other. Sharing our joy along the way would only make things that much sweeter in the end.

Mr. Riley, the president of the Raystown Home for Orphan and Friendless Children, looked as important as his title. A tall man with graying hair at his temples, he wore a dark suit, the only hints of light being the white of his shirt and the glint of a gold chain draped across his middle, holding his pocket watch.

Hazel led us all into the office but stood close to the wall, leaving Mr. Riley and me face-to-face.

"Miss Sillsby." His eyes and voice softened. "Sadie. On behalf of the board of trustees of the Raystown Home, I'm honored to offer you the position of matron."

Even knowing the words were coming, they lifted me into ecstasy. I wet my lips and took a deep breath. "I'd be happy to accept the position, Mr. Riley."

The words thrilled and terrified.

Hazel beamed at me as Mr. Riley reached into his satchel and pulled out a piece of paper and a pen. "If you'll sign here"—Mr. Riley pointed to a place on the page—"it will all be official."

My hand inched across the indicated space, careful not to smudge the ink flowing from the fountain pen, the first one I'd ever used. *Sarah Eleanor Sillsby.* I handed the pen back to Mr. Riley.

"Miss Brighton has assured us that you can commence your duties immediately." Mr. Riley's pointed gaze held mine for a moment. My eyes sought Hazel's.

"I'll be close enough to answer all your questions, Sadie." Her quiet words calmed the panic that clouded my joy. Of course she wouldn't leave me alone, but I never imagined she'd let go of us with such tranquility.

Mr. Riley cleared his throat. "I believe Miss Brighton has agreed to stay until you make a decision about your assistant."

I blinked. My assistant. The first big task.

"Will I need your approval before I hire someone?" I squeaked.

Mr. Riley shook his head. "We are here in an oversight and advisory capacity. Just as with Miss Brighton, the children and staff are under your direction. And since the assistant's salary is already in the budget, it doesn't require an extra approval. Which reminds me, your salary will increase to twenty dollars per month. Starting today."

Twenty dollars. Twice what I'd been earning as Hazel's assistant. I glanced down at my cheap shirtwaist and drab skirt, then over at Hazel in her tailored outfit. My salary hadn't left much for luxuries like pretty clothes. Especially when I didn't have the time to sew them for myself. Now my mind imagined a new suit. Businesslike and fashionable, as befit the matron of the Home for Orphan and Friendless Children. After that, I could save toward helping Blaine with the land.

"Two other items of business, Miss Sillsby."

"Yes?" I pulled my attention back to Mr. Riley.

"First, the board would like to host a reception here to honor Miss Brighton's years of service."

"I think that's a wonderful idea!"

Hazel blushed, then tried to frown away the idea, but her lips twitched upward and I knew it pleased her. "I'll tell Mrs. Fore to begin planning immediately."

"Good. Each of the board members is donating five dollars toward the event. And speaking of money, we would appreciate a full financial report from you at our next meeting, the third Thursday of the month. We have been concerned, as I assume Miss Brighton has informed you, and would like to evaluate how things stand."

I opened my mouth, but my lungs refused to inflate. For a moment, I felt as if I were drowning. Not in water, in numbers. A report full of figures. I squeezed my eyes shut. I could do this. I had to do this.

My eyes flew open again. I pulled my shoulders back and met Mr. Riley's curious expression. "I'll be prepared."

"Good." Mr. Riley clasped his satchel shut. "I speak for the entire board when I say that we are thrilled to have you, my dear. I know you will be as diligent as your predecessor to care for the hearts, minds, and souls of the children entrusted to your care. And that you will continue to be frugal in your management of day-to-day life."

Tears blurred my vision as Mr. Riley shook my hand. I remembered all the times he'd joked with me as a girl during his visits to the Ramseys and wondered if he, too, felt the poignancy of this moment. "Thank you, Mr. Riley."

He hurried into his coat. "If you ladies will excuse me . . ." He slapped his hat on his head and departed.

Hazel gripped my hands with a squeal. "Let's tell the others!"

I held back. "No, wait. I haven't told Blaine yet. I don't want him to hear it from anyone else."

"But we need to tell them, Sadie. Don't worry. We'll swear them to secrecy."

Hazel's laughter spilled out again as she pulled me after her. "No one would spoil your surprise."

I expected her to drag me to the kitchen first, since the scritch of brush bristles over wood confirmed Miranda hard at work in the parlor. But Hazel stopped there anyway. Miranda looked up from her hands and knees, scrub brush in hand, face red.

"Good news, Miranda! Sadie's our new matron!"

Miranda rocked back on her heels, but before she could reply, Hazel yanked me toward the kitchen.

"Mrs. Fore!" Hazel let go of my hand. I stumbled to a chair at the worktable and let its solidness catch me. Mrs. Fore's knife peeled the brown skin from a potato and let it plop into the sink.

"There isn't a fire, is there?" she asked, another strip of brown peel curling under her knife.

"No, no fire. An announcement. Sadie is our new matron!"

Mrs. Fore set down her potato, a wide grin stretching her lips. She took my face between her pudgy hands and planted a kiss on my forehead. "You'll do a fine job, Sadie. You'll make us all proud."

I circled my arms around her ample waist and squeezed. "It helps to know you're here," I said.

She waved away my words, then stopped. "But what did Blaine say to this good news?"

My gaze cut to Hazel, then back to Mrs. Fore. "I haven't told him yet. It'll be a surprise when he visits tomorrow night. You won't say anything before then, will you?"

Mrs. Fore's deep chuckle scattered my momentary fear. "Of course not. I'll make his favorite pie, though. An announcement like this deserves a special treat."

My mouth watered at the thought of a flaky crust topped with creamy butterscotch custard filling and finished with sweet, fluffy meringue. Blaine would think he'd died and gone to heaven. A pie with so many eggs rarely made an appearance in the winter.

Then my conscience smote me. "What about breakfast?" I said softly. Though we didn't always feed the children eggs, we did on occasion. I hated to take away even a small pleasure when they had so few.

"Don't you worry about that. Oatmeal suits us just fine." She patted my hand. "It's not every day a girl gets named to an important position like matron. Or has her beau to celebrate with."

My eyes turned wet once more as I silently thanked the Lord for His abundant gift of people who loved me.

Blaine usually visited after supper on Fridays, when Hazel took the evening off to spend with the professor. We'd play parlor games with the children before I put them to bed. Then we had the first floor to ourselves.

But the clock ticked toward bedtime and still no sign of Blaine.

A game of Parcheesi ended. I instructed the children to put it away. We straightened the room and I pointed them upstairs. Moans answered my directive.

"But, Miss Sadie," Henry whined, "won't we even get to see Blaine at all?"

"You can see him Sunday. At church." I glanced at the clock. A half hour earlier than their normal bedtime. But Blaine's unexplained absence had left me shaken. Had his horse thrown a shoe? Had it been spooked by an automobile? Was Blaine lying bloody and helpless in a ditch somewhere?

Imagination twisted my insides. But as I climbed the stairs behind the children, I told myself he would arrive at any moment, and with a perfectly simple explanation of his lateness. Until then, I'd use the extra moments to freshen up. I even considered donning my Sunday dress. But no. That might make him suspicious. I wanted my news to take him completely by surprise.

Back downstairs, I tossed a small shovelful of coal into the heater in the parlor before heading to the kitchen.

"It's all on the table, dear." Mrs. Fore rubbed her eyes.

The silver company tray held two wedges of butterscotch pie on china plates. Then I noticed the silver coffeepot and china coffee cups, as well—things usually reserved for visits from board members or potential parents and donors. Or the preacher and his wife. I glanced up at Mrs. Fore.

She shrugged. "Just a little something special."

I smiled as I lifted the heavily laden tray. Thanks to Mrs. Fore, the evening would be perfect. Walking carefully to the parlor, I wondered where such fine things had come from. Heaven knew the Home didn't have extra funds to purchase such niceties. They must have been donated long ago. China cups rattled against saucers. I gripped the tray more tightly. It wouldn't do to bring them back in pieces.

Sitting alone in the parlor, I felt quite formal all of a sudden. Even wished I'd followed my instinct and changed into my best dress.

Then the thud of horse's hooves on the road outside sent me rushing to the front door. I flung it open and ran out onto the porch. Hugging the column at the top of the steps, I watched the familiar chestnut mare trot up the dark lane, Blaine's ancient black buggy rolling behind. By the time he reached our hitching post, the cold had seeped through my dress. I rubbed my hands over my arms as he jumped from his perch and twisted the reins around the iron stand.

Bounding up the front steps in two strides, he wrapped his arms around my waist, picked me up, and twirled me around.

When my feet hit the ground again, knives of cold slashed at my chest. "Blaine! Someone will see!"

"I don't care who sees." His hands cupped my face. "I want the whole world to know you're my girl."

I giggled. "I think that's been apparent for a while now."

"But this is different." Even in the darkness his eyes gleamed like the mahogany bannister after a polishing, the excitement on his face more indicative of Carter than of Blaine. "I got it, Sadie. I got the farm."

Chapter 5

Blaine whipped a sheaf of papers from the pocket of his coat and placed them in my hands. "See? The land is mine. All mine!" He lifted and spun me again.

I fought free of his arms, my fingers still gripping the pages I couldn't read in the darkness. I tottered, dizzied by the twirling—and the news.

Please, no. The Home's matron, like a teacher, wasn't permitted to be married. I'd signed my name to a contract, just as he'd signed his. My teeth chattered as I shook from head to toe.

He pulled me inside, sat me in front of the heater in the parlor, and shoveled more coal into its cast-iron belly. Then he captured my face between his work-worn hands. His lips brushed mine, sending a tingle down my spine. "I've known I wanted you to be my wife since I was twelve. Over a decade of waiting."

Blood pounded in my ears, my heart jerking and twisting beneath my shirt.

His breath whispered against my cheek. "Mr. Sorrel's moving to Pittsburgh with his daughter. He offered to sell me the farm for far less than I ever imagined he would. The Lord has heard my prayers, Sadie. Now I can have you with me every day." His voice sounded far away, as if I'd fallen into a pit and he was calling down to me.

Deep laughter rang through the room as he rocked back on his heels. "Are you surprised?"

Surprised wasn't the word. Bewildered. Flummoxed. I blinked, then glanced down at the papers in my hand and examined Blaine's name on a bill of sale. Instead of elation, my stomach threatened to give up its supper. I pressed my hand over my mouth as I stared at the final page. It wasn't like the others. This sheet held numbers, not words. I couldn't make sense of them.

"What's this?" I thrust the paper in his face.

His Adam's apple bobbed in the center of his thick neck. "A mortgage. I told you, I couldn't wait. He needed to sell quick. If it wasn't me, it would have been to someone else."

I sucked in a breath and held it. The enthusiasm in his eyes sizzled and died. I pressed my hands against my middle, wishing I could draw in more oxygen, but my corset remained tight against my ribs.

The sofa sagged as his weight descended beside me. He leaned forward and poured us each a cup of coffee from the tall silver pot. "I've shocked you." He handed me a cup, and I took it without thought. "This has been in process for a couple of weeks, but I didn't want to say anything in case it didn't work out." He handed me a plate of Mrs. Fore's butterscotch pie.

I twirled my fork through the meringue, brought a bite to my mouth, and then set it aside. If I forced it down my throat, I feared it would come right back up. How in the world could I tell Blaine my news in light of his?

"Three hundred acres of good farmland," he continued. "A place for us to live, to raise a family. And no one can take it from me." He shrugged, then gulped down a big bite of pie. "At least not after I pay what I owe."

I exploded to my feet and retreated to the opposite side of the room, arms crossed over my chest, trying to keep my anger inside. We'd never discussed anything but full payment for his land. That was the reason it was taking so long, the reason we'd waited to marry. If he'd not had a problem with a mortgage, we could have been together years ago. Then I never would have been offered—and accepted—the position that fulfilled all my yearnings.

With my back to him, I let my arms fall limp, then laced my fingers together and squeezed tight. I pivoted slowly around to face Blaine again.

He shoveled more pie into his mouth, not even noticing my silence. My announcement would surprise him as much as his had me. I braced my hands on the wall behind me. "Hazel came home with some news of her own the other day."

"Did she?" He plowed into my unfinished pie before pouring himself more coffee.

"She's finally accepted the professor."

His full lips spread into a wide grin. He set down the now-empty plate, picked up his cup, and leaned back on the sofa. "That is good news. I'll admit, I never thought she'd do it. But then John Stapleton is one persistent old cuss."

With the toe of my worn boot, I traced an arc on the floor. "Hazel asked me to be her bridesmaid."

"That's nice." The clink of china told me he had set his cup down.

I crossed to the window behind the sofa, fingered the fading petals of my daffodils before noticing a stray thread dangling from the seam of my skirt. If I yanked, would it break away or begin to unravel? "She asked me something else, too."

"What was that?" He twisted to see me as his mouth stretched into a yawn.

"She asked me to take the position of matron."

He sat so still I wondered if he'd heard me. I chewed my lip. Waiting. Waiting. Waiting.

The clock chimed. A door closed somewhere in the house. When silence descended once more, he rose, jaw ticking. "And what did you tell her?"

I stared at my hands. "I knew of no reason to tell her no," I whispered.

"You took the job?" The disbelief in his voice rubbed against my heart like new shoes on bare skin.

My gaze met his. "I love this place—and these kids. As do you. Of course I accepted the position. I had no idea—"

"So now that you know, you'll tell her you're not interested in the position anymore, right?" His eyebrows crunched toward his nose. His mouth flattened into a firm line.

My heart pounded. I gripped the back of the sofa. "I've already signed the contract. I wanted to surprise you."

He rounded the sofa and took my shoulders in his massive hands. "You'd rather work here than become my wife?"

My resolve faltered. I stared at the floor. I hated to disappoint him. "Yes. For now. They need me, can't you see that?" I whispered through the thickness in my throat.

His hands found my fingers. "I want to marry you, Sadie Sillsby. Now. I thought you wanted that, too."

I looked down to where his hands dwarfed mine. Rough palms. Jagged fingernails, some with dirt beneath their tips. He'd been fixated on owning land since before I'd known him. Now that he did, he expected me to drop everything and join his dream. But I had dreams of my own. Fledgling dreams I couldn't just abandon.

I shut my eyes and ground top teeth into bottom, searching for words to make him understand.

"Mama Ramsey always told me the Lord had something special planned for my life. I never let myself believe that before. Not really. And now this. How am I supposed to walk away from it?" My voice broke along with my heart. "Don't you see? It's not forever. Just for . . . a few years."

"Years?" His dark eyebrows rose. He stepped away. My hand fell from his and suddenly turned cold. "Am I just supposed to wait around until you decide you want a life with me? We've always planned for a place of our own. A farm. It's what God made us to do."

Arms across my chest, I chewed my lip. I hadn't asked for this position, didn't seek it out, had never even dreamed it would one day be mine. The Lord had opened the door for me. My heart yearned to help these children just as Blaine's heart yearned for land.

I pulled back my shoulders. "What if God made me to be the matron of this Home instead?"

His chin dropped to his chest, but not before I witnessed

the stark pain shooting from his eyes. It felt like a palm across my cheek.

He ran both hands up his face, over his head. His fingers laced at the back of his neck as he blew out a long breath. "Please, Sadie. Think about what you're saying."

His complete bewilderment twisted my heart. I reminded myself he wasn't a man given to quick change. He needed time to think things through. He would never let something like this drive a wedge between us. If I could count on nothing else, I could count on that.

Couldn't I?

I thought of how Hazel had staved off Professor Stapleton's attentions for so long, putting the needs of the children and this place before her desire to have a home and family of her own. The professor hadn't abandoned her. She must have learned some secret, some way of expressing how she felt to encourage his patience. Or was his love for Hazel stronger and deeper than Blaine's love for me?

The thought set my knees trembling. Perhaps in our youth and naïveté we'd misjudged our feelings for one another. Maybe what we felt wasn't love at all, only infatuation borne out of friendship and shared experience. If we didn't have the same dreams, how could we ever be happy together?

My eyes burned with tears. Had this been what Jesus meant when He asked His followers to deny themselves, to leave their families behind? I had no family anymore, now that both Papa and Mama Ramsey had gone to heaven. Only Blaine. If being a missionary to these children meant sacrificing that relationship, I'd have to trust the Lord to accomplish what concerned me.

I lifted my chin. "I know exactly what I'm saying, Blaine. I'm saying I can't be your helpmeet. I have . . . other things I need to accomplish."

His chest puffed out, eyes blazing with hurt. "Don't expect me to sit around and wait until you decide you're ready for a husband. If you can't be satisfied with the life I'm offering now, I fear you never will be. And I'm not willing to take that chance."

Fisted hands flew to my hips. "Just because you own a square of ground doesn't give you the right to possess me, as well."

We stared at each other, neither of us blinking. Then I pivoted. He stepped past me. I focused on the wall, on the need to keep my chin from quivering and my knees from giving way. My jaw tightened until it birthed a pounding in my head.

His footsteps faded. The quiet click of the front door unnerved me more than if he had slammed it shut.

Chapter 6

I woke from a fitful sleep, threw back the covers, and stared into the mirror. My brown eyes were puffy and red. I dabbed a bit of powder on my face to cover the ill effects of the night. As long as I didn't look anyone in the eye, I ought to be fine.

But the stutter of my heart begged to differ. Had Blaine and I really parted ways? Was our relationship over forever? I covered my face with my hands, waiting for the tears to cascade down my cheeks and leak through my fingers. But this time, they didn't come.

I stumbled through the morning, avoiding everyone. Much easier on a Saturday morning than a school day. I wandered into the empty parlor. From the windowsill, the fading splendor of the daffodils mocked me—yet another reminder of Blaine's hasty words. I poked the soil around the wilting stems. Dry crumbs of dirt clung to my finger. Dry as my eyes. Dry as my heart.

Brushing my hands clean, I determined to keep the flowers alive. I might not have Blaine, but I wouldn't disparage his gift, especially when it might be the last one I ever received from him.

And yet, could I really wish for anything different? I felt the call of God to this position. To accept Blaine's proposal now would feel . . . selfish. As if my personal happiness mattered more to me than the lives of these children.

I lifted a prayer to the Lord, a request to still my anxious heart and remind me that He had orchestrated this path. For both of us.

"Do you mind taking them back alone?" Hazel asked as we exited the church the next morning.

"Not at all." I looked up at the cold blue sky, deciding to give the children a bit of time to visit with their friends. But after a few minutes, I was ready to go. I counted heads, missing one.

Henry.

I couldn't see him in the churchyard. Had he gone to the outhouse? I headed to the back of the church. Then I spied Miranda and Mrs. Fore sitting on a bench in the side garden, their backs to me.

I stopped, holding my breath. It wasn't like Mrs. Fore not to hurry home and have dinner on the table. And Miranda. She rarely stayed longer than to shake Pastor Uland's hand.

Mrs. Fore patted Miranda's arm. "There now. It's for the best, I'm sure."

Miranda slumped, pressing a hand over her eyes. "I could've done that job. I know it."

I sucked in a breath. I knew she didn't care overmuch for me, but had she been looking for another job already?

"And maybe you could have, I don't know." Mrs. Fore shifted. I whirled around and stepped into the shade of the church building, hoping I blended into the gray wall.

"Hazel didn't even give me a chance. When I asked her about it, she said she was sorry, but the board of trustees would never approve me."

My mouth dropped open. Was that why she'd been so cantankerous? Miranda imagined *she* should be matron of the Home?

Mrs. Fore didn't answer.

"She's had everything. I've had nothing. This was my only chance."

"Not everything, dear. Remember that before she had the Ramsey family, she lost her own. She was a child like these we love."

Miranda's eyes flashed at Mrs. Fore. I pressed myself against the cold stones, trying to remain perfectly still. They stood and walked away from me, toward the street, words fading to silence.

Henry trotted around the corner of the building. I hustled him away before he could say a word, wondering if I'd be interviewing candidates for two job openings next week.

"I didn't notice Blaine at church this morning." Hazel handed me a cup of coffee before she joined me on the parlor sofa that evening. "We're not still sworn to secrecy, are we?"

The corners of my mouth tugged downward. I wanted to reclaim the elation I'd felt when I'd written my name on the contract. But I couldn't. Not until I'd swept Blaine from my heart and mind.

"Tell anyone and everyone," I said, forcing my lips to curve upward.

Hazel tilted her head and studied me with narrowed eyes.

I squirmed under her scrutiny. I'd never hidden my feelings well, though I'd tried harder in the past few years.

"Sadie." Her chiding tone set my heart aching.

Setting aside my cup, I hopped to my feet, pondering the question I'd asked myself all day. After circling the room, I stopped at a chair, my hands braced on its high back. "Do you ever regret taking so long to accept Professor Stapleton?"

"No." A quick answer, followed by a faint pink tinge to her cheeks. "Well, maybe a little. Why?"

"Blaine and I, we . . ." I shrugged, then clamped my lips shut. Tears still hovered too close to the surface to trust my voice. If I could have both Blaine and the Raystown Home, I would. But it wasn't possible.

"Did you argue?"

Air streamed from my mouth in a long sigh, trying to dislodge the lump in my throat. "More than that. We . . . parted ways."

Concern cloaked Hazel's face. Her voice softened. "Did you have plans you didn't mention?"

I shrugged, then stared at my upturned palms. "We had a 'someday' understanding. He refused to consider a formal engagement until he owned a farm outright."

"And you didn't think that would happen anytime soon."

My head shook. Tears welled. I pressed a finger under each eye, determined to keep them from falling. "Before I could say a word about my position, he announced he bought the farm he's been leasing."

54

"Oh, Sadie." Hazel crossed the room, grabbed my hands, and held them tight.

"He didn't tell me until the transaction was complete. Of course, by then my position was official, too. He couldn't understand why I wouldn't simply give up the job and marry him." Instant fury dried my tears. So much easier than sorrow.

Hazel gripped my shoulders and tried to look into my face, though I kept my head lowered. "You can say no, Sadie. Even now. We'll find someone else, and you won't hurt my feelings."

Slowly, my head lifted, until I looked directly into her eyes. "I don't want you to find another person. Like you, I believe God placed me in this position. You put off your own personal happiness to serve these children. Is my decision any different?"

"No." The word stretched long, and her hands fell away, as did her gaze. "Just make sure this is really God and not some overindulged sense of duty. I can explain to the board. They will find someone else."

"Not someone who knows and loves this place the way I do."

Hazel rubbed her forehead and frowned. "I'll admit the board and I are both relieved to have someone who can facilitate a seamless transition."

Pride puffed my chest. The Home needed me. Lily Beth, Cynthia, the other children—they needed me, too.

Blaine would survive on his own.

Or he'd find someone else. If only that thought didn't crush my heart. . . .

"I'm off to bed. You coming?" Hazel rose.

"I'll lock up first."

"Thank you." Her smile looked weary. "And don't worry. If the Lord has called you here, He'll provide all that you need. In every way."

I locked the front door, then returned to the parlor to click off the lamps. The sagging daffodils drew me. I brushed my finger over the petals, the leaves, thinking of the Giver of living, growing things. Of color in the midst of drab winter.

Babying my flowers back to life would only prolong the pain, not assuage it. Best to make a clean break, to focus on my new task. I picked up the oval pot before plunging the room into darkness. Then I hurried to the kitchen and eased open the door.

A chill wind swooped up my skirts, reminding me not to dawdle. With one flick of my wrist, the faded flowers landed on the frozen ground next to the stoop, roots shooting into the icy air, free from the crumbling clods of dirt that had been their home. A sob rose in my chest. I forced it down. Blaine and his daffodils would no longer be a part of my life.

Mrs. Fore looked at me queerly when I rushed into the kitchen with the children in the morning. I gave my usual greeting, received a harrumph in reply, and brushed it aside. Likely she hadn't slept well last night. Best stay out of her way until lunchtime. She'd feel better by then, with the children off to school.

I bundled Lily Beth in her coat, wrapped a scarf around her neck, and tweaked her nose. She smiled. The girl had adjusted well. As if she'd been here weeks instead of days. Fourteen-year-old Sylvia took her hand today as they followed the rest of the children out into the cold morning.

Mrs. Fore clanged one pot against another. I jumped and turned. When she looked up, I froze, heart battering my chest.

"You had a row over it, didn't you?" she asked.

My stomach twisted. I glanced around the kitchen, thankful for no audience. "What makes you think that?"

Mrs. Fore's wide shoulders rose and fell. I looked away, knowing she would see the truth in my eyes. I wasn't ready to talk to her about Blaine. Not yet.

Then I noticed Miranda staring at us from the doorway, scrub brush and bucket in hand.

She sniffed as if a bad odor rent the air. "I'll thank you all to stay off the stairs this morning. The floors always take longer to dry when it's cold."

"Of course. I'll inform Hazel." I started to follow Miranda from the kitchen.

"Your posy." Mrs. Fore's quiet words stopped me. "Dumped in the yard."

I swallowed moisture before I turned, but no matter how hard I tried, I couldn't meet Mrs. Fore's steady gaze. "Oh, that. I finally gave up on it. I guess I don't have a green thumb after all."

Before she could form a reply, I fled to the sanctuary of the office.

"The first thing you need to do is hire an assistant." Hazel paced down the side of the room. "We'll get the advertisement written this morning, and I'll take it to the paper this afternoon. But until you start interviewing candidates for that job, I thought it might be helpful to go over a few things you might not have picked up over the past few years."

My insides wiggled. How much didn't I know?

Fear must have been apparent on my face, for Hazel laughed. "Don't worry. You've helped with almost everything. You know more than you think you do. But I want you confident at your first board meeting next week."

The board meeting. I needed bucket loads of confidence before then.

"Of course you know that the matron is not only responsible for the children who pass through and live in the Home, but also for every single financial detail." Hazel occupied the chair behind the desk now. I brought a straight-backed chair closer and sat. "It seems a daunting task, to be sure, but it's simple arithmetic. Nothing complicated. As long as the numbers in the ledger match those in the bank book, we're fine." She cocked her head. "As long as that number isn't zero!"

Her laugh trilled like a small bell as she handed me a stack of bills. I didn't join her merriment. I gulped down a yelp. How would I manage to do my job if it involved so many figures?

"This is our financial book." She pulled another ledger from a drawer. "Record the expenditures and the receivables in the appropriate columns. I find it easier to total them each week rather than leave them too long."

The back of my neck grew damp. I tried to keep the panic from my eyes.

"From these records, I write up our financial reports for the board each month. Oh, and don't forget to note when you refill the cash box. I usually make sure to start each month with at least ten dollars there for trolley fares and other sundry items. Does all that make sense?"

I nodded, but my chest constricted. All those numbers. And they had to be right. Should I mention that math didn't come easily to me? I opened my mouth, but Hazel had moved on, explaining the meetings already on her calendar that would now fall to me. I swallowed down my protest. I could do this. I could.

I pressed my fingers into my temple and concentrated on Hazel's words.

I'd lived through hard things before. Agonizing physical pain. Lingering illness. But those had ended. Peace had come. Then friendship. Then a family. I had to believe the Lord would continue to supply all my needs.

Chapter 7

The telephone rang early Friday morning. Hazel waved me off and answered it herself. I hid a grin. She was acting as my assistant these days—answering the phone, writing correspondence, arranging interviews.

All that would soon be done by a person I didn't yet know. Today's examination of candidates for my old job took on new import and sent me scampering to the office to sort through their applications.

Hazel scurried in, eyes wild. "I completely forgot about this!"

I jumped to my feet, heart pounding as she scattered a stack of letters, searching until she held only one. Her eyes skated over the paper, then she passed it to me. "Read it for yourself."

A neat, flowing script filled the page.

Dear Miss Brighton,

Thank you for contacting us in regard to the possibility of associating our organization with your Home for Orphan and Friendless Children in Raystown, Pennsylvania. We understand that you serve the children of Huntingdon County as well as the surrounding counties.

We are very interested in considering an association between your home and the Children's Aid Society of Pennsylvania. As you know, our stated purpose is to provide for the welfare of any destitute children who may come under our control, to establish and maintain for the public a Bureau of Information concerning charities, and to aid and cooperate in the protection of children from cruelty. It seems as if your organization has much the same philosophy.

If it is convenient for you, we would like to send one of our representatives to tour your facilities and observe for a week or so. That way we can evaluate your accomplishments on behalf of children in need with the express purpose of determining if we can help each other. We look forward to hearing from you soon as to a convenient time for this evaluation to take place.

> *Sincerely,*
> *Mr. Edwin D. Solenberger*
> *Secretary, Children's Aid*
> *Society of Pennsylvania*

My forehead puckered. "What does it mean? How can the Children's Aid Society help us?"

"Information. Connections. The CAS has a much larger base of operation, so they can assist with our funding as well as provide other support."

My heart beat faster. "Would an association with them change things here?"

"Oh, no. And even if they can't help us, it never hurts to

build relationships with others whose mission is much the same as ours."

Relief slowed my pulse.

"It would be a very good association, in my opinion," Hazel continued. "And I'm sure you, of all people, can persuade them of that."

"Me?"

Her eyebrows rose toward the tiny curls at her hairline. "You *are* the matron, Sadie."

"Oh, yes. Of course."

"The reason I remembered the letter is that the telephone call was from the CAS. Their representative will arrive a week from Monday. He will observe our operation and gain a more thorough understanding of our history, our budget, our needs—those kinds of things."

I looked down at my shirtwaist, my skirt. Would I have time to get a new suit before the man arrived?

"Of course, this makes it crucial for you to choose a new assistant today. You'll need a few days to get her comfortable enough to handle things while you attend to the CAS's inquiries."

I knew she was right, but I'd hoped for more time to consider my decision, for the thought of entrusting the day-to-day care of the children to another person troubled me. Would I find someone to be patient with Janet's math problems and Cynthia's fear of speaking? To handle Carl's penchant for mischief and George's clever way with words? Would she hug the children before they left for school in the morning and say prayers when she tucked them in bed at night?

A knock sounded at the door. Hazel patted my hand. "Just

the first of many new journeys of faith, Sadie. You'll do fine."
Then she went to let in the first candidate.

Five hours later, I pressed my fingertips into my forehead
and rubbed. After six interviews, I didn't feel sure about any
of them. Hazel returned to the office after seeing the last
interviewee to the front door.

"Are there any more applicants?"

"One more," she said. "After that, you'll have to choose."

I nodded, smoothed back my hair, and took a deep breath.
"Send her in, then."

Hazel disappeared. I glanced at the two pieces of paper
on my desk. One contained a list of questions to ask each
candidate. The other remained blank, ready to record the
answers given. I dipped the nib of the pen into the inkwell,
let the excess drip away. It wasn't that any of the women had
been unqualified, exactly. They just weren't . . .

I sighed. Perhaps I was asking for the impossible. I wanted
someone who could step in and take charge of the children,
see to their needs without coming to me to make every decision. But then it wasn't fair to judge these women by my
own experience. I'd lived here even before I began working
as Hazel's assistant. I knew how things were done.

The door opened. I looked up. Miranda's gaze roamed
from wall to wall as she brushed at her skirt.

"Did you need something, Miranda?"

Her usual haughtiness had vanished, leaving her unfamil-
iar. She stumbled into the chair in front of the desk. "I'm
here for my interview."

I looked down at my paper, trying to quell my confusion. Of course she wanted my old job. She'd wanted the matron's position, hadn't she? I guessed she imagined being my assistant was the first step in that direction. But how on earth could I consider her? We'd tolerated each other, for sure, but little more. With Miranda, there would be no possibility of friendship to soften the long hours of hard work.

Besides, she seemed to have no qualifications other than that she'd cleaned the place. I knew she had quit school young. Could she even read? Write? How could I turn over correspondence to her if she chicken-scratched her letters like Henry or had trouble with simple arithmetic like Janet?

And me.

I ignored that thought as I wrote *Miranda Jennings* at the top of the blank page.

I couldn't give her the job. But if I turned her away, would she leave us altogether? Would I be searching for and training both an assistant and a maid? I wanted to scream. Instead, I thought of Hazel, her placid countenance as she'd faced all manner of trouble. I would emulate her.

"So you're interested in becoming my assistant?" I held the pen poised over the blank page.

"Yes." She looked down and fumbled with her hands. Then her head rose again, the usual defiance lighting in her eyes. "I can, you know. In spite of what you think of me."

I set down the pen and folded my hands on the desk. "And what do I think of you, Miranda?"

The bravado flickered and died, leaving only . . . desperation?

"You think I'm nothing 'cause I don't have an education. But education ain't all in school, you know." Her shoulders pulled back, and her chin lifted just a touch. "I've been takin' care of people almost my whole life. I can take care of the children here. I *want* to take care of these children."

I shook off the softening of my heart. I had to make decisions with my head. Miranda wasn't qualified for this job. She knew it. And she knew I knew it.

Proceeding with my list of questions, I jotted a few notes. When I looked up again, I returned to playing Hazel. "I'll tell you the same thing I've told the other candidates. This job carries with it not only a lot of responsibility to me, to the board of trustees, and to the donors of this institution, it requires a great deal of patience and an overabundance of love. I will make my decision by tomorrow and let you know." I stood and held out my hand.

Miranda stared at it a minute. Then her hand grasped mine in a firm shake. As she pulled the door shut behind her, I plopped back into my chair, arms and legs akimbo. Children were so much easier to understand than women like Miranda.

And men like Blaine.

Chapter 8

Behind the office door, Hazel sat unperturbed as I paced. "You have to choose, Sadie."

"I know." I pressed my warm palm against the cold window glass. Too many choices in a short amount of time. I wished she could just tell me what to do.

"Either hire Miranda or don't. You'll have challenges no matter what. But if I could offer one piece of advice . . ."

I returned to the chair behind the desk. "Yes, please."

"Don't assume you know all there is to know about Miranda. She's never let me get close to her, either, but I suspect there are things within her that, if nurtured, would produce a great harvest of good."

The heels of my hands pressed into my eyes. I'd asked for her advice. Wanted it. But I simply couldn't envision working closely with Miranda. Besides her often disagreeable nature, I still doubted she possessed the skills needed to perform tasks required of the position.

No, it wouldn't work, no matter how hard Hazel wanted me to try.

Hands back on the desk again, I glanced down at the three

names still on my list. I picked up the pen and drew a line through Miranda's name, leaving two from which to choose.

Back and forth, weighing one candidate and then the other, I kept returning to Viola Brown. The youngest of all the applicants. Yet I had been even younger when I got the job. Hazel hadn't held that against me. And Viola came from a respectable family. Given my own shadowed past, perhaps her family's stellar reputation would keep my stains from showing. I closed my eyes, breathed a quick prayer for wisdom. Then I stood, confident of my decision. "Viola Brown. I'll telephone her immediately."

Hazel nodded, no condemnation in her eyes. "She should be a fine addition to the staff here."

"Yes, but now I dread telling Miranda. I fear she'll quit the job she has. Then I'll really be in a bind."

"You'll manage." Hazel's smile seemed sincere. "That's what the matron does—manages. Ask the Lord to guide you—and trust in that guidance. Release control to One higher than yourself."

"I will. I promise. I couldn't have had a better example of that than you have been." I pressed my cheek to hers, then headed for the telephone, praying Miranda wasn't anywhere in the vicinity when I made my call.

Viola Brown accepted on the spot. I knew the news would travel fast, so I trudged off to find Miranda, wandering the house in search of the scrape of the broom, the scratch of a scrub brush, the bump and slosh of a bucket of water. If Miranda took the news hard, we—Mrs. Fore, Viola, and

I—would all have to pitch in until I could secure another housemaid. I hoped it wouldn't take long.

I mounted the stairs. The shimmery creak of a metal bed moved out of its place caught my ear. I hurried to the boys' room, then sat on one of the neatly made beds. "Miranda, I need to speak with you."

Her broom stopped mid-sweep, then started again at a faster pace. "You can talk while I work."

I stared at my hands. "It was a difficult decision, but I felt I needed to pick Viola Brown for the position."

Her broom kept moving. Neither of us spoke. Would she wait until she left for the day to give her notice—or quit outright? Maybe she simply wouldn't arrive for work Monday morning. I opened my mouth, then closed it. No use trying to pull the words out of her. She'd do what she pleased. Perhaps it was best not to stoke the fire.

I made a quick stop in my bedroom to pin up a stray wisp of hair. Fixed again, I was at the second-floor landing, ready to descend, when I heard a muffled sob.

Miranda? I dismissed the thought even as I inched toward the sound. I'd never known her to cry. And certainly not where I might hear.

Another strangled sob. A few sniffles. I held completely still. Then the scritch of the broom bristles across the wood floor.

I raced down the stairs as quickly and quietly as I could, knowing I'd made the best decision for the Home, for the children. Miranda would get over it. But I had little doubt this would be her last day in my employ.

I couldn't still my quaking knees as I led the children over the frozen ground to the stone church on the corner of College Avenue and Chesterton Street, only a block and a half from the Home. My heart squeezed at the thought of encountering Blaine on this familiar ground.

Would he avoid me? Could I avoid him? Would it be easier to endure that first awkward meeting in public or in relative private? I longed to see him. And yet I didn't.

My mittened fingers clung more tightly to Cynthia's and Lily Beth's, my gaze searching for distraction from the disquieting thoughts in my head.

Carl scooped up a handful of snow and worked it between his hands.

"Don't you dare throw that snowball!" I called.

Carl's fingers opened slowly. The packed globe plopped to the ground. Carl grieved his abandoned weapon with a longing look.

"Scoot!" I gave him a playful swat on the behind. He rubbed and glared as if he'd felt my hand through his coat and pants and wool union suit. I shook my head as I surveyed the churchyard, trying not to search for Blaine. But my traitorous eyes sought him all the same.

I didn't find him. Not his person or his conveyance.

Entering the high-ceilinged sanctuary, I frowned. No familiar head of black hair towering over the other worshipers. It wasn't like him to be absent from church, and he'd missed last week, too.

But his whereabouts weren't my business. Not anymore. For all I knew, he'd decided to attend the Presbyterian congregation. Or the Methodist. There were any number of churches in town that would welcome him. He didn't have to be at this one, even if he always had been before.

A few pews ahead of me, Mrs. Gretson leaned over and coaxed Wilma to sit down and face the front. But the smile I'd seen on the little girl's face before she turned warmed me more than if a hot brick had nestled near my feet.

Ten months ago, Hazel had found Wilma keeping vigil near her dying mother. A little bit of a thing. Not even ready for school. Her mother implored our assistance, which we willingly gave. When her mother passed on, Wilma found a home with the Gretsons, a kindly family with three almost-grown children.

I surveyed our current charges. It was now my responsibility to search out more families that would imitate the Gretsons' generosity. The weight of that task dropped on my chest. *Help me to communicate the need, Lord, so that each child might find their place. Put them in loving homes, just as You did for me.*

And Blaine.

My throat tightened. Would he forever invade my thoughts?

A small hand sought mine as organ notes resounded through the room. I looked down, smiled at Janet, and received back her gap-toothed grin. Breath flooded back into my chest. I had much more important things to think about than a broken heart.

When Pastor Uland finished his benediction, I motioned my little flock toward the open doors. In spite of the frigid temperature, a bright sun illuminated the blue sky. Each of our children shook hands with Pastor Uland before skipping down the steps and onto the sidewalk.

"A wonderful sermon as usual, Pastor." I extracted my hand as quickly as possible, hoping to pull on my mittens before my fingers froze.

His eyes twinkled just a bit. "I see you are taking to your new position. They were quite well behaved today, weren't they?"

"Yes. At least during the service." I glanced at the scattered children, some talking with friends from school, others with children they'd known in the Home.

"Even a small victory is a victory, Miss Sillsby."

I nodded and moved forward, stopping to speak with those long connected to the Home and its children, receiving their congratulations. Did I notice a new respect in their eyes, their manners, or did I just imagine it?

The crowd thinned. A commotion of boyish voices drew my attention. The familiar head jutting above them sent my chin downward, my eyes intent on the frozen ground. Did I want to encounter him here? Now?

"Aw, Blaine. It's not that cold."

"We played baseball and everything yesterday."

"You said we could dig up all that old stuff and make a bonfire. It'll be more fun while it's winter."

My stomach somersaulted as I lifted my gaze and studied the man who'd held my heart for so many years. His smile didn't come as quickly as usual—and it didn't reach his eyes. I wondered if my expression looked the same. The ache of missing him nearly caved my chest. If we couldn't be husband and wife, couldn't we at least remain friends?

I could act as if nothing had changed. He'd either follow suit or—

I couldn't contemplate the "or."

A deep breath solidified my determination. I sauntered to the outskirts of the small group. "How are you, Blaine?"

His head snapped in my direction. Wary eyes finally softened to unease over a forced smile. "They want to start work on the garden."

I smiled, then grimaced, remembering the stack of bills Hazel had given me to enter into the cash book. Expenses up. Donations down. Would Blaine continue his generosity or would it be curtailed by my choosing the Home over him?

A new thought froze my heart. His mortgage. No doubt he'd need to sell his surplus, not give it away. Especially considering it was winter. He'd have no real income until fall's harvest. Would Blaine consider his work in our garden his freewill offering? Just this morning, Mrs. Fore had pointed out her dwindling supplies and wondered aloud when we'd see Blaine again.

If he didn't bring us food this week, we'd have a higher grocery bill. Not a good thing, according to Hazel. The budget had so little room for error.

I wanted to voice our need for him to continue his generosity, but I feared it would sound different now that I held the title of matron. What had been a gift of the heart might now be considered coerced.

His gaze remained glued to mine, though he spoke to the boys. "I'll be around in another week or so. We'll see if the ground's thawed enough for you to break up the frozen soil."

Hoots and whistles joined the hurrahs. Blaine cupped my elbow and angled me away from the boys.

"Congratulations." It was spoken through a crooked smile, but it sounded more like condolence than felicitation.

I tried to grin, as if the word put us back on more normal footing. But it didn't. I felt unstable, as if I were walking across a frozen pond. My mouth tightened, but I refused to let the smile fall away. We needed to talk, to clear things between us.

"So you haven't changed your mind." His words knifed through me. I shook my head. His hand fell from my arm and found his pocket.

I didn't want to ask the obvious question, but it stole into the air anyway. "You haven't, either?"

He shook his head but didn't look up.

"Oh, Blaine. I don't understand." Tears gathered behind my eyes, warming my face.

"I can't say I do, either. But it's where we are, isn't it? I have my land. I won't give it up now. If I can't have you and it . . ." He ran a shaky hand through his hair. "I don't understand how you can ask me to wait indefinitely and expect me to be happy about it."

"And I don't understand how you can want to marry me one moment and not the next."

He blew out a long breath and looked beyond me. "I didn't say I didn't want to. I said I couldn't. There is a difference."

"It doesn't feel any different."

His shoulders hunched. "To me, either," he mumbled. Then his gaze again locked onto something behind me. I turned to search for what had grabbed his attention.

Carter was slouching along behind four little girls. His head turned in our direction. Blaine raised a hand in greeting. Carter pulled a knit cap lower over his ears before he turned away, climbing into the back of the wagon without a hand to any of the little girls.

Blaine shook his head. "Too much of his father in him. He'll make life difficult for himself, I'm afraid. In spite of all we've tried to do for him."

I hugged my arms tight around me as I sidled a glance at Blaine. The same curve of the jaw and shape of the eyes as Carter, in spite of their opposite build and coloring. My chest constricted. If only Carter could have lived peaceably with him out at the farm. But that experiment hadn't worked any better than the two previous foster homes.

Tears blurred my vision. Maybe Blaine could give up on Carter, but I couldn't. To do so would be to deny everything within me. "He doesn't have to turn out like his father, you know."

Blaine's head traveled a slow road back and forth. "I haven't given up on him—just resigned myself to letting him test the reality he believes to be true. He's had his chances. Good homes, every one. And he's despised them all."

I agreed that Carter needed stability. But since he'd been with the Comstocks, he seemed more settled than before.

Didn't he?

When the team of horses pulled into the road and headed out of town, Carter looked back. From where I stood, his expression looked wistful. Longing.

I frowned. We tried to check on all the families that opened their homes to foster children, but the days didn't always lend themselves to timely visits. Had Hazel talked with the Comstocks recently? If not, I needed to bump them to the top of my list.

Chapter 9

Oatmeal roiled in the pot and bread crisped in the oven when I arrived in the kitchen Monday morning. Today we would say hello to Viola, and a new era would begin. A change of season—like the cold outside giving way to the warmth of spring. By July we'd have forgotten winter temperatures. In just the same way, it would soon seem to everyone as if I'd been matron for years.

Or so I hoped.

"You're up and about early." Mrs. Fore stirred the oats as the steam reddened her cheeks. "Anxious about the new girl?"

"Not much." I poured a cup of coffee, sipped it black, and hoped it would quell the churning in my stomach over Miranda. I begged God to let her slip through the door as usual. I needed to be available for Viola on her first day, not scrubbing floors and walls in preparation for Hazel's goodbye reception a week from Friday.

Lifting my chin, I told myself to take courage. No matter what Miranda chose in regard to her job, I would meet the challenge.

I set my cup aside and joined Mrs. Fore in the breakfast preparation. "Did Miranda say anything to you on Saturday?"

"About what?"

"I don't know. Anything . . . unusual?"

"Not as I can recall."

I carried bowls and spoons to the dining room, then brought out the large trivet for the steaming pot of oatmeal I would place on the sideboard. Viola would do these tasks tomorrow morning. A niggle of regret warned me that I'd miss interacting with the children, but I tamped it down. All of us would get used to the new arrangement. Even me.

Viola and her mother arrived to set up Viola's new room while the dining room table filled with children. Miranda still didn't appear. I tried to ignore my disappointment, though I'd believed it would turn out this way. No courtesy of a formal resignation. Just abandonment.

I gathered empty bowls and stacked them, still fuming over Miranda. I charged toward the kitchen. "Mrs. Fore, I'll need—"

Movement caught my eye. I turned. Miranda bustled inside, teeth chattering. She wriggled fraying mittens from her hands and shoved them into her coat pocket before glancing at me. Then she sat to a bowl of oatmeal Mrs. Fore set on the table.

A tight-lipped smile stretched my face. "So glad you're here this morning, Miranda."

Her head jerked up, spoon suspended in midair. "I'm not late."

"I didn't say you were. I'm just . . . surprised to see you."

Her eyes narrowed. "Why?"

I lifted one shoulder, let it drop again. "After our conversation Saturday, I wasn't sure what you meant to do. You left me no indication."

Her spoon clattered against the table. "You thought I would quit?" Her head wagged back and forth. "You don't know anything about me, do you?"

"Miss Sillsby?" Viola stepped into the kitchen, fresh-faced and eager.

My mouth tugged upward. "Just call me Sadie."

Viola's whole face lit with elation, as if I'd handed her a platter of gold bars instead of a gesture of friendship and equality. She did seem young. Had I appeared so to Hazel the day I'd moved in as her assistant? And if her youth startled me, what must Mrs. Fore and Miranda think of Viola's honey-gold curls and wide eyes?

I cleared my throat. "Miranda, Mrs. Fore, please meet Viola Brown, my new assistant."

Mrs. Fore gushed; Miranda grunted. Exactly as I'd expected.

I hooked my arm through Viola's, praying she'd be easier to handle than Miranda, and that perhaps I would come to call her a friend.

The next afternoon, I bundled up Lily Beth as soon as she'd swallowed her after-school slice of bread. I left the others to Viola. It would do them all good to begin to learn to get along without me.

Hazel hadn't agreed with my decision to let Dr. Lawson evaluate Lily Beth's condition, but I was willing to take the chance. I needed to know if something—anything—could be done to fix the girl's eyes. I'd worry about the money to pay for it later.

Lily Beth and I skipped and sang until we rounded the corner to Dr. Lawson's office. His home, really. A large sandstone structure with a wraparound porch and turrets, putting me in mind of a castle from a fairy tale. At the steps of the imposing structure, Lily Beth pulled back.

I knelt in front of her, my hands cupping her tiny waist. "Dr. Lawson just wants to look you over, love bug. He's a nice man. I promise." I tugged her forward.

She didn't resist. At least not outwardly. But her angelic face took on a downcast quality.

We approached the side door that led directly to the rooms where Dr. Lawson saw patients. In the small anteroom, we removed our coats and waited. Then an inside door opened and Dr. Lawson beckoned us into an examination room.

He lifted Lily Beth onto the table. "And how are you today, little lady?"

The girl's expression softened.

Dr. Lawson talked with her throughout the examination. Ears, nose, throat, reflexes—and eyes. When he finished, he opened the door that led into his personal domain. "Mrs. Lawson?" he called out. "I have a patient who very much needs some bread and jam."

Gwen Lawson appeared, her smooth face alive with a radiant joy as she held out her hand to Lily Beth. Thin and elegant, I guessed her to be in her forties, though she resembled a much younger woman. Why didn't she and the doctor have any children of their own? Had anyone ever asked them if they'd be interested in taking one of ours?

Dr. Lawson shut the door, concealing them from view, leaving me to desert my musings in light of his serious expression.

"She's in fine health."

I nodded. "I'm more concerned about her eyes."

"The vision doesn't seem to be greatly affected."

"I understand, but don't you think straightening them is still a good idea? Or is that even possible?"

He blew out a long breath. "I'd need to take her to Philadelphia and allow a specialist to evaluate the correct treatment. If there are serious issues, surgery would be required, but often a simple set of eyeglasses will draw the pupils into correct alignment."

"I see." My heart sank toward the floor. Funds didn't exist to travel to Philadelphia or consult a specialist. Hazel had tried to explain this to me, but I still couldn't wish I'd listened. If there was a way to help Lily Beth, I'd find the money somewhere. Could I do any less than what had been done for me?

Dr. Lawson rubbed a hand down the graying hair on his chin. "Let me make a few inquiries and see what I can discover. I'm not promising anything, but don't despair yet. We may be able to help the girl in some way."

I accepted Dr. Lawson's warm handshake and encouraging smile. Then I went to find Lily Beth. I wouldn't mention anything to her yet. For now, she remained content. But I wanted her to have things she couldn't conceive of—like eyes that didn't make others turn away or poke fun, that wouldn't put off potential foster families considering opening their homes.

Lily Beth believed her mother would return for her, but I

had no such illusions. If we didn't care for this child, no one would. And I refused to let that happen.

I took my noon meal with Viola, Mrs. Fore, and Miranda, just as Hazel had always done. Miranda's brooding eyes stared at me over the top of her spoon. But in spite of her attitude, I couldn't fault her work at all. I sipped my soup, grateful to do something I knew how to do already.

"The cellar shelves are growing empty. I'm still on the lookout for Blaine." Mrs. Fore's statement cut off Viola's ceaseless chatter.

The girl blinked at the interruption. Her gaze rounded the table, stopping at each one of us before she found her tongue again. "Who's Blaine?"

I winced, then nudged my spoon into the hot broth and brought it to my mouth. Soon the mention of his name wouldn't rip away another piece of my already shredded heart. But today I could barely swallow. My spoon clattered against the side of the bowl.

"Not to your liking?" Miranda's expression challenged as boldly as her words.

I shifted my focus to Mrs. Fore but faltered beneath the unspoken questions in her piercing eyes.

"It's perfect, as usual. Just right for a chilly day." I bit into a slice of bread, eager for a reason to keep quiet.

Miranda's eyes narrowed before her gaze drifted to Viola's bewildered expression.

"Who's Blaine?" Viola asked again, this time tugging at Mrs. Fore's sleeve.

"Hush, dear." Mrs. Fore patted Viola's hand as she spoke, but she was still watching me.

I pressed my napkin to my lips, scooted my chair away from the table, and rose. I'd need to tell Mrs. Fore the truth soon. But with the financial reports due to the board, and the visit from the Children's Aid Society's representative looming, I had no energy for personal explanations. For the next week, I'd just do my best to avoid Miranda's hostility and Mrs. Fore's curiosity.

While Viola was writing some letters in the next room, the house quieted. I drew the ledger and several blank sheets of paper in front of me and stared at the numbers on the Expenditures page. All I had to do was make sense of them the way other people did. With just a glance, my classmates could add, subtract, multiply, and divide. But not I. I held my fingers in my lap and counted out every number in every function. It took longer that way, but I managed.

Mama Ramsey had always helped me with my math, even before she took me into her home. She would breeze into the parlor late each afternoon, her gentle voice calming my frenzy as we talked through the problems on the page. She never called me stupid, like the other children did. She never frowned, like my teacher did. No, Mama Ramsey smiled and explained, explained and smiled. Finally, she taught me to count on my fingers, then draw a line on the page every time I reached ten. Then I could count the tens and come up with the right answer.

Sometimes.

I read through the list of bills, a dollar amount accompanying each one, and groaned. I'd need to follow Hazel's example of totaling the expenditures weekly if I wanted the numbers to remain somewhat manageable. Already I'd let it go too long. The column stretched halfway down the page.

Holding my lip between my teeth, I counted on my fingers until I ran out and had to write the number down. Ten. Twenty. Thirty. Forty. I blew out a long breath, started again. Two hours later, my paper filled with chicken scratches, I found two numbers the same: $73.25.

That had to be right.

Relief loosened the tightness in my shoulders. With a deep breath, I held my pencil over the ledger book. Then I became aware of laughter, squeals, and shouts drifting in through the windowpanes. My children were home.

I scribbled $37.25 beneath the long column of expenditures. I held my breath and glanced at the facing page with its income notations. Hazel had added those before she left. My finger found the total: $52.37. I held up five fingers, then three. Yes, we'd brought in more than we'd paid out. I shut the book with a thud and gave a happy sigh.

Nothing at all to worry about.

Chapter 10

I t's almost seven o'clock, Sadie!" Viola's voice carried up the stairs.

I twisted, trying to see myself in the mirror at every angle. Just my best Sunday dress. This would be the last time I'd appear so shabby. At least the lace at my throat added a touch of elegance.

No longer needing to save for the future, I'd spent sixteen dollars of the twenty I'd collected in the jar on my dresser for a suit of my own. Almost one entire month's wages. It was extravagant, but I wanted to make a good impression on the Children's Aid Society representative on Monday, as well as in my other public dealings. But the suit wouldn't arrive until tomorrow.

What would Blaine think to see me dressed so fine?

I huffed out a sarcastic laugh. When I donned my suit on a Sunday, likely he wouldn't even notice. My bravado wilted. Maybe I just hoped he wouldn't notice. It hadn't been as easy as I'd imagined to erase him from my daily thoughts. Or my nightly dreams.

I tried to shut off thoughts of Blaine and focus on my first meeting with the entire board of trustees. With a financial report to present. I pressed a hand to my stomach, unable to decide if I'd eaten too much or not enough at the supper table.

"Sadie! Mr. Riley's here."

Setting my old hat on my head, I jabbed the pin in place before racing down the stairs. Hastening into my coat and gloves, I grabbed the stack of reports from Viola before hurrying out the door and into Mr. Riley's large touring car. In the front seat, the supple leather felt as soft as warm butter. A fitting conveyance for the owner of the largest lumber mill in the area—and a far cry from Blaine's ancient buggy or his rickety wagon.

Squeezing my eyes shut, I focused my thoughts on the meeting as Mr. Riley maneuvered the vehicle through narrow streets. I'd known Mr. Riley since my childhood. He attended our church and had been friends with Mama and Papa Ramsey. But the seven other men that comprised the board—one representative elected from each congregation in town—I knew only by name and occupation. Once more, I ticked off the list in my head.

Gerald Brumbaugh. Undertaker.

R. L. Findlay. Gas company manager.

Sinclair Baker. Hotel manager.

Daniel Delp. Banker.

Harold Wise. Farmer.

Ben Sheeder. Merchant.

Max Philpot. Butcher.

All upstanding men in their churches and the community. Men who would scrutinize the new matron and her work.

I clasped my gloved hands in my lap and bowed my head, asking the Lord to calm my agitation. I wanted to present myself well, didn't want them to regret accepting Hazel's recommendation. Their impression would reflect on her judgment as much as on my own character.

A few minutes later, we arrived at the Abbey church, with its tall steeple and ivy-covered stones. The heavy wooden door closed behind us with a hollow thud that echoed through the building. Red carpet muted our steps as we made our way past the sanctuary, down a hall, and into what I surmised was a Sunday school room.

Mr. Riley took my wraps, then motioned me to a chair at the front. The rest of the men took their seats. Mr. Riley opened with a prayer. Then business commenced.

"Our objective this evening is to evaluate the financial state of the Raystown Home. After our last quarterly report, several of us had concerns." He turned to me. "I assume you've brought the information we asked for, Miss Sillsby?"

I stumbled to my feet and handed the page of figures copied in Viola's neat hand to each member. I pulled in a deep breath.

Yesterday, I'd been satisfied with my work. Today, I wasn't nearly as sure the numbers were correct. All the moisture left my mouth and seemed to find its way to my palms. I rubbed the dampness down the sides of my skirt. I'd looked over the totals Viola had transcribed. Even with my limited understanding, I knew things didn't look good.

Mr. Riley scratched his head and frowned. "I confess, I had hoped to see quite a different story when we looked at the year so far."

Other men murmured agreement.

Dampness spread to my forehead and the back of my neck. What if I'd done something wrong? Would they see it? Point it out? Then I realized I'd never actually compared my answer to the amount in the bank book.

Mr. Findlay stood. "While this month seems to be more on target, it doesn't supply the shortfalls of the previous one. Over the course of eight months, only two have managed a surplus. That, gentlemen, does not make for a sustainable operation."

Mr. Philpot rose. "As much as I hate to say it, I believe we must consider the viability of continuing this ministry."

I sucked in a sharp breath and sat hard in my chair. Continuing? Had I understood correctly?

"Excuse me." My voice squeaked like an iron hinge. All heads turned in my direction. "May I ask exactly what you mean, Mr. Philpot?"

The man's face reddened. "I mean if we cannot find the appropriate funding, we may have to cease operation of the Home."

"Cease operation?" I jumped from my seat. "But the Raystown Home has been serving the children of Huntingdon County for almost twenty-five years!" My feet carried me from one end of the room to the other. "Children who have nowhere to go need us. If we close our doors, who will be Jesus to these lost and hurting little ones?"

Mr. Philpot's pallor returned to normal, but his expression remained grim. "I understand and applaud your passion, Miss Sillsby, but if the Lord wants this work to continue, He'll have to provide the money to sustain it."

I tried not to notice several of the men staring at the floor, but they were impossible to ignore. I clasped my shaking hands together and willed my eyes to stay dry and my voice strong. The Raystown Home must continue to exist. If it didn't, what would happen to children like Cynthia or George or Lily Beth? I had to make these men see reason.

"If we close, these children will have to leave the county, leave any sense of continuity in their already topsy-turvy lives."

"But don't some of the children already leave the county—and even the state? Through adoption or fostering?" Mr. Brumbaugh asked.

I pressed my lips together, not wanting to acknowledge the truth but finding no way around it. "Yes, though the number is quite small."

"Still, those children adapt."

"Yes, but—"

Mr. Riley stepped in front of me. "I think most of us can see the wisdom in such a consideration."

Mr. Wise, a white-haired gentleman, faced the group. I returned to my seat, feeling small beneath his towering height. "What if we set a fleece to help us decide what it is the Lord desires us to do?"

A throat cleared. Men shifted in their chairs. I sat tall and straight. And perfectly still.

Mr. Wise let the room quiet again. "Perhaps the only true test would be to raise the entire amount of next year's operating budget. That way we could work from an amount we have rather than from an amount we guess at for each year's budget. The funds raised during a year would then supply the need for the following one."

Several men mumbled their assent. I didn't even flinch, though my heart tumbled over itself like a rock rolling down the side of a mountain.

"How much money does it take to keep the Home going for a year?" Mr. Baker looked at the paper I'd handed him.

Mr. Riley arranged his spectacles closer to his eyes. "Looks like close to forty-five hundred dollars. That is assuming no unexpected expenses crop up."

"Extra funds could be sought for special projects," Mr. Delp said. "I agree with the idea of raising next year's budget now. Otherwise, we fall further and further behind. What point is there in raising money that is used to pay off old shortfalls? People prefer giving to present or future needs, not past ones."

Mr. Riley pulled out his pocket watch and snapped open the gold cover. Then his thumb pushed it shut again. He took a deep breath, as if he didn't want to say the words he had to say. "Let's put it to a vote, then. All in favor of continuing our present course if we raise the 1910/1911 operating budget before July 1, the start of our new fiscal year, please raise your hand."

Hands crept into the air as I looked from one man to another.

Mr. Riley lifted his hand last, his shoulders slumping in defeat as he did. "The vote is unanimous. We must have forty-five hundred dollars in hand before July 1 or we shut our doors and assume the Lord has other plans. And I think it best that we do not advertise our fleece. Let us each go about raising support for the Home as usual and see what the Lord provides."

Each man's nod shoveled a heavier weight onto my chest.
"Are you agreed, Miss Sillsby, to keep this between us?"
Reluctantly, I added my consent.

"Good. Then let us pray for His will to be done."

I bowed my head along with the rest, but I hardly heard
Mr. Riley's prayer. I already knew God's heart in the matter.
He desired us to continue our mission—to take in children
and place them out, to offer them salvation of body and soul.
I lifted my chin. I, for one, would be expecting a miracle.

Chapter 11

I closed the front door of the Raystown Home, then clicked the lock with as little noise as possible. Leaning against the door, I listened for Mr. Riley's automobile to putter away. On legs flimsy as string, I tottered into the dark parlor and slumped onto the sofa.

Deep cold sank into my limbs, like the dark, dank corner where I had curled in a ball and tried to ignore the pain in my legs, the discomfort in my belly.

I trembled at the memory. Would the Lord give me the responsibility of this place and then snatch it away? I'd never believed Him to be capricious, but now I wondered. Such an enormous mission from the board, then muzzled like an undisciplined pup.

Covering my face with my hands, I breathed deeply. Not that I'd want to tell Mrs. Fore, Viola, or Miranda anyway. I didn't need them frightened into searching out other work before it was truly necessary. Perhaps for now the mandate of silence was for the best. At least here.

But, oh how I wished I could talk it over with Hazel. Or Blaine.

No, not Blaine. I couldn't bear the thought of any smugness on his part. It would be too humiliating to tell him. As if I were begging him to renew our former understanding.

Dragging myself off the sofa, I headed to my bedroom. To think. To pray. At the top of the stairs, I heard a child's muffled cry and hesitated. Viola would attend to things, wouldn't she? Or had her senses not yet become attuned to the children's needs?

I waited. No sound stirred behind Viola's door. I didn't want to see another living soul at that moment, but better a child than Viola.

Creeping into the girls' room, I wondered if I'd imagined the noise. Then a sniffle and a hiccup sounded from the bed in the corner. Lily Beth's bed. I knelt down and pulled the little girl around to face me.

"What's the matter, love bug?" I whispered.

Stuttering breaths as she shook her head. I smoothed back her puffy wisps of hair. "Do you miss your mother?"

Her little teeth appeared over her bottom lip, but then she shook her head. Once.

At least she was honest.

"Bad dream?"

This time she nodded. I scooped her up, carried her into my bedroom, laid her in the middle of my bed, and pulled the extra quilt over her nightgown-clad body.

"See? I'm here. And everything's fine. You go on back to sleep and I'll carry you to your bed later." Whatever had frightened her would likely flee after a few minutes in the light.

Her mouth twitched into a smile that disappeared as quickly as it had formed. I sat on the edge of the bed and stroked her head. She closed her eyes, those pitiful, lopsided eyes. I leaned down and kissed her forehead, heard her sigh.

As I plaited my hair into one long braid, her breathing grew even. I shed my clothes, my corset, and shivered into my flannel gown. I stood above her for a moment and prayed that she would find rest, that the Home would find donors, and that each of the children in our care would know God and live lives worthy of Him.

Quilt and all, I carried her back to the girls' room, back to her bed. She moaned, turned, but stayed asleep.

If only everything in life were fixed as easily as a child's nightmares.

"Miss Sillsby!" The reedy voice called from across the churchyard after the service on Sunday, a gloved hand waving in my direction. I directed Viola to watch over the children and proceeded to the outskirts of the lawn.

I'd made as much peace as I could with the board's directive since Thursday night, convinced that constant prayer teamed with constant work would meet the need—or at least impress the CAS representative who would arrive tomorrow.

Miss Pembrooke's withered face stretched into a smile at my approach. Once my teacher, now the teacher of those under my care, she wrapped her pencil-thin arms around my waist and patted my cheek. "So nice to hear of your good fortune, my dear. Such an honorable place you've achieved."

My chest swelled with pride. I needed those words, needed the confidence they gave me for Monday's meeting with the Children's Aid Society representative. I opened my mouth to thank Miss Pembrooke for her kindness, but she continued on.

"Now that you're in charge, dear, I feel there are some things you ought to know."

My heart sank. There were those in town who delighted in revealing the shortcomings of our children, but I hadn't expected Miss Pembrooke to be one of them. Remembering our need, I worked to keep a smile on my face and honeyed my reply. "I'd be happy to hear whatever you have to tell me, Miss Pembrooke."

She darted a glance across the scattering congregation and then grabbed my arm, pulling me closer. "It's that Wellsmith boy."

"Blaine?" My head whipped around. Blaine stood talking with Pastor Uland. My heart twisted. Still, I didn't see why Miss Pembrooke would have issue with Blaine. Or take up that issue with me.

"Not him," Miss Pembrooke hissed. "The other one. The younger one."

Slowly, I turned to face her, my heart pattering fear. "Carter?"

She gave a decisive nod. "That's the one. My friend Mr. Williamson, who teaches at the high school, told me that the boy is truant as often as not. And running with an unsavory crowd. Troublemakers, every one."

I seethed as her eyes gleamed with the thrill of being the one to inform me of things I obviously didn't know, but I kept a smile on my lips and kindness in my voice. "I appreciate your concern for the boy, Miss Pembrooke."

Gossip always blew things out of proportion. Likely things

were much less serious. Best to allow her to feel she'd done her duty and move on. "I'll investigate the situation immediately."

"Looks like you have your chance now." She nodded toward something—or someone—behind me. I turned. Mr. Comstock was charging in my direction, red-faced. Miss Pembrooke disappeared from my side.

I braced myself for an onslaught of displeasure, then decided to take the upper hand. "How are you this fine morning, Mr. Comstock?"

He stopped so fast he almost toppled over. "Not as well as you, apparently."

My stomach sank. "I'm so sorry."

"You should be."

My breath caught at the ferocity of the words.

"That boy, that dadblamed boy." He almost growled.

I wanted to cower under his anger, but to do so would be to admit defeat before a fight. I pulled back my shoulders, determined to be everything a matron ought. "How may I assist you, Mr. Comstock?"

"He didn't come home until almost daybreak. Daybreak! And me with impressionable girls asking where he'd been all night. Tomcatting, I imagine. Leastwise, I hope he's not been doing worse."

Oh, Carter, how could you? "I'm so sorry, Mr. Comstock. I'm sure if you talk to him—"

His cheeks puffed out as his face grew redder. "That boy won't listen to talk! I've tried! The good Lord knows I've tried. I think he'll have to lea—"

"Wait." I held up both palms and swallowed hard. "What if—what if I talked with him?" I needed Carter to stay with the Comstocks. After the failed attempt of living with his own brother, the board wouldn't have much more patience with him. Carter was almost out of options.

Mr. Comstock hummed as he considered. "I'd need to know he'd really heard what you said, make sure he seemed willing to try—really try—to fit in with our family, our rules."

"Of course. Absolutely. Why don't we all sit down together—you, your wife, Carter, and me—and talk this out? Is there a day this week that would be convenient for you?"

More grumbling, but his fury seemed to have faded to frustration. "Thursday after supper would do us."

Relief trickled over my tense limbs. At least I could deal with the CAS man before I managed this tangle. Then I noticed Blaine inching in our direction, eyes narrowed, face stormy. I hurried my words, trying to get Mr. Comstock on his way.

"I believe we can get things worked out in the best interest of everyone."

Mr. Comstock tipped his hat, bid me good-day, and stalked off toward his wagon before Blaine reached my side.

"What was that all about?" His deep voice both composed and unnerved me. I couldn't answer, not without revealing the whole truth.

His hand gripped my elbow. "You'd tell me if Carter was in trouble, right?"

I let my head nod once. My conscience pummeled me for the lie.

On Monday morning, I dressed in my new clothes. The single-breasted light green coat skimmed past my hips over a matching gored skirt with kilted pleats at the knees and trim to match the coat. I twisted my hair up the back of my head rather than wrapping it in a knot at my neck and surveyed myself in the small mirror.

Very respectable.

Then I ran a hand across my forehead, down the side of my face. Did I look anything like my mother? I had no idea. While I could still remember the darkness, the stench, the chill of that place, I could not remember her face.

Perhaps that was best. I didn't know. All I knew was I'd been rescued. I could do nothing less for these now living beneath our roof. I lifted my chin. Though the amount we needed to raise was daunting, nothing was too big for my God. I'd seen the things He'd done for friendless children. Children like me. And I refused to believe He'd abandon us now.

Today I would be the face and voice of the Raystown Home for Orphan and Friendless Children. At this moment, nothing else mattered.

Sleepy voices drifted from the hall. I smiled. Viola had indeed done her job in rousing the children. Passing through the rooms after her, I prodded those still abed. Before I reached the stairs, I peeked into the girls' room once more. Lily Beth sat on the edge of her bed, all dressed, feet swinging above the floor.

"Let's go to breakfast, sweet girl." I held out my hand. Her fingers found mine. I squeezed. She squeezed back. No, it wouldn't be hard to represent these children and their needs to the CAS—or to the world.

Mrs. Fore looked up as we entered the kitchen. "You look pretty as a picture!"

I lifted an apron from a peg on the wall.

"Oh, no. You'll not sully those fine clothes on my account. You put that right back."

With a frown, I did as she said.

"Sit at the table and keep me company while I finish up with breakfast." She pulled out a chair. I sat.

Miranda drifted through the back door, hung her wraps, and took the bowl of oatmeal Mrs. Fore had ready for her. She sat down next to me, her gaze sidling in my direction before darting away again.

Viola whisked in and out of the dining room. Janet and Cynthia skipped into the kitchen hand-in-hand a few minutes later, followed by several of the younger boys eager to fill their stomachs. I stood, needing to be busy, not to sit and think about the day ahead.

The back door flew open, pinning me against the window. I grabbed the handle, ready to shut out the icy air.

"Blaine, you sweet boy," Mrs. Fore called. "Get inside and put your things down."

I held my breath, wanting to close the door but wanting to hide behind it at the same time. Why this morning? The chilly air swirled in around us. My teeth chattered. I secured the door with a silent click and tried to blend into the wall.

"Thought since I was coming this way, I'd deliver your order from the grocer, as well." A burlap bag and a box of canned goods thudded onto the table as Miranda skittered away to her work.

Mrs. Fore patted his cheek.

A blush colored his face, sending my heart reeling in his direction. Oh, to be able to rest my head on his broad chest, to let him soothe away my worries about today. About Carter. About money. With great effort, I reined in my desires. I needed to leave. Too much depended on this day, on my clarity of thought. If I could inch along the wall behind him, maybe I could escape without detection.

One silent step. Then another. Just a bit farther and I'd be there.

"And doesn't our Sadie look lovely this morning?" Mrs. Fore wiped her plump hands on her apron.

Blaine shifted around. My foot stopped midstride. I drew up as tall as possible and forced myself to smile right at him.

His gaze traveled from my eyes to the hem of my skirt. I clasped my hands behind my back, trying to still the trembling. Waiting for him to speak made me as nervous as a bird in a barn full of cats. Even now I cared what he thought, though I wouldn't let him know it.

His jaw clenched. "You look . . . good, Sadie."

I nodded, not trusting myself to speak, but the silence set my fingers twitching.

Mrs. Fore sent gawking children into the dining room. I blessed her in my head. Neither Blaine nor I moved. I stared at the floor. He cleared his throat. I looked up. The concern in his eyes captured mine. If only I didn't long to lose myself in the dark depths of those eyes, or didn't remember the touch of his lips against mine.

He stepped toward me, his hand almost touching the soft green fabric of my skirt, his breath flowing warm on my neck. "Please don't shut me out, Sadie. Not when it concerns Carter. I want to know, even if he doesn't want me to know."

How could I resist such a plea? Too many secrets crowded my head. I glanced toward the dining room, then pulled Blaine into the small storeroom.

"I don't know much myself. I'm meeting with the Comstocks on Thursday—"

"I'm coming with you."

"No." I stepped away from him, my hand on the doorknob. "You can't. It isn't your job. It's mine."

He studied me for a long moment, the war between inserting himself into the situation and holding himself back visible on his face. Sadness framed his eyes. "Yes, I guess it is."

I spun around, returned to the kitchen, and busied myself stacking empty pans in the sink. I had to focus on winning over the CAS representative. Dealing with Carter. Hosting our public farewell to Hazel. Finding good homes for our children, and raising thousands of dollars in three months.

In the midst of all that, I had no time to nurse a broken heart.

A few moments later, a blast of cold air slapped my back.

Chapter 12

Just before two o'clock, I secured my hat on my head and shrugged into my coat. Viola looked me over and pronounced me quite fit for the task at hand.

"Any questions about what I need you to do while I'm gone?" I asked.

Viola's eyes grew wide. "I just glanced through the mail. Thank-you notes, mostly. A few inquiries as to whether or not we can take another child." Her smile turned to a frown. "How do you want me to answer those?"

I cringed, knowing the truth was more desperate than she imagined. Yet how could we turn away any child in need? Wasn't that the very reason we existed?

"Leave those to me."

The clock chimed twice. Viola almost pushed me out the front door. "Go on, now. You'll be late."

A few minutes later, I climbed aboard the electric trolley for the quick trip into the center of town. Alone in a back seat, I prayed for something to go right this week.

The railroad tracks ran beside the Juniata River, the water sharpening the cool air as it blew across the current. I crossed my arms. The train station's waiting room would be warm, but I needed the sting of cold in my face to keep me attentive. I paced the covered platform in the company of a few others until the arriving engine chugged into view. Smoke billowed from its stack. Wheels squealed to a stop.

Through the railcar windows, I saw passengers stand, ready to disembark.

I smoothed my coat, wishing it didn't hide my new suit. A strand of loose hair brushed my face. I tucked it back into place.

How would I know the CAS representative? Hazel had given no indication of what type of man to expect. Likely she didn't know herself. I imagined he'd fall within the range of our board members—a businessman of middling age. Or perhaps he would more resemble Professor Stapleton, a man in his thirties, slight and bookish.

People on the platform united with those stepping from the train. Others disappeared into the depths of the railcars, valises in hand. I craned my neck in search of someone searching for someone.

The spill of people slowed as I made my way toward the front of the train. Then I changed direction.

A man was standing near the ticket office, his back to me, a satchel hanging from one hand, a carpetbag from the other. I looked around. No one else took note. Could this be him?

I moved closer, reached out to touch him on the arm, then changed my mind. I cleared my throat. "Excuse me."

The man turned. I tried to cough back my gasp. Golden

hair slicked down over a perfectly proportioned face. Classically handsome, with eyes the color of maple syrup and just as sticky. Surely this couldn't be the man I'd been sent to meet. He couldn't be more than twenty-five years old!

His head cocked to one side, and his eyes narrowed just a bit. "Miss Sillsby?"

I nodded, breath catching in my chest as a slow grin lifted his perfect lips into a wide smile.

I'd never seen so handsome a man. Had I dreamed him to appear more comely than he was? I blinked, but he remained the same.

He set down his carpetbag and held out his hand. "Earl Glazier, Children's Aid Society of Pennsylvania."

I shook his hand and chided myself for not spitting out words of welcome, but my mind couldn't seem to form them.

"I believe there is a hotel close by?"

My tongue finally loosed. "Yes. In the next block. I'll take you there first, let you get situated."

"Wonderful." We walked side by side, the soles of our shoes scuffing against the wooden sidewalk in opposite beats. We turned onto the street, the redbrick hotel rising on our left, his head twisting from side to side as he took in Raystown. "Nice little town."

"Not much compared to Philadelphia, I imagine."

His laughter rang out as if I'd told a joke instead of made an observation, but it coaxed a smile to my face all the same. Perhaps working with this man wouldn't be as difficult as I'd imagined. At least the scenery would be pleasant.

We turned in at the hotel. Sunshine streamed through the large picture windows, brightening the ornate lobby furniture.

I accompanied him to the long, polished counter, then felt the awkwardness of my presence.

"I'll wait over there until you get things arranged." I moved away.

"It won't take long," he called. Heads turned, looking for the source of such a public conversation.

Heat crawled up my neck. I pressed my lips into a tight smile before locating a seat behind one of the large columns near the back of the room. I unfastened my coat, wishing for a piece of paper to fan my face. I fingered one of the black buttons on the jacket of my suit. So far this day hadn't gone the way I'd imagined, but I was glad I'd splurged on a new outfit in which to face it.

Very glad indeed.

While Mr. Glazier arranged his things in his room, I had time to adjust my expectations to reality. I definitely preferred this reality. Someone young and committed to the cause of helping abandoned children had to be a kindred spirit.

"I'm all yours, Miss Sillsby." Mr. Glazier stood before me, arms spread wide. The volume of his voice drew furtive glances from others milling around the lobby. I jumped to my feet, buttoned my coat, and steered him out the door of the hotel.

His gaze roamed over my face, sparking heat I knew reddened my cheeks. "I must say, I never expected the matron to be quite so . . . youthful."

Neither did I. I tried to think of something to say as we walked the half block to the trolley stop, but we arrived there with quiet still between us.

He shoved his hands into his pants pockets and rocked forward on his toes. "Quite a bit of bustle for such a small place."

I looked around with fresh eyes, trying to see Raystown as a stranger would. On this cobblestoned street alone stood a dry goods store, an undertaker's establishment, a tailor, a confectionary, and a furniture store. A prosperous town, even if it was smaller than Philadelphia. My throat tightened. This place, the town and the orphanage, meant so much to me. I wanted this man to understand that.

"It's not all that small, really. The borough sprawls out a good bit north of the Juniata River. There's a power plant and the glassworks, a brick factory not far away, and lots of lumber and farming interests. Not to mention the other businesses that spring up in a good-sized place. There's a hospital being built, and a dam, as well."

His eyes found mine again. "And how long have you been living here, Miss Sillsby?"

I sucked in the chilled air. "You mean here in Raystown—or at the Home?"

"So you grew up in the area?"

"Yes, I did. I—" Did he need to know I'd been an inmate of the Home in my younger years, or would it be prudent to keep that fact unrevealed? I stepped forward, looked up the street for any sign of the approaching trolley.

"Ah, a local girl. And how long have you been in your current position?"

"I . . . well . . ." I fumbled with my handbag, wondering how to answer. Then I caught myself, stilled my hands, and looked him straight in the eye. "I've recently taken over for Miss Brighton. She's to be married next month."

His grin widened. "New leadership, then."

At the clack of trolley wheels, we both stepped away from the street. The car stopped in front of us. I drew coins from my purse for our passage and deposited them before taking an empty seat on the third row. I expected Mr. Glazier to take the seat across the aisle, but he didn't. He sat down right next to me, his leg and arm pressed against mine.

It felt awkward to sit in such close quarters with a stranger. Although he didn't act with the formality of a stranger. Was that a trait of city dwellers—or just Mr. Glazier?

The trolley swayed as it wound its way through the streets of town, up toward the college. When we reached our stop, I stood. He did the same. Once the car continued on its way, he took my hand and secured it in the crook of his elbow.

"Lead on, Miss Sillsby." His arm rose in a gesture much like the actors I'd once seen at the theater in town. He wasn't like any of the men I knew, but I liked his flamboyance. It was interesting. Amusing. So different from the people I normally encountered.

"This way, sir," I said, joining in his gaiety. "But please, call me Sadie."

He stopped. I jerked backward just a bit. He placed his hand over his heart and bowed from the waist. "Only if you will address me as Earl, dear Sadie."

I raised my hand to my mouth to hide a giggle, wondering if he acted this way with everyone or just with me. If nothing else, it would be an entertaining few days.

But my laughter died as I remembered that Earl Glazier's visit had serious implications. We needed his recommendation, needed the Home to be aligned with the CAS, to gain some assistance in our current financial turmoil. I doubted his respect would be secured with childish behavior on my part. I was the matron now. I had to act as such.

My feet picked up the pace, eager to introduce him to my domain. There I could observe his interaction with the others and then adjust my conduct accordingly. I didn't want to be deemed young and silly. I needed him to like me. I needed him to take back a glowing report to his superiors at the Children's Aid Society and bring a great wave of funding our way.

Chapter 13

Here we are." I stopped at the bottom of the Home's steps, peering up at the high gable of the roof. Beautiful in my eyes, in spite of peeling paint on the eaves and the weathered wood that formed the porch. The square structure had been adequate when built in the early 1880s, but by the time I arrived a decade later, children crowded the rooms. When Blaine and Carter arrived a few years after me, before the century turned, the additional wing was under construction, jutting out like the long side of an L from the original building. It contained a large dining room downstairs and a spacious boys' room overhead. The kitchen had been attached to the house the year before I took the position as Hazel's assistant.

I frowned, seeing it anew. It could use some brightening up. Perhaps if I planted something with colorful blooms to draw the eye away from the shabbiness of the exterior. But that couldn't be done until spring peeked through the lingering winter.

The smell of baking ham greeted us as we came through

the front door. Earl breathed deeply before shrugging out of his coat and hanging it next to mine.

"We'll conduct our business in here." I opened the office door, turned, and bumped into Earl.

He motioned across the hall. "The parlor, I assume?"

"Double parlor, actually. And the kitchen was brought inside not very many years ago. It sits behind the office, though the staircase cuts through the space between, of course."

Earl nodded as he turned a slow circle. "Four bedrooms upstairs?"

"Yes. A small one for me, one for my assistant. Two large rooms for the children. One was created by knocking through the walls of two rooms; the other is part of the wing added a little over ten years ago."

"Yes, the wing. I noticed it when we walked up. Your organization owns the building outright, then?"

My jaw clenched as I pictured the column of expenditures. The largest of our expenses covered repayment for the construction and renovation. An immovable expense, according to Hazel. One that would remain for at least another decade.

Would Mr. Glazier—Earl—find fault with us over that? Or would our need recommend us to him all the more?

"Why don't we meet the staff?" I led Earl toward the kitchen. Mrs. Fore stooped over the open oven door, spoon in hand, stirring baked beans laced with brown sugar and bacon, sending even more flavor into the air.

Earl took another deep breath. "Smells mighty good, ma'am."

Mrs. Fore eyed him for a moment before straightening.

I stepped into the gap. "Mrs. Fore, please meet Mr. Glazier, from the Children's Aid Society of Pennsylvania."

"A pleasure, Mrs. Fore." He bowed in her direction. "I imagine it will be even more so after I make the acquaintance of your cooking."

I flinched, knowing Mrs. Fore's distrust of flowery, flattering words. She preferred Blaine's bluntness. Sure enough, she responded with a sniff instead of a thank-you before lifting the lid of the large roasting pan.

The spicy scent of cloves overpowered the sweet of the beans. I wondered briefly how much the ham had set us back. A question for another moment.

A thump overhead alerted me to Miranda cleaning upstairs. But where was Viola?

The back door burst open. Three breathless children raced inside.

"Shut the door, please," I called over their commotion. Cynthia rushed straight toward me, then threw her arms around my waist and buried her head in my middle. I placed my hand on her head, tipped it back so I could see her face. "What's wrong, sweet pea?"

"Teacher made me say my piece today. Only I couldn't say it. You forgot to help me. Everyone laughed." Her face returned to my clothing. My new clothing. Now being dampened by teary eyes and a runny nose.

How could I have forgotten? I lowered myself until I could peer straight into the girl's hazel eyes. "I'm so sorry, honey. Truly I am. Can you ever forgive me?"

She nodded. I pulled her close, squeezed her tight. I had forgotten her, but hadn't I instructed Viola to help her in my absence? Where was that girl, anyway? I shoved aside my irritation and focused on Cynthia's tear-streaked face.

"Don't worry, sweetheart. Viola will help you. And the next time teacher calls on you to recite, you won't be afraid. I promise."

She nodded. I patted her head as the little boys stomped into the kitchen. The bigger boys raced in only long enough to leave their books and return outdoors for the few chores that awaited them. Nancy and Sylvia whispered together, stealing glances at Earl and giggling.

Finally, Viola sauntered into the kitchen. Hands on my hips, I lifted my eyebrows toward the ceiling.

"Oh! I didn't realize the time." Her blue eyes went wide, and a blush found its way across her ivory cheeks as her gaze fixated on Earl. "Come along, children, and tell me all about your day." She threw a coquettish smile over her shoulder as she corralled the younger ones into the dining room, slices of bread in hand.

I stood dumbstruck. Had Viola just made eyes at our guest?

"You handled that child beautifully," Earl whispered near my ear. "No one would guess you haven't been ensconced in this establishment for years."

"That's because—" I clamped my lips shut, startled that the words had almost flown from my mouth without thought. "It's because I worked as Hazel's assistant for so long. Five years. Since I graduated from high school."

"Then that accounts for it, I guess."

I guess. I ducked my head and led him back to the office, determined to keep the past tucked inside dusty ledgers. At least for now.

As we waited for supper to be ready, I told Earl the history of the Home, how in the midst of a spiritual revival at the Brethren College, a group of students and professors began feeding and clothing indigent children. Then they realized the need for a more permanent place to house those left on their own. Not an institutional residence, but a place of transition, a home in which to wait while loving families were found to care for each child.

The land was donated, the house built. Families came forward to help.

Earl crossed one leg over the other. "An unusual history. Ahead of its time, really. This is the very model we wish more to employ for children in such situations. I attended the White House Conference on the Care of Dependent Children last year. President Roosevelt is very committed to exploring more effective ways to help children who find themselves in great need. In fact, we hope to create an agency in Washington to oversee all such operations that provide care to these children."

He continued on, describing the pending legislation for establishing a Federal Children's Bureau. I drank in his words, imagining the thrill of participating in such a meeting, helping make decisions that would affect so many children's lives.

"I forget, did you say earlier that the building is owned outright?"

I blinked. He'd switched back to our particular situation. It took me a moment to adjust my thinking.

"Yes. And no." I tried to keep my forehead from puckering,

my lips from curving downward. "Though our board of trustees felt the addition necessary, they had trouble raising the funds to build it. After much debate, they took out a loan, and then another for the kitchen attachment. We make a small payment to the bank each month with a larger payment at the end of each year." I wondered if the men who sat on our board now would have plunged us into such a precarious situation. I doubted it.

A low whistle skimmed from his lips. "Hard to run a place like this with that kind of fixed expense."

I peered out the open door, listening hard for Mrs. Fore's invitation to supper. The discussion of money made me uncomfortable, as if revealing the true state of things betrayed the board's confidence. But I knew that wasn't true. He'd come here to learn facts such as these. I'd simply been asked to withhold the total amount the board hoped to secure.

"Miss Sadie!" Cynthia's copper curls bounced as she stood in the office doorway. "Mrs. Fore says supper's ready."

I laughed, glad to see she'd forgotten her earlier angst. "We're on our way."

Earl grinned as the child raced away. My stomach fluttered. If I could keep him smiling, maybe everything would turn out fine.

When our plates sat empty and Viola and the children had been excused, Mrs. Fore bustled in and cleared the table.

I dabbed my napkin to my lips, then set it on the table. "Did you want to continue to work this evening or go back to your hotel and start again tomorrow?"

I pictured Hazel's calendar. Tomorrow I was supposed to speak to the women's club at the Methodist church. "Actually, I do have an engagement in the morning."

Earl turned serious. "Oh?"

I tucked a swatch of hair behind my ear and swiped my tongue over my bottom lip. "Part of my position requires me to expose our need to the community. Tomorrow, I'm speaking to the Women's Missionary Society at the Methodist church. They help fund our work here and like to have a yearly update."

He nodded, then pulled a small notebook from his jacket pocket. "Then let's continue for an hour or two more this evening, and I'll accompany you to your engagement in the morning."

I blinked. "You want to go with me?"

"Absolutely. Seeing every aspect of your work—not just the ledgers and your care for the children, but out in the community, too—will give me a better foundation for writing up my report." His lips curved into a full smile. "Besides, I can't think of a more pleasant proposition than accompanying a pretty lady and applauding her success."

My arms and legs tingled. A man who understood and appreciated my calling. Did it take such a simple thing to undo me?

Miranda stood in the doorway, cleared her throat. Her gaze focused on a point somewhere over our heads. "Mrs. Fore wants to know if you desire coffee and cake."

I jumped into the silence. "Mrs. Fore makes the best pie—"

"Cake today, miss."

My exuberance wilted faster than my daffodils. Of course Mrs. Fore wouldn't make pie. Blaine wasn't here.

"Just coffee, please." Earl's cultured cadence shoved Blaine from my thoughts. "And if you don't mind, I'll take my cup to the office while we plan for tomorrow." He smiled at Miranda. She blushed and looked away.

Was there a female in my employ not besotted with this man?

Oh yes. Mrs. Fore.

"Make that two cups, Miranda." I passed her without a glance.

"Thank you, miss," Earl said from behind me.

To my utter astonishment, Miranda gave a civil reply.

Chapter 14

Earl knocked on the front door just after the children bounded off to school the next morning. He swept his hat from his head and placed it over his heart.

"Are you ready, dear lady?"

His open expectation roiled my stomach. I hadn't been nervous about my speech, but suddenly I was. My mind raced to Cynthia. Was this how she felt when she stood before her class? I'd have more sympathy for her from now on. Attempting to talk myself into calm, I set my hat atop my head, tilted it just a bit, and pinned it in place.

I had nothing to fear from these ladies. I only had to speak from my heart, appeal to their already generous natures.

Twenty minutes later, Mrs. Jones, an elegant woman many years my elder, clapped her hands to be heard over the buzz of conversation. "Ladies, please be seated."

Seventeen women occupied the chairs arranged in rows in the small room in the basement of the Methodist church. Earl stood against the wall in the back. I perched on the edge of my seat, facing the group.

Mrs. Jones motioned toward me. "As you all know, one of the local charities we support each year is the Raystown Home for Orphan and Friendless Children. As you probably read in the newspaper, the Raystown Home has announced a new matron, Sadie Sillsby, who is with us today."

I smiled at the group as I pulled at the wrists of my gloves and stood before the gathering. "Good morning. I'm so happy to be with you today. I see many familiar faces, but a few new ones, too, so please indulge me as I relate a general overview of our mission."

The words flowed as I recounted our history and our heart for needy children. I explained how each church in town appointed one member to serve on our board of trustees, how we raised our financial support through freewill offerings, how the Home functioned in regard to the duties of the matron and her staff. Then I told the story of Wilma's placement in her foster home a few months ago. Of Joseph Dickens' adoption by a Centre County couple just last month. Of children who had been reunited with their parents and were doing well.

"In this past year, we have seen no decrease in the number of children who need assistance. Though we all consider this a ministry, it still requires money to feed and care for the children, keep up the facility, and pay our small staff. You have been a generous group in the past. I sincerely pray you will continue to allocate a portion of your funds for us in the future."

Earl's handsome face grinned from the back of the room. My smile widened. "By supporting the Raystown Home, you not only give a child in need a chance at a better future, you extend the necessities of life in the name of our Lord and

Savior. I know that each of you in this room desires to be a part of that kind of work." With a nod, I stepped back to my seat, accompanied by a polite smattering of applause.

A few minutes later, Mrs. Jones dismissed us to the refreshment table set up in the adjoining room. Earl appeared beside me, his hand lighting on the small of my back, like Blaine used to do. I shied away for a moment, willed my heart to slow its frantic pace. Earl only meant to be gentlemanly and kind.

"Fabulous," he whispered near my ear as he guided me into the next room. I thrilled to my toes.

My mouth held its easy grin as I milled through the throng of women, chatting with one and then another. Earl brought me a glass of punch and a plate with two small cookies, but he didn't intrude on my conversations. He stood back, observed. All while a smile played at his lips and his eyes almost danced.

Mrs. Allison swooped in, kissed my cheek. "Oh, Sadie. I know Cecilia Ramsey would have been proud. You've turned out so well."

My bubbling joy faltered. Would Earl read any of my history in those words? My gaze skated in his direction, but his attention had been captured by Mrs. McNeil. He smiled at the sour-faced old woman. I thanked heaven she'd decided to talk with him instead of me.

"Bless you, Mrs. Allison." I pressed my hand to hers. "I'm more grateful than you know."

She leaned in with a whisper. "And don't worry about the money. I'm treasurer of our group this year. I'll make sure we give as much as before, if not more."

"Thank you." I couldn't say more without releasing the tears that stood in my eyes.

The women drifted away in clusters until finally Earl led me out the door and to the trolley. Neither of us spoke until we reached our stop.

I wanted to skip ahead, wave my arms in the air, release my joy. If being matron meant more moments like today, I wanted to be matron forever.

Clutching Earl's arm, I tried to temper my excitement. "I had it straight from the treasurer's mouth that they will give at least their usual donation. Maybe more."

Earl laughed. "I'm not surprised. Part of what made your presentation so winsome is your passion. You obviously believe in what you are doing."

"Oh, I do!" The old image surfaced again. A disheveled, dirty little girl carried into a parlor by strong arms. Mrs. Fore and Mrs. Dilly, a widow who was then matron, soothing her with soft words, warm food, a soaking bath. Clean clothes. Kisses on sallow cheeks. I believed in that kind of love, that kind of care. Because I'd lived it.

"One woman did make an interesting comment, though." Earl slowed.

I moderated my pace, as well. "Oh? What was that?"

"Something to the effect of 'Blood will always tell.' I suppose she meant she didn't believe children from less than virtuous parents could be what their parents were not." He sighed. "I know there are many who hold to that way of thinking. The whole eugenics movement, for example."

How could I be so full of joy one moment and so empty of it the next? Eugenics. The belief that men and women without intelligence or moral character should be stopped from having children, for they would issue forth children with the same shortcomings.

Lily Beth would draw their scorn for both her mother's character and her own physical defects. Carter's behavior seemed to reinforce their theory, too. But there were other children who did not. Sally Johnson now lived in Philadelphia, married to an attorney, a mother of two bright and charming children. Harold Winston, a blacksmith in Belleville, had just been elected to the town council.

Myself. Matron of the Raystown Home.

And yet even as I rehearsed our successes, condemnation camped heavily on my shoulders.

I shuddered, remembering a ladies' tea, all the other guests having gone, Mrs. McNeil's shrill voice raised above its normal volume. I had trembled outside the parlor, listening.

"That girl will turn out just like her mother, you mark my words!"

"Now, Bertha. You can't know that." Mama Ramsey's voice remained calm. I strained to hear her words. "You're just upset. And with good reason. But you cannot impute the mother's sin to her child. Not if you claim to follow Christ."

Mrs. McNeil charged out the door. I jumped from her path, hid in the shadows. She never confronted me openly, but her rancor remained clear.

I wanted to sit down and weep but had no desire for Earl to see me like that. Yet I had to say something. Not only to him, but to myself. "People like that don't take into account the saving grace of Christ." I clung to my own words, desperate to believe them true.

"No, they don't. And they don't take into account wonderful people like you who give themselves to help change a child's world." His grin returned with no hint of suspicion.

I relaxed, then matched my stride to his. Mrs. McNeil had evidently kept my history to herself. For now. But I trembled to think that at any moment she could remind the world that the blood running in Sadie Sillsby's veins was that of a common prostitute.

Earl laced his hands behind his head and leaned back in his chair, a look of satisfaction on his perfect face. Voices drifted in from across the hall. Viola and the children. I hoped she'd made Cynthia practice her recitation. And Janet always needed special attention. Did Viola notice Lily Beth or overlook her? And what about the boys? How did she handle their energy?

"Where are you, Sadie?"

"What?" My attention whipped back to Earl.

He leaned forward, draping one arm across the edge of the desk. "We've been working quite diligently these past two days. Why don't you and I go out for a quiet dinner tomorrow night, sweet Sadie?"

My forehead scrunched. Dinner? As a friend or a colleague? Or as a man and a woman?

The questions whispered across my mind, startling my spine straight. An open cheerfulness characterized his face, as it always did. My gaze pinned itself to a paper on my desk as my lips twitched into a smile.

What would it be like to be alone with this handsome,

sophisticated man? Without Viola hovering around the edges, Miranda blushing to her fingertips whenever he appeared, or Mrs. Fore's thinly veiled dislike lingering like a bad smell?

"So is that a yes?" His head tipped to one side. "I've heard there are a few restaurants in town."

Tomorrow. I groaned. "I'm sorry. I can't. Tomorrow night I'm scheduled to meet with Carter and the Comstocks. They've had some . . . misunderstandings between them."

Earl's thin eyebrows arched over those gold-dusted brown eyes. "A foster child and family?"

"Yes. Carter came to us when he was four years old, along with his older brother, Blaine. This is our third try at placing Carter with a family. He's sixteen now, and if this doesn't work out, I don't know that the board will approve us taking him back in. The Comstocks are good people; Carter just hasn't adjusted well."

"Some never do. But you say he has an older brother? What about him?"

My chest tightened. Why had I mentioned Blaine? I picked up a pen, rolled it between my fingers and my thumb. "Blaine did fine with a foster family. He's grown now. Has—" My throat closed over the words. I forced them free. "He has his own farm."

"And the boy can't stay with him?"

I hesitated, not wanting to expose their history, yet knowing Earl cared only in a professional capacity.

"We tried that a couple of years ago, after Carter had issues with his second family. But it didn't work out. They didn't get along, though Blaine tried hard to—" My lips clamped shut. Earl didn't need to know all the details. "Anyway, that's what I'm doing tomorrow night."

He stood, then gathered his coat and hat and satchel. "I'll tag along, if you don't mind."

I rubbed a spot near my temple, hoping I didn't have wet ink on my fingers. "I don't know. I'm not sure—"

His laughter cut off my words. "I won't be taking notes, Sadie, but I might be of some help. I do hold a master's degree in sociology from the University of Pennsylvania, so I have a bit of knowledge to share."

He did have more education, if not experience, than I did. Could I benefit from some of his wisdom? Could Carter?

"Thank you for wanting to help. I'd love your assessment of the situation. The Comstocks live outside of town, so I have a horse and buggy reserved at the livery."

"Perfect. I'll drive you there and back and won't say a word unless you ask my opinion." He pretended to turn a key over his lips. I laughed. He did, too.

For the first time since Blaine and I had parted ways, my load felt bearable again.

Chapter 15

Carter slumped in a chair at the Comstocks' kitchen table, arms folded across his chest. His clear blue eyes studied Earl with suspicion one moment and wistful admiration the next. And no wonder. The man exuded a suave confidence, not to mention he cut a fine figure in his stylish attire.

Mr. Comstock grumbled as he took the seat at the head of the table. Pale Mrs. Comstock filled coffee cups all around and then retreated into the background.

Earl did as he'd promised—sat silent.

"I'm so thankful we can talk things through. Now, Mr. Comstock, would you please tell us what you expect of Carter when he lives with your family?"

The man shifted in his seat, but his gaze remained steady on mine. "I want him to be home at a decent hour, to do his chores, and to be respectful when he speaks—to us and to our daughters."

"Perfectly reasonable requests, Mr. Comstock. Nothing more than we would require of him if he lived at the Home instead of with you."

Carter scowled, looked away. I could see he wasn't going to participate willingly in this conversation. If I didn't come up with some sort of plan, Mr. Comstock might insist Carter leave with me this evening.

Wisdom, Lord. I need the wisdom of Solomon. And then it came to me. Mr. Comstock was used to small children. Almost-grown Carter wanted a bit more freedom. What if Mr. Comstock could give him some within the confines of what he asked the boy to do?

"Carter, what if Mr. Comstock gave you a list of chores to be done each day but allowed you to determine the order and time of day in which to do them?" I held my breath, waiting for Carter to grunt away the suggestion or Mr. Comstock to dismiss it.

Carter studied his fingernails, then finally raised his head and looked me in the eye. "I could do that." Then he glanced at Mr. Comstock, as if challenging him to be the one to reject my proposal.

Mr. Comstock gave me a curt nod. I hadn't realized until that moment that my shoulders had been hunched up around my ears. I let them recede to their usual place as my fingers stretched long on the table.

"Good. Carter, I expect you to be diligent in completing your tasks before evening. And Mr. Comstock, please let him know if there is a reason something needs to be done by a certain hour. Carter is man enough to take your direction, I am certain. Just as certain as I am that he is responsible enough to carry out your wishes once you have made them known for the day."

"What about him coming home at dawn? I won't have that in my house. Nothing good happens in the dark hours."

"I agree, Mr. Comstock." I turned to Carter. "You must abide by Mr. Comstock's curfew while you live in his house. Will you do that? For me?"

For a moment, I spied the scraggly little boy peeking out from behind his brother's back. Fearful. Uncertain. Clinging to Blaine's hand. I'd tempted them both into the warm kitchen, fragrant with the smell of fresh bread. Inch by inch, Carter approached, until he sat in my lap gulping down a second cup of milk.

Now I wanted to press the almost-man's face between my hands and force him to obey. Couldn't he understand I wasn't here to condemn but to help?

He pulled his gaze from mine, looked at Earl, and then at Mr. Comstock. He slouched deeper into his chair before nodding.

"Thank you," I whispered.

We all stood. I shook hands with Mr. and Mrs. Comstock, then threw my arm around Carter's shoulder and led him outside. Earl readied the horse and buggy while Carter and I stood a distance away. "I'm proud of you," I said, pushing up on my toes to see straight into his eyes.

He flipped up the collar of his jacket, then sank his hands deep inside the pockets.

"Stay out of trouble?"

He nodded. The horse whinnied behind me. I stepped toward the buggy, toward Earl. "I'm praying for you, Carter. As always."

He raised his hand in farewell, then ducked his head and took long strides toward Mr. Comstock's barn.

Earl helped me into the buggy, my shoulders heavy with the

strain of the evening. Now that we'd sorted things out with the Comstocks, Carter would calm down. I had to believe that. For if he continued on the path he'd set for himself, I feared the dire prophecies of women like Miss Pembrooke and Mrs. McNeil—even of his very own brother—would come true.

Fat drops of rain splattered the clean window panes the afternoon of Hazel's reception. Even Mrs. Fore's pies couldn't rouse the somber mood of all gathered to say good-bye to Hazel.

All except Professor Stapleton.

A lopsided grin covered his usually serious face as he chatted with board members and their wives, his eyes seldom moving from his bride-to-be. My heart cinched at the sight, almost driving the breath from my body. I'd hoped Blaine's love for me would be that steady, that sure. That obvious to the world.

But I couldn't think about Blaine. I needed to mingle, to encourage those who supported this ministry to give generously. If I let the Home down, I'd have allowed my heart to be rent in two for no good purpose.

I sipped coffee and wandered among the clumps of guests at the far end of the parlor. Earl would arrive soon. Perhaps he could help me encourage generosity.

Conversations hummed around me, some giving me hope of future contributions. Craning my neck, I searched for the Comstocks, knowing that all the foster families had been invited. But the burly man and his sickly wife didn't seem to be in attendance. Which meant Carter wasn't there, either. Disappointment wrestled with concern. I needed to make time for another visit soon.

The front door opened. I scooted closer to the breath of air, away from the press of people within the house.

"I'm just in time for the party, I see." Earl peeled off his coat and draped it over a chair in the office.

The merriness in his face coaxed the first genuine smile of the day to my face. I rested my hand in the crook of his arm. "Let me take you around and introduce you."

Back in the teeming parlor, I sought Mr. Riley—or any other board member. Instead, my gaze slammed into Blaine's. He lifted a cup of coffee to his full lips as his eyes let go of mine and locked on Earl.

Earl closed the small gap between us, his shoulder brushing mine before he pressed his hand against my back. Questions ambled through Blaine's eyes. My heart turned circles like a puppy chasing his tail. I wanted to run, but my feet wouldn't move.

"Blaine, meet Mr. Glazier from the Children's Aid Society of Pennsylvania. Mr. Glazier, Blaine Wellsmith. Blaine has a farm and a greenhouse just outside of town and often supplies us with fresh produce." It didn't hurt to remind Blaine of our need and his previous generosity.

Earl stretched out his hand. Blaine set down his cup and returned the gesture. "Wellsmith. Carter's brother?"

"You've met my brother?"

"I have. I accompanied Sadie when she went to help smooth out the boy's issues with the Comstock family."

Blaine's eyes darted to mine. Guilt slithered through me

at the lowering of his eyebrows. He thought me disloyal. But taking Earl with me had no bearing on Blaine.

"Mr. Glazier, I presume?" Mr. Riley clapped Earl on the shoulder. The two men shook hands, not needing me to introduce them further. When I looked back, Blaine had gone.

"Sadie? May I speak with you?" Dr. Lawson stood at my elbow. I followed him into the foyer, where fewer people gathered. He fumbled in his coat pocket, pulled out a slip of paper, and handed it to me. "My friend Dr. Jonas is willing to evaluate Lily Beth's condition."

My eyebrows rose at the Philadelphia address. "Free of charge?"

He hesitated. "The evaluation, yes. As a favor to me. But you'll have to find the money for any treatment he recommends."

I'd known Dr. Lawson long enough to understand what he hadn't said. He'd cover his colleague's fees from his own pocket. And even that, I knew, pushed the bounds of his generosity. Although he thought his good deeds went unnoticed, I'd seen them firsthand when it came to our children. And I knew he and Mrs. Lawson barely existed on the money he received for his medical services. He didn't have the heart to charge what he ought.

I peeked into the parlor. Lily Beth was sitting in a chair in the corner, her little legs dangling above the floor. My heart filled to bursting. I so wanted to fix her.

"When can you take her to Philadelphia?" he asked.

My mouth pressed into a firm line. If only I didn't have so many things vying for my attention. "I can't get away right now. Miss Brown has only been here a few days. But if you can accompany her—"

Dr. Lawson shook his head. "I can't get away at present, either."

I considered the board members, but they each had their own business to tend. Perhaps one of their wives?

Hazel's delicate laughter rose over the conversation, and I smiled. She had much to do as she prepared for her wedding, but perhaps not so much that a short trip would put her behind. Besides, she might need things she could only find in the city. "I'll ask Hazel if she'd be willing to go."

"Splendid idea. Let me know what she says. I only have to give my friend a few days' notice." He seemed to know, as I did, that Hazel wouldn't refuse the request.

"I can't thank you enough, Dr. Lawson." Emotion hushed my voice.

"That little girl deserves the same chance at a productive life as the rest of them." His mustache lifted as he grinned. "Besides, my wife would strangle me if she knew I hadn't tried to move heaven and earth to help the child. She's quite stolen Gwen's heart, you know."

"As she has stolen mine. I only hope we can find someone willing to pay the cost of whatever is needed to fix her eyes. I can't bear the thought of not doing for one of these little ones the same as was done for me. We have to care for their bodies as well as their souls."

A bump propelled me forward. Dr. Lawson caught me, held me upright. I turned to scold but found myself staring into the stormy dark eyes that haunted my dreams.

"Sorry," Blaine mumbled, making sure I held steady, then

disregarding me altogether. "Dr. Lawson, could I speak with you?" The two men walked out onto the porch. I strained to hear their conversation, but nothing reached my ears.

Then an arm circled my waist. Earl. My heart hitched for a brief moment. If only I knew him well enough to successfully interpret his playful demeanor.

Whisking me back into the parlor, Earl chased away my curiosity over Blaine and Dr. Lawson with an amusing story and boisterous laughter. New guests arrived. New conversations ensued. I disentangled myself from Earl's side, mingling with families and patrons. Until Blaine's deep chuckle drew my attention again.

I excused myself, followed the sound. In a shadowed corner, Blaine's back was to me. Who had coaxed laughter from him? I stepped around Mr. and Mrs. Brumbaugh.

Viola stood with her back pressed into the wall, cheeks colored with a delicate blush. A vision of youthful loveliness in her lavender Sunday dress. An enticing smile bloomed as she glanced up at Blaine through downturned lashes. She giggled, covering her pert mouth with a gloved hand.

I wanted to snatch her by the ear and march her upstairs. Instead, I stood behind Blaine, my eyes just visible over his shoulder.

Viola's gaze locked onto mine. As slowly as the hands on the face of a clock, Blaine turned. The longing in his eyes stole my breath and captured my heart—until I remembered who'd stood beneath that smoldering expression. My heart froze solid as I clutched Viola's arm and pulled her away.

"I don't believe you've met Mr. Riley, Miss Brown." I spoke through clenched teeth, my eyes shooting fire at the man who'd once declared his undying affection for me. His desire to marry me. I hadn't known his heart was so fickle.

Viola twisted back, saying good-bye to her new friend, no doubt. I surged forward, forcing her to keep up. By the time we stopped in front of Mr. Riley, I knew I'd made a mistake. Earl stood at his side, setting Viola's eyelashes fluttering anew.

Earl responded with his usual charm but threw a mischievous grin at me, as well, as if we shared a secret amusement over the girl. He understood, at least. A man of the world could spot a flirtation. Unlike Blaine, who had obviously been flattered by her attention. I hoped he recognized Viola's actions for what they were. Perhaps I ought to make certain.

I turned. Blaine no longer towered above the others. Maybe he'd retreated to the kitchen. Or maybe he'd gone home. Either way, at least he was no longer flirting with my new assistant.

Chapter 16

A yank at my sleeve pulled my attention downward. Henry stared up at me, eyes wide. "Mrs. Fore needs you in the kitchen."

"Of course. Thank you." I wound through the maze of people.

"Is there a problem, Mrs. Fore?" I stopped face-to-face with Blaine.

My head turned one direction and then the other. Where had all of Mrs. Fore's helpers gone? I swallowed hard. "I was told Mrs. Fore asked to see me."

"I was told the same." The pleasant rumble of his deep voice wrapped around me like an old quilt. I shook the feeling away, picturing his recent tête-à-tête with Viola. I cleared my throat and hoped he'd take the hint to excuse himself.

Instead, he stepped forward, his hands hovering near my waist. I didn't recoil, but I didn't invite his touch.

I glanced down at my own hands, biting back words that longed for escape. About Carter. The board's fleece. Lily Beth's eyes. About how I dreamed of him almost every night and missed his arms holding me close. But I needed to keep distant from him now. At least until my heart remembered what my head never forgot: We had chosen separate ways.

"How is the farm?"

He shrugged. "It'll be better when summer comes. I told Mrs. Fore I was sorry I hadn't been by, but things have changed. Should I talk to her about that—or to you?"

I sucked in a quick breath and prayed I didn't look worried. Would he quit donating his surplus food and expect payment from us instead? And why wouldn't he? He had a mortgage to pay. My heart hardened just as Earl's laughter carried from the front of the house.

Blaine's eyes narrowed. "That Mr. Glazier seems a bit of a dandy."

My eyebrows arched. What right did he have to critique my colleagues—or my new friends? "My new assistant seems to meet with your approval, though."

His face reddened. Was he embarrassed that he'd been flirting with her, or that I'd seen it?

"And how is my brother?" Now it was his turn to look haughty.

I blew out a steadying breath.

"I met with him and the Comstocks yesterday. I think we have things worked out."

Some of his tension seemed to abate. "Good. I want the best for him. You understand that, don't you?"

He sounded like my old friend Blaine again, but was he saying what he thought I wanted to hear or had his feelings about Carter changed since we'd talked last?

"I'm . . . not sure what to think."

He stepped closer, towering above me. "Stating a fact isn't the same as losing faith. I fear where he's headed, but that doesn't mean I won't do all in my power to help him steer right."

I nodded, my throat clogging. I did know that. But it was easier to make my heart forget him if I pretended otherwise.

Mrs. Fore bustled into the kitchen, a wide smile creasing her face. She hooked her empty arms around us, placing herself in the middle. "All better now?"

I held my breath, focused on the tip of my toe.

"Don't pay me any mind," she said as she hurried away again.

"I guess you told them?" The hard edge on his words made me flinch.

"Hazel knows, but—" I glanced over my shoulder— "she just . . ." I shrugged. I had no idea what Mrs. Fore thought at this moment.

"Sadie, I—" He reached for my hand. I pulled it away and stared up into his face. Counted the ticks of his jaw. One. Two. Three. Four.

"Sadie?" Hazel's gentle call.

"I'd better go." I raised my hand in farewell, wishing the forlorn look on his face didn't twist my heart into knots.

Earl and I walked out behind Hazel and Professor Stapleton and Mr. and Mrs. Riley, but he held me back as we reached the bottom of the porch steps.

"I have to leave in the morning."

"I know. Thank you for coming. For considering us."

"It was my pleasure. Truly. In fact, I'll give a glowing report to the others in Philadelphia. I think we can assist you in running your operation more efficiently. Perhaps we can interest some of our donors in supporting you, as well."

"Oh, that would be wonderful." This week had been difficult on so many fronts, but Earl's hope infused my own.

"In fact, we often send someone to consult for a few weeks in these situations. Would you have any objection if I came back?"

Everything went still. Earl's desire to return meant good things for our ministry, but I wondered if he could help me, too. Distract me from Blaine until my heart remembered it beat only for the Home and its children. "I'd like that very much."

He grabbed my hand and squeezed. "That's what I wanted to hear." Then his eyes cut to the others. Before I could blink, he pressed his lips to my cheek and then bounded to Mr. Riley's automobile for his ride to the hotel. My chilled fingers grazed the warm spot on my flesh in wonder.

The house finally cleared. Viola, Miranda, and I helped Mrs. Fore clean up. When I mounted the stairs, intent on bed, Mrs. Fore held me back. "Didn't you get your spat worked out?"

I sighed. "It's more than a spat, Mrs. Fore. It's a complete separation." Exhaustion birthed a sob that hiccuped in my throat.

"There, now." Mrs. Fore patted my shoulder. "I'm sure it can be mended."

I shook my head, swallowed down my tears. "But it can't. He purchased the farm, and I took this job."

Mrs. Fore rubbed a pudgy finger across the wrinkles in her forehead. "I don't understand."

I gulped in a breath. "He wanted me to give up my position and marry him, but I feel like I'm supposed to be matron. He says God made him to till the land. I say God made me to run this Home."

She shook her head and tutted. "'And ne'er the twain shall meet.'"

"Something like that." Saying it out loud again lessened some of the anguish. I laid my hand on her arm. "It's for the best. Really, it is. I'm sorry I didn't explain sooner."

She waved away my apology. "No one can tell what the future holds."

The twinkle in her eye disturbed me, for I did know my future. This place. These children. I didn't have room for anything more.

Every time I closed my eyes that night, two men vied for my attention. Earl's chiseled good looks and playful demeanor. Blaine's soulful eyes, our long friendship, his practical nature. I punched down the feather pillow and turned over.

I'd never considered the attentions of any man besides Blaine. Yet the contrast between him and Earl was too stark to ignore.

Blaine seemed uncomfortable when he saw me in my new tailored skirt and jacket, while Earl's eyes lit with greater appreciation when I dressed the part of matron. With Earl, there would be no rough exterior, no work-worn hands, no ground-in dirt from taming the earth. Even this evening, I'd noticed that Earl held the china teacup firmly in between his fingers instead of cupping it from view, as Blaine did.

I ought to dream about Earl, a man of knowledge, understanding, and patience—a man more like Professor Stapleton. He understood my work as the professor had understood Hazel's. A man like Earl would not abandon plans over a hiccup, or run after the first young miss who batted her eyes at him.

And yet, I wavered. Did those outward differences reflect the inner man? I didn't know Earl well enough yet to be certain, didn't know if I ever would. But if Blaine could flirt with Viola right in front of me, why couldn't I at least explore the possibility of Earl?

Chapter 17

On Monday morning, I went to Dr. Lawson's office with the news that Hazel would take Lily Beth to Philadelphia the following week.

"Wonderful. I'll make the arrangements with my friend." One of his bushy eyebrows cocked in my direction. "Do you need money for her train ticket?"

My mouth dropped open. I hadn't even considered that expense. I fumbled with my handbag, knowing I had but a few coins in the bottom, and those were reserved for trolley travel.

Dr. Lawson waved his hand. "No matter. An anonymous donor has offered to pay for her travel and cover up to fifty dollars of the cost of her treatment."

I sat hard in the nearest chair, tears of gratitude filling my eyes. I grabbed the doctor's smooth hand. "Thank you."

He chuckled, then gently pulled away from my grasp. "It isn't me. I promise. Though Mrs. Lawson would have insisted had . . . this person not contacted me. Go on now. I'm glad that little girl will have a happy ending."

Lily Beth would get her eyes fixed. That would only be

the beginning of her happy ending, as Dr. Lawson called it. And I intended to do everything in my power to ensure all the other children had happy endings, too.

Two meetings and a quick shopping trip later, I trudged up the hill from the trolley stop. Mrs. Alcorn planned to talk with her husband, a carpenter, about taking a boy into their home as a son and an apprentice. Mr. Treehorn, owner of the theater, agreed to consider a benefit performance when the next traveling show came through town. Three women at the milliner's had given five dollars each "for those poor orphans." I didn't bother to correct their assumption that none of our children had living parents.

In fact, all of my conversations had been successful. No one had refused my requests outright, thrilling me to my toes. This really was the perfect job for me.

Viola met me on the porch, chattering like a two-year-old as she walked backward in front of me all the way to the office.

I pressed my fingertips into my temple, trying to stave off the pounding. I should have stopped to eat something, but I didn't want to spend the money. "When the children come home," I told her, "I'd appreciate you keeping the interruptions to a minimum. Preferably none at all."

Viola blinked her long lashes and brushed a curl from her forehead. "I'd never disturb you while you were working, Sadie."

I bit my tongue. No, she only popped in and out of my office every three minutes after the children arrived home, peppering me with questions. If I had a dime for every time she opened my door, I'd be able to cover all our budgetary shortfalls.

"Be sure Cynthia practices her recitation today. I know she wiggles her way out of it most days."

"She said you were going to help her. Oh, and Janet cried all through breakfast because she'd made a mess of her knitting. Can you help her straighten that out?"

I held a smile on my face, though I wanted to scold. "It's your job to take care of those things, remember?"

Viola scrunched her nose as if she'd smelled an odor. "I'm not good at speaking pieces. And knitting? The yarn always gets tangled in my needles."

Of course it does. With a sigh, I dropped my handbag beside the desk. "Would you ask Mrs. Fore to bring my dinner in here? I have some paper work to catch up on."

She clapped her hands. "Like a picnic. We'll have such fun!"

Before I had a chance to say I'd only meant *my* dinner, she scampered away. Did I have that much energy at eighteen? I plopped into the chair, wishing I could crawl into my bed and sleep for an hour or two. But I had work to do.

I rubbed my forehead in earnest now. I had reports to finish for the next board meeting, over four thousand dollars to raise before July 1, and a family to approve before I could place a child in their home.

That family had to take precedence. Even over the money.

A few minutes later, Viola returned. She set a tray of food on the desk between us. "Oh, and guess who came by this morning."

My ears pricked, but I didn't bother answering since she jabbered on.

"Mr. Wellsmith." Her eyes widened as she took a bite of her stewed chicken.

I set down my fork, unable to force food into my mouth.

"He brought vegetables. He's not a grocer, is he? He doesn't look like one." She shoveled a bite of cooked carrots into her mouth, her jaw working as fast as the legs of a rabbit on the run.

My stomach turned over. "He's a farmer, actually. He supplies us out of the surplus in his cellar—and his greenhouse. Sometimes he stops in town and picks up our groceries, as well."

"And he's not married."

The chicken I'd just put in my mouth caught in my throat. I coughed, choking it down all the way to my stomach. "No, he isn't married."

"And neither is that nice Mr. Glazier. I imagined they'd both have been caught by now."

"Mr. Glazier?"

She nodded. "Of course he's much more showy than Mr. Wellsmith. And he makes a girl feel . . . special when he talks to her." Color stole into her cheeks. "At least that's how he made me feel when he was here. Anyway, I came right out and asked if he was married. He laughed and said he hadn't found the right girl yet. Then he changed his mind and said maybe he had. What do you think he meant by that?"

The girl's audacity stifled any thought of a reply. But although the conversation silenced, Viola's expression revealed thoughts in continuous motion. Whatever she was concocting, it wasn't any of my business. Blaine and Earl were grown men. They could handle Viola and her interest.

But could I?

I pushed away my half-eaten dinner and determined to return to more certain footing. "So you'll see to Cynthia this afternoon?"

Viola's expression puckered, as if she'd just sucked on a lemon. "That girl is impossible."

I lowered my head to hide my twitching lips. I could have said the same of her. "Be patient and keep trying."

With another dramatic heave of breath, Viola stood. "If you say so. But it won't do any good."

She flounced away, leaving the office door wide open. I started to close it, then paused. Perhaps the sound of the children would be the motivation I needed to finish my paperwork.

"He brought our order from the store. Nothing more." Mrs. Fore scrubbed at a spot on a dish but didn't look up at me. I sensed her confusion. And her disappointment. I dared not admit my own. If Blaine no longer brought us produce, I'd have to find a way to replace it. And cheaply.

"I'll go into town and talk with Mr. Knutz about our groceries. I need to squeeze a bit more out of our budget."

"Stop by the butcher's, too, then. Beef was too dear the last time I checked, and we do need meat from time to time."

I stiffened. Blaine had always brought venison from his smokehouse, too. And rabbits when we needed them.

A bell tinkled overhead as I pushed open the door to Mr. Knutz's store. My eyes adjusted to the dim interior as the warmth of the stove in the corner wrapped around me. Mr. Knutz waved from his place behind the counter as he chatted with another customer. Canned goods lined the upper shelves. Fresh produce spilled over the baskets below. A barrel of pickles. Coffee. Oatmeal. So much that we needed. So much we struggled to afford.

Lifting an orange to my nose, I pulled in the exotic scent. Then I set it back in the pile. When I'd lived with the Ramseys, we'd had such delicacies on occasion. And not just in our Christmas stockings. I sighed, remembering.

But I hadn't come here for me. I'd come for my children. Turning a slow circle, I surveyed the abundance. *Won't You soften his heart, Lord? Just a little? Surely a few dollars a month wouldn't come amiss. And we are in such need.*

The woman at the counter turned. My smile faltered. Mrs. McNeil.

Then I remembered the light green suit that hugged my shoulders and hips. I need not be ashamed of my appearance or my character. And yet beneath her piercing gaze, I felt like nothing more than a little girl playing dress-up.

A curt nod as she passed. I let out a long breath, stepped to the counter.

"And what can I do for you today, Miss Sillsby?" Mr. Knutz's salt-and-pepper beard bobbed as he spoke.

Suddenly my request seemed as bold as Viola's inquiry into Earl's marital status. But I had to continue. I had no other choice.

"I need a favor, Mr. Knutz."

He chuckled, setting his beard waggling again. "Why do I have a feeling this will cost me something?"

My fingers tightened on my handbag as heat surged into my face. "It's just that . . . you see—"

"You need more time to pay on your bill?"

I shook my head, my mouth as dry as cotton.

"Want some penny candy thrown in?" His eyes laughed as I squirmed. I wiped a damp palm down the side of my new skirt, then chided myself. I wasn't a little girl begging for a handout. I was a woman seeking compassion for orphaned and friendless children.

I raised my chin. "We need to increase our monthly order and I'd like to negotiate a better price since we will be purchasing a larger quantity."

"Is that so?" The bell tinkled. Mr. Knutz glanced over my head and nodded, but I refused to be distracted.

"So can we work something out or shall I take my business elsewhere?" And I would. If I had to. I could canvas the local farms looking for a better price. It would require time and effort, but if it would save money, I'd do it.

Mr. Knutz shook his head as he reached into his pocket. "Here's a donation to your cause, Miss Sillsby, but I can't commit to a long-term business deal."

He pressed a bill into my hand. Five dollars. I wanted to spout off the Bible verse about what happens to those who do not heed the cry of the poor. They would find themselves unheard in their time of need. But I clamped my lips shut and kept it inside. He was a kind man doing what he could; he didn't need a sermon from me.

I shoved the bill into my handbag and mustered a smile. "Thank you ever so much, Mr. Knutz. Your generosity knows no bounds."

The bell over the door tinkled again. Heavy footfalls pounded the floor behind me. I whirled to leave.

Blaine towered over me.

"Oh! I—" My gaze lowered to the crate of produce in his massive hands. Food that used to come to us, free and clear. Did he sell it to Mr. Knutz now? Would Blaine's harvest still find its way into my kitchen, but at a much higher price?

"Making a profit, I see?"

Blaine refused to meet my eye.

I glanced back at Mr. Knutz and raised my voice a trifle. "I can't promise to pay what he's paying, but I feel sure you and I could strike a bargain for the supply of food to the Raystown Home, Mr. Wellsmith."

He angled away from Mr. Knutz and lowered his voice. "Sadie, I—"

"You don't have to explain. You can't just give things away anymore. I understand. But if you'll tell me what he's paying you, I'll see if I can find it in our budget to match it."

Blaine skimmed a glance toward Mr. Knutz. "Let's talk about this outside." He stepped toward the door.

"If you walk away, Wellsmith, you'll never sell to me again!"

I held my breath, praying Blaine would choose the Home over Mr. Knutz but knowing money held the final sway.

Or did it?

Pressing my hand against his arm, I looked into his face. "Please?"

He strode out the door, leaving Mr. Knutz sputtering and me running to catch up.

I sailed into the kitchen and threw my arms around Mrs. Fore.

"Blaine will continue to supply our cellar." The turn of events thrilled me. I'd secured a break in our budget, and I'd get to see my friend from time to time. It would be painful, but I wasn't ready to let Blaine go completely. Not yet.

"Well now. That's some good news." Mrs. Fore chuckled, her ample belly shaking beneath her apron. In spite of her mirth, the words gave me pause.

"Has there been bad news?"

Mrs. Fore's eyebrows scrunched toward her nose. "Not bad, exactly."

A high-pitched wail came from somewhere nearby. I grabbed Mrs. Fore's arms as my heart tried to escape my chest. "What is it? *Who* is it?"

She chuckled and shook her head. "No need for alarm. It's just Cynthia. She and Miss Viola don't get along too well, it seems."

"Oh." I breathed deeply. My heartbeat slowed. Now seemed the perfect time to take pity on Cynthia and hear her recitation myself.

"I can't, Miss Sadie. I just can't!" Cynthia hid her freckled face in her arms on the dining room table as she sobbed. I laid a hand on the girl's head and prayed for the right words to say.

"I know it seems hard, sweet pea, but you can do this. I know you can." The open book caught my attention. It wasn't the words themselves that gave her trouble. She could say them by heart. Just not to anyone but me.

She continued to weep, but it grew quieter. I reached across and tipped one edge of the book until it met the other with a muffled thump. Even as my heart ached for the child, my mouth twitched upward. Cynthia was a performer. She just didn't realize it yet.

The tear-stained face rose, bottom lip trembling. "But what if I can't? What if everyone laughs at me?" The final word came out in a wail as she hid her face again.

The girl needed to overcome her fear of being in front of people. I didn't want it to haunt her all her life, just as I didn't want Lily Beth's crossed eyes to define her. If only Cynthia had a more interesting venue than her classroom to compel her to recite. But where?

A memory tickled at the back of my mind. We used to give entertainments at the annual fund-raiser picnic. We could implement that again. Having the children perform might even increase donations. And if I put Viola in charge, perhaps she and the children would bond more quickly.

"Cynthia?" I found her chin, tipped it up. "What if we worked on a shorter piece for you to recite at the picnic on Decoration Day?"

Her eyes grew round and her lip quivered.

"Not just you, honey. The other children would participate, too. A program."

A finger tapped my shoulder. "I could say my poem from last year." Janet's solemn face melted my heart. I pulled her into my embrace.

"See? Your friends will all be with you. Doesn't that sound fun?"

"I don't know, Miss Sadie. I still don't think I can."

"And that is your problem, little miss. If you think you can, you will. But we won't worry about this today. We have weeks to work on it. Right now, I want you to wash your face and help Mrs. Fore get the table ready."

Cynthia sniffed, wiped one arm across her nose, and bounded away with Janet.

Yes, showcasing the children would not only help Cynthia overcome her fear, it would be the perfect draw to our picnic. After the performances, I'd give my plea. My passionate plea for the children. And maybe, just maybe, we'd raise all the money the board sought.

Chapter 18

Aw, c'mon, Miss Sadie." George threw the baseball into his mitt, grabbed it, and threw it again. Every time it landed with a muffled thud in the leather. "You always used to play with us on Saturdays."

"That was before. Why don't you ask Viola?" I shuffled papers on my desk, wishing he would leave me alone to finish my work. Earl had written that he'd be back in two weeks. Before he arrived, I needed to sort out these figures that refused to match. I'd copied and added more bills and more donations over the past week, but none of the numbers matched the bank account total. Not even close.

George scowled. "We already did. She said she'd sit on the stoop and watch, but she didn't want to get dirty."

"I see." I pressed my fingers to the sides of my head. The pleading look in his eyes tugged at my heartstrings. What other twelve-year-old boy still wanted a big sister of sorts to join in his games? We'd be in the back of the house, away from prying eyes. It wouldn't be as if the entire town would witness the matron's momentary departure from dignity. And it wouldn't hurt to enjoy the beautiful April day for a short time.

149

I pushed away from the desk. "Just a couple of innings, agreed?"

The grin on his face could have spanned the sky like a rainbow. "I'll tell the others," he called as he ran off. I shook my head and followed at a slower pace. Viola didn't know what she was missing. Maybe I could show her.

She'd picked up on her tasks well enough, but the children hadn't taken to her yet. I wanted that to change. I needed that to change. They still ran to me when they were upset or afraid or frustrated or sad. And while it cheered my heart, it increased my workload, negating the whole reason I'd hired Viola.

"Hurry, Miss Sadie! You're up first." Carl hopped from one foot to the other as he waved me over.

I stepped around Viola, her hands clasped around her knees, her gaze fixed somewhere in the distance instead of on the game.

Taking the homemade bat from Carl, I approached the stone designated as home plate. I crouched down, bat held over my shoulder, ready to swing. Just like Blaine had taught me.

My knees straightened. The bat sagged. A lump lodged in my throat as I remembered his arms stretched around me, putting my hands in the right position.

"Get ready, Sadie! He's going to throw it!"

I shook off the memories, bent my knees, focused on George. The ball flew across the plate. I held my ground.

"Strike one," a neighborhood boy shouted from his crouch behind me.

My team argued to no avail. George wound up again. This time I kept the ball squarely in my sights as it sailed toward me. I reared my arms back and swung.

Crack!

The ball sailed high in the air.

"Run, Sadie! Run!"

I lifted my skirt and raced toward the rock indicating first base. The boys in the field chased after the rolling ball. I rounded the base and headed for second. A chorus of cheers accompanied the boys jumping along the third-base line.

"C'mon! C'mon!"

Third base beckoned, though Henry stood unwavering, foot on the rock, hands outstretched, ready for the ball. Could I make it? I urged my feet faster. Just a little farther. Right—there.

My foot touched the flat stone just as Henry moved for the ball. My body bumped his. His bumped mine. I reeled backward, praying my skirt wouldn't end up over my head. I sat hard on the ground, with a most undignified *oomph*. Then the small thud of the ball hitting the ground drew my attention. I scrambled to get one hand on the base.

"Safe!" Blaine's deep voice carried across the yard, then bellowed laughter.

"Hooray! Hooray!" The boys on my team jumped and cheered. I kept my head down, wishing my face would cool and my breathing would slow.

Blaine's large hand reached into my line of sight. His eyes danced with amusement as he pulled me to my feet. I let go of his hand, dusted off my skirt, and tried to brush back hair that had flown free of pins.

Viola strode into view, hands behind her back, lashes lowered. I wanted to give the girl a good smack.

She's young, I reminded myself. *She needs a good example.* I forced a smile. "See what fun you've missed, Viola?"

Her slim figure swayed back and forth as her eyes lifted toward Blaine. "I'm afraid I wouldn't know how to play such a rough game."

The back door opened. Miranda stepped onto the back stoop. A few of the boys ventured in her direction.

A hand on my elbow, a voice close to my ear. "Are you hurt? Would you like to sit down for a while? I can take your place."

I gently removed my arm from Blaine's grasp. "I'm fine, thank you."

He pulled a handkerchief from his pocket and rubbed at a spot on my cheek. "There. That's better."

All words fled my head.

The boys came back across the yard, the housemaid in tow. "She'll run for you, Sadie, if you're done in."

I glanced first at Blaine, then Viola. "Yes, I think that would be best."

Miranda passed me without making eye contact and stood on the rock I'd just abandoned, while Viola sidled up to Blaine, wriggled her small hand between his arm and his body, and led him toward the house.

Hazel and Lily Beth left for Philadelphia early Tuesday morning, Lily Beth in a dress Mrs. Lawson had sewed for her, complete with a matching bow for her hair. Hazel seemed as giddy as a schoolgirl on holiday. Lily Beth was the one with the serious demeanor. After the train pulled away, I walked to the Comstock house, but no one was home.

I lifted another prayer for Carter. For Lily Beth. For all the children.

Viola and I accomplished quite a bit over the next three days, even with Miranda glowering in the background. I ignored her, going on with our work. Viola was a bit flighty, but she seemed to be settling down some.

I even managed enough quiet time to finish entering our latest expenses and add them up, finally arriving at two identical sums. The donations proved a bit harder to keep up with. Some, like Mr. Knutz, had handed me cash. Others had brought foodstuffs, clothing, bank drafts. The cash and bank drafts concerned me most. I had to remember to note them—or deposit them in our account. But if my figures were accurate, we'd made a slight bit of progress. Not in extra money saved toward our goal of forty-five hundred dollars, but at least in covering what we spent in monthly obligations.

If only I could find a way to cut expenses further. But heating costs had been especially high this past winter. The telephone had become a necessity. Salaries were already thin. At least Blaine had agreed to sell us fresh produce at a rate less than the grocer's. Even with my limited math skills, I knew that our agreement meant the difference between finishing the month with money in the bank and not. Perhaps I could forgive him for charging us at all.

Friday afternoon, Viola flitted around the parlor, excited as a bumblebee in a summer garden, fussing over six-year-old Timmy's clothes and hair.

"Where are his things?" I asked, looking for his small bundle of possessions.

"Miranda is seeing to that."

I frowned. "That really isn't her job, Viola. It's yours."

"She doesn't mind." Viola tried again to smooth down an errant swatch of blond hair just above Timmy's ear.

"Viola—"

The knock on the door sent her flying to usher in the Goff family. Viola really did have a good heart. I needed to remind myself of that more often.

The Goffs' nine-year-old twins cooed over Timmy as if he were a new puppy. One of their skinny girls threw both arms around the boy's pudgy waist and strained to lift him off his feet. Face red, she leaned over instead and chattered in his solemn face. Laughter overcame any thought of tears as we waved good-bye to the smiling family.

Mrs. Fore sighed and shook her head. "I do believe that is my favorite part."

"It's what we're here to do." I nodded toward the auto pulling out of the yard. "That boy will have a chance now."

I wrapped my arms around the porch post and thought of Carter. Three different homes, yet I couldn't shake the feeling that he still hadn't received the chance he needed.

After supper, I caught the trolley downtown. Then I wandered around the train station, unable to keep still. What treatment had the doctor prescribed? And would the anonymous donation cover it?

The shrill scream of the train whistle sent me running onto the platform. Almost the moment the iron giant stopped, Lily Beth hopped down the steps in front of Hazel and threw

herself into my arms. Hazel's smile drooped a bit below somewhat haggard eyes.

"Anything wrong?" I asked.

She shook her head, hefted her bag. "Just tired. We walked
all over Philadelphia, didn't we, Lily Beth?" She stroked the
child's flyaway hair.

Lily Beth nodded into my shoulder.

"She missed you." Hazel's energy seemed to be returning
a bit as her gaze roamed the area. Then she looked behind
her. The professor quickened his step. She threw herself into
his arms in much the same way Lily Beth had with me.

I lifted Lily Beth's head from my shoulder so I could look
into her face. "Did you see the nice doctor?"

She nodded, one serious eye fixed on me, the other wandering off over my shoulder. A heaviness lodged in my stomach.
Shouldn't she be excited? We were going to fix her eyes, make
her look like other children.

"John will take us all in the motorcar. Let's hurry. It's cold
again." Hazel's quick steps left us behind. The professor took
Lily Beth from me and carried her to his automobile.

A few minutes later, we sat in the parlor, coffee and cookies on the tray in front of us. Miranda volunteered to tuck
Lily Beth into bed. Viola agreed before I could protest, then
perched herself on the edge of the sofa, eyes bright.

Hazel finished a cup of coffee and poured another. I couldn't
choke down even one of Mrs. Fore's melt-in-your-mouth short-
bread cookies, though they disappeared just fine under Viola's
hands. The professor didn't notice anyone or anything but
Hazel.

The china cup and saucer in my hand rattled. I set them

aside. What was Hazel not telling me? I glanced at the clock on the mantel. After eight. If she didn't speak soon, I feared I'd scream.

Hazel breathed deep. "There. I feel more human now." She pressed her hand on Professor Stapleton's and grinned. I wanted to shake the news out of her now.

Viola darted a glance among the three of us. Then she cleared her throat. "What did the doctor say?"

Bless you, Viola!

Hazel blinked, then looked at me. "Dr. Jonas was quite helpful. He determined that a special pair of glasses would train her eyes straight."

"A pair of glasses." I let out a long breath. "How expensive . . . ?"

"The money Dr. Lawson gave me more than covered the cost." She fished the spectacles out of her handbag and gave me the tiny wire frames that held round pieces of glass, the arms curved at the end to fit over Lily Beth's elfin ears. "Now it's just a matter of making sure she wears them. We were both so tired, I didn't want to force the issue right away."

I made eye contact with Viola, hoping she understood that this fell under her responsibility. I'd make it clear to her later.

"Will she require another trip to Philadelphia?"

Hazel shook her head. "Not now. I brought back a letter for Dr. Lawson. He can evaluate her progress."

I closed my eyes, lifted a heartfelt *thank-you* to the Lord. "That's wonderful news. And how long will it take to correct her eyes?"

"Anywhere from a few months to a year."

I felt the blood drain from my face. A few months. A year.

If Mrs. Ashworth returned for her daughter, could she be trusted to keep Lily Beth in the glasses? Surely if she cared enough to come back for her daughter, she'd make sure her daughter's eyes were trained to normal. But for some reason Mrs. Ashworth didn't strike me as the kind of woman who would take the time to notice her daughter's well-being.

"What is it?" Hazel asked just before she yawned again.

"I don't know. I—" No one else had seen what I had that day. No one understood my fear for Lily Beth should her mother return.

Hazel stood to leave. Professor Stapleton jumped to his feet.

"Thank you." I hugged her. "I know it wasn't easy for you to leave right now. I appreciate your sacrifice on Lily Beth's behalf."

Hazel squeezed my hand. "You know I'd do anything for these children, even if I have agreed to run a different kind of home now." She pressed her cheek to mine, then gazed up into the eyes of her fiancé.

I had to look away from the intensity of their devotion. If only my focus hadn't found instead Viola's starry eyes shining over hands clasped beneath her chin.

Chapter 19

That night I dreamed of the tender look that had passed between Professor Stapleton and Hazel, only in the haze of sleep the faces resembled Blaine's and Viola's. Fighting through the fog, I slid into a world of Mrs. Ashworth's shifty eyes, then Miranda's haughty ones. I searched for Lily Beth's spectacles to make them all disappear. But the glasses tumbled out of reach, always out of reach. I called for help, first from Earl, then from Carter. Then I stumbled and fell, the edge of some high cliff drawing closer.

And I woke. Blinked into the semidarkness. Blew out a long breath. I needed something to clear my head. Some task to keep me too busy to think. I climbed from bed, then stood at the window, hugging my arms around my body as the day dawned.

My gaze found the hydrangea bushes along the back of the property. They looked so forlorn, a mass of bare branches poking up from the earth. With the warmer weather, they would fill out with leaves. By June, great globes of color would break out over the branches.

But Blaine had mentioned the hydrangeas needed a place with less sun now that the big oak that threw its shade their way had come down due to a bolt of lightning last autumn. I could do that today. Trim them back and replant them in the front of the house, where everyone who passed by could admire their beauty, where their bright blossoms would cheer all who entered our door.

Those plants needed my help today, just as Lily Beth and the others needed my care. And I found myself anxious for time outside the house. Donning my oldest skirt and shirt-waist, borrowing an apron from Mrs. Fore, I headed for the storage shed out back.

The weathered door creaked as I opened it, shafts of mote-filled light crisscrossing the dark, dank space. Rakes and hoes stood orderly against the wall, baskets of smaller instruments lining a crude table.

I picked out a pair of long-handled pruning shears, along with a spade and the short-handled pruning shears, and set them all in the wheelbarrow. Pushing the unwieldy thing in front of me, I wandered to the back fence.

The sun spilled warmth into the day as I clipped and snipped the branches. Here. There. Top. Bottom. Until each bush re-sembled a neat square of twigs. The shouts and laughter of children accompanied my work, sweet as music to my ears.

"Sadie?" Viola trotted around the corner of the house.

"Over here." I rocked back on my heels, rubbed an arm across my forehead to sop up the perspiration, and peered up at her. Time to enlist some help digging the bushes up.

"Oh good. I found you. I need—" She paused. "I didn't know you gardened."

I stretched my back, then my arms, and rolled my head around on my neck. "I decided these hydrangeas would look much better up by the front porch."

"Oh." She nodded, mouth turned down. "Aren't you supposed to let hydrangeas grow out? Not trim them back?"

I brushed dirt from my hands, avoiding her questioning gaze. "I don't think so. Why?" I set the shears in the wheelbarrow's basket.

Her pert nose scrunched and wiggled. "It's just that my grandmother would never let my pap anywhere near her hydrangeas. Said if you cut them back they wouldn't bloom."

"I think you are mistaken." I grabbed the handles of the wheelbarrow to cart it around to the front of the house. I needed to prepare the spots where the bushes would be planted.

"But, Sadie—I need to know if we allow the boys to climb up on the roof of the house."

"What?" The wheelbarrow's legs collided with the hard earth.

Viola pointed to the opposite side of the house. I lifted my skirt and ran in that direction. George and two of the other boys were holding the tall ladder from the tool shed against the place where the roof sloped low, over the kitchen.

"What do you think you're doing?" I shouted.

With one foot on the bottom rung, George hung his head. The others looked anywhere but at me.

I jammed my fists to my hips. "Put it back. Now."

A chorus of *Yes, ma'am*s answered. My foot tapped as they complied, but truth be told, I had a hard time keeping back a snicker at the sight of their crestfallen faces.

Viola giggled behind me. I turned. She clamped her hand over her mouth, eyes wide.

I grabbed her arm and led her around to the front of the house. Then I burst into silent laughter. "Oh my. Those boys do beat all. But you have to school yourself so as not to encourage their outrageous ideas."

Viola sighed. "I'll try to do better. I promise I will."

For the first time since Viola had arrived, I had hope for her success.

Viola stood on the porch while I patted down the damp soil around the replanted bushes and added more water.

"I really don't know why you had to go to all that trouble, Sadie. We could have just bought new ones and had them planted."

"I wanted these plants. Not new ones." I reminded myself that she knew little about our finances here. She came from a well-off home. Likely they could simply go out and buy new ones. "These will bloom nicely. A bit of morning sun, then the house shading them the rest of the day."

I swiped at a drip of perspiration on my face.

Her lips twitched. She pulled a handkerchief from her sleeve and held it out to me. "Down the side of your cheek."

"Oh." I took the square of fine linen and rubbed it on my face. When I tried to hand it back, she refused.

"Keep it. I guess I'd better make sure they got that ladder put away." She stopped, raising a hand as if greeting someone. I turned.

Blaine was striding up the walk, his gaze settling on my

newly planted bushes. I pulled back my shoulders, let the pride of accomplishment fill my voice. "We'll have an abundance of color come summer."

Blaine's head wagged back and forth. "Not from those plants you won't."

I pressed my lips together and huffed through my nose. "Blaine Wellsmith, you are determined to find fault with me."

"No, Sadie, I'm just telling you the truth." Blaine pointed at the neatly shaped mass of branches. "You've cut them back. Now they won't bloom."

"See? I told you."

"Go tend the children, Viola," I snapped. She threw Blaine a grin and sauntered away.

What did either of them know about flowers?

I grabbed the wheelbarrow handles and trotted with it toward the shed. Blaine plodded along behind me.

"Let me do that." His hand closed just above mine. I jerked away. The wheelbarrow tipped, fell to the ground. I let go. He picked it up. Now I was the one following.

"I don't need your help." I stood in the doorway of the shed, blocking the sunlight.

"Appears to me, you do."

I wanted to pound my fists against his chest, tell him to go away and let me learn to live without him. But it wouldn't do any good. I'd end up in frustrated tears, wishing again to be sheltered in his strong arms. I stomped my foot, growled, then stalked toward the house. If Blaine and Viola knew so much about hydrangeas, maybe they deserved each other.

By Sunday morning, I'd recovered from the planting, both from the soreness in my limbs and grumpiness in my spirit. It helped that Viola hadn't heard Blaine and me argue. Somehow that would have made it worse. But even though I felt better, I suddenly dreaded seeing Blaine at church. Would he still sit in his usual spot—across from my old place, where Viola now sat?

The thought niggled like a stone in my shoe the entire walk from the Home to the church. But when I looked in the usual direction, I didn't spy Blaine.

Good. At least he wouldn't distract me from drinking in the peace and presence of the Lord. The music, the sermon. My heart composed itself.

But as we exited the pew after the service, a touch on my arm made me jump.

"Mrs. Comstock," I said. "How nice to see you."

She twisted a handkerchief in her hands. "I don't know if you'll think it nice or not."

My stomach dropped. What had Carter done now?

"Why don't we sit?" I motioned her into the back pew of the almost-empty sanctuary.

She walked to the farthest end. I followed. When she sat, her thin lips remained in a solemn line and the handkerchief continued to twist. "My husband found Carter in the barn late last night with some other boys." One narrow shoulder rose, then fell. "Men, really. They were drinking and playing cards." Her head snapped up, her eyes intense. "He could have forgiven that, but not the smoking. One small spark could have destroyed all our seed for planting this spring."

My jaw tightened. This was more serious than a few chores

left undone. This was a threat to a generous family's livelihood. "Where is Carter now?"

Her gaze faltered. She looked away. "I'm not sure. They argued. Both of them refused to come to church this morning."

Oh, Lord, give me wisdom. Then I thought of Earl. One more week. If I could keep Carter with the Comstocks until he returned, Earl might see a solution I didn't.

I pressed my palm over Mrs. Comstock's hands, stilling them. "If things aren't reconciled when you get home, Mrs. Comstock, please ask your husband to contact me."

She nodded, stood. "I wanted you to know, in case Mr. Comstock's pride gets in the way."

I tried to smile, but it didn't last. "Or Carter's. Thank you for telling me."

But oh, how I wished she hadn't.

Chapter 20

By midweek, Mr. Comstock still hadn't contacted me. Did that mean he and Carter had worked things out or, as Mrs. Comstock had said, had his pride kept him from admitting there was another problem?

What was my duty? I didn't want to jeopardize Carter's situation, but neither did I want to put the Comstocks in an awkward situation. I stopped at the desk, shifted the scattered papers, and pulled Earl's letter to the forefront. He'd be here on Monday. I bit my lip and wondered if the situation with Carter could wait until then.

The plod of a horse's hooves accompanied the creak and jangle of a wagon. I peeked out the window. Blaine. Delivering food, I imagined. He likely knew nothing of Carter's latest antics. And I had no desire to tell him just yet. Not until I'd handled the situation.

I snatched up my handbag and flitted into the foyer for my light cape. The moment his deep voice reverberated from the kitchen, I snuck out the front door and hurried to the trolley stop. Viola would find the note on my desk eventually. And I did need to take the latest donation to the bank. I just hadn't planned on doing it this minute.

Stepping across the threshold of the bank, I quailed, as if the large solid building could sense my inadequacies. But here was the one place I needn't worry. They kept our balance with perfect precision. Why hadn't I thought to check with them before?

At the barred window, I chatted with the teller, an old schoolmate of mine. He took the deposit and smiled.

"And could you write down the total in our account as of this transaction?"

"Absolutely, Sadie." His eye twinkled with humor. "Or do I say 'Miss Sillsby' now that you're in charge?"

I replied with a playful smirk. If he only knew how much that small comment meant to me. I hoped the number he gave me would further lighten my spirits.

He shook his head, then pushed a square of paper toward me. "There you go. Enjoy this beautiful day."

"I certainly will." And I would—as long as this number matched the one in my ledger back home.

I arrived back at the Home to find it empty of Blaine but full of Viola.

". . . and then he said he'd see me again next week. What do you think he meant by that, Sadie?"

"I imagine it meant he'd see you when he brought more from his cellar." Because heaven forbid a man would walk through our doors and Viola wouldn't be there to greet him.

Her expression drooped. "You don't think he meant anything else? I asked Mama if I could bring my graduation dress back with me when I visit her this week. I thought it might come in handy."

My eyebrows rose of their own accord. A frilly white graduation dress in an old house full of children?

Viola picked up a stack of letters to answer, sighed, and flounced out the door. If only she'd put as much thought into her job as she did into Blaine's passing comments. Then we might make some progress.

I shook my head, took the paper from the bank out of my handbag, and smoothed the page against the desktop. Then I reached for the cash book, praying the totals would at least be close.

There was $62.15 in the bank.

And $239.42 in my ledger.

Oh no.

I laid my forehead in the middle of the open book. If only the information would simply seep into my head and arrange itself. But it didn't. It wouldn't. Now I'd have to admit my deficiency to the board and risk dismissal and . . .

Unless. What would it hurt to just change the total in my ledger? The bank's figures were correct. I'd obviously made an error somewhere. I could easily rectify that. The totals would match. Everyone would be happy.

I erased my number and substituted it with the bank's. Then I shut the book, folded my hands over it, and smiled.

Dressed in my freshly pressed green suit, I assumed the role of the dignified matron once again and prepared to meet with Mr. and Mrs. Stratmore about becoming foster parents.

Mrs. Fore set a tray of coffee and cookies in the parlor. I wanted the Stratmores to feel comfortable. There would be time later for details to be set forth in an office setting, but much would depend on a comfortable connection now. As we talked, I could ascertain their fitness as parents, both from their actual statements as well as through my intuition. In a town this small, it wouldn't be hard to discover any blemish on character or reputation once I did a bit of research.

Viola escorted the couple inside. The feather in Mrs. Stratmore's hat tickled my nose as I shook her hand. A tiny woman in stature but not in size. The old settee creaked under her weight as she reached for Mrs. Fore's treats and started eating.

Mr. Stratmore didn't stand much taller than his wife. Or any less stout. His round cheeks bobbed with laughter as he shook my hand.

At least they seemed jovial souls. And given their substance, I assumed feeding a child wouldn't be a problem.

We chatted, Mrs. Stratmore's eyes shining with unshed tears when she talked of her now-grown offspring.

"We have all that space in the house, and I so miss the pitter-patter of little feet." She lifted the cup to her small mouth.

I cocked my head. "Are you interested in becoming foster parents or in adopting a child?"

"Not adopt." Mrs. Stratmore looked at her husband, who gave a curt nod. "Just a temporary arrangement that would help a little one and bring us a bit of joy, too."

I smiled, though if I'd been able, I would have covered my eyes and groaned. Too many misunderstood the nature of our placements. "We prefer to place children in homes where they will be part of the family. We hope they can stay in one place until they are old enough to be out on their own."

"Oh yes. Yes, of course." Wariness crept into her eyes.

"And as for the 'pitter-patter of little feet,' the youngest child currently under our care will be eight next month."

"Oh." Her mouth puckered like a bow beneath her bulbous nose. "I see." She dabbed a napkin to her mouth.

"What about an older child?" Mr. Stratmore reached for his third cookie.

I relaxed. Perhaps I'd judged their motives too quickly. I'd assumed they longed for grandchildren, wanted a stand-in until their own children provided the real thing.

"We're always looking for good homes. I have a boy, George, who is close to thirteen. He's been here over two years and I would love for him to find a place to feel at home until he graduates from high school. He's quite intelligent, but not bookish. Very considerate and helpful, too." I forced myself to tell the truth, even knowing that if they agreed to take George, I'd miss him more than most. "We have several children here between the ages of eight and fourteen who need a home. A few others are waiting for their parents' situation to change, so they are not ones we place out."

Mrs. Stratmore clapped her pudgy hands together, her eyes lighting up like a child's on Christmas morning. "May we see them?"

As if she were picking out a pretty from the mercantile.

I rose. "Before we get to that point, there is paper work to fill out. And I'll need to come and visit your home."

"Of course." Mr. Stratmore stood, took the cup from his

wife's hands, and set it on the small side table. "We're at your disposal, Miss Sillsby."

With a nod, I led them across the hall to my office. As I rounded the desk, a quick rap sounded on the front door. I called for Viola.

No answer. Not from her, Mrs. Fore, or Miranda.

I started to call again, but the knocking turned insistent.

"Please be seated," I said to the Stratmores. "I'll be right back."

The pounding intensified. "I'm coming," I muttered, then pulled open the door.

"Mr. Comstock!" My heart stumbled over its regular beats.

"Miss Sillsby." The man's ruddy face burned bright red as he gritted the words through clenched teeth and crushed his hat between his hands.

My stomach dropped to my knees. "Please, come in."

He stomped past me, then paced the small entry space. I inched toward the office, hoping to pull the door shut. But before my hand touched the knob, his bellow filled the air. "He's run off!"

I shut the office door with a bang, but not before I saw the shocked expressions on the Stratmores' faces.

I grabbed Mr. Comstock's arm and directed him toward the back parlor. "Let's talk in here, where we'll have some privacy." I shut the pocket doors, dividing the room in half, then whirled to face him, my fingers splaying against the door behind my back. "What happened?"

He tossed his crumpled hat on the sofa and dropped down beside it. "I don't know." His head shook. "We started out fine after that talk with you. The boy's a bit lazy, but nothing that couldn't be worked out of him. Then there was the smoking in the barn." He looked up at me. "My wife told you about that."

I nodded.

He stared at the floor again. "Things got tense between us again, but we managed. Then the principal called. He's been skipping school. When he came home yesterday, I confronted him. He didn't deny it. I informed him that we wouldn't have truancy in our house. This morning, we thought he'd left early for school and we were encouraged. But when my wife went upstairs, she found his room swept clean and all his clothes gone."

I dropped into the nearest chair and closed my eyes. *Lord, please be with Carter.*

When I opened my eyes again, the man's angry face softened. "I like the boy. Truly I do, Miss Sillsby. There's something so . . . winsome about the lad—most days. But I can't spend all my time trying to hold him in a place he doesn't want to be."

I rubbed my forehead. "Of course, you're right. We'll alert the police. When they find him, we'll bring him back here until we can sort things out."

He stood. I did the same. He stuck out his hand. I shook it.

"Thank you, Mr. Comstock. For trying."

He smoothed the brim of his hat, then placed it on his head. I slid the pocket doors open and followed him outside. I held in my sigh until Mr. Comstock stepped from the porch. Then I glanced through the window into the office.

The Stratmores had gone, too.

I'd lost one foster child and two foster families, all in the span of a quarter of an hour. All while Viola had disappeared like dust under Miranda's broom. Slow steps took me to the kitchen. Miranda sat at the table, peeling potatoes with Mrs. Fore.

"Anyone seen Viola?" Sweetness laced with a hard edge.

Mrs. Fore glanced out the window, then back down at her task. "I think she's out back, digging in the garden."

"I guess I'll talk with her out there, then." I yanked open the back door and charged down the steps.

Viola looked up from her place on the ground. "Oh! Did you need me?"

"We have a problem. Carter Wellsmith has run away from his foster home."

"Wellsmith." Her face brightened. "Is he related to Blaine?"

I took a step back, startled that she was on a first-name basis with my—with Carter's brother.

Both of the Wellsmith boys had broken my heart.

Chapter 21

As soon as I hung up with the police, I knew I needed to telephone Mr. Riley, but I feared he'd refuse to help Carter at all. Three foster homes in the past twelve years. Would the board of trustees allow me to give him one more chance?

After a prayer for mercy, I made the call. Mr. Riley didn't react as vehemently as I'd feared, but I could hear exasperation in his voice.

"And no one knows his whereabouts now?"

"No. I sent Miss Brown to talk with the principal at the high school, but she hasn't returned yet. I've telephoned the police, too. I just thought you should know."

"Please keep me informed."

"Yes, sir." I hung up and sat at my desk to await Viola's return.

No one at the school had seen Carter since Mr. Comstock had spoken with him. Mrs. Fore came into the office and sat across from me, patting my hand, calming me as I jumped at every knock on the door, every jangle of the telephone.

On top of the sick feeling that I'd never see Carter again sat the guilt that I hadn't called Blaine.

By nightfall, my concern over Carter had grown to screaming fear. Sitting in bed, I pulled my legs up to my chest, arms holding them close.

"Please, Lord. Keep him safe. Bring him home." For all his bravado, Carter was simply a scared little boy, a boy who had been through more difficult times than most. He was like me in many ways—putting on a confident face while living with the desperate fear of never overcoming the ghosts of the past.

I rested my forehead on my knees and prayed some more.

On Friday, I sent Viola and Miranda to complete other tasks while I helped Mrs. Fore with the dishes, mostly to steady my nerves. I stacked the dry plates, then lifted them to their place on a cabinet shelf. The handle of the back door jiggled.

"Oh, bother." Mrs. Fore wiped her hands on her apron. "Must have stuck again."

I stiffened. It would be Blaine, of course. Anyone else would come through the front door. By now, someone would have told him. After last week's encounter over the hydrangeas I had no desire for another altercation. Yet if I admitted the truth to myself, an argument wasn't what I feared most at that moment.

"Dear boy!" The catch in Mrs. Fore's voice caused me to turn. The tin cup in my hand clattered to the floor.

"Carter!" I rushed to embrace him. His blond hair fell over his eyes as usual, and the half smile conveyed a sheepish request for forgiveness.

Mrs. Fore patted his cheek and smoothed back his hair in the manner teenaged boys allowed only grandmotherly types to do. "We've been so worried! Where have you been?"

"I—" His eyes cut one direction, then the other. One shoulder lifted and fell. "Around."

"Sit right down there," Mrs. Fore instructed. "I'll fetch you some dinner."

He seemed eager to comply. I sat beside him, drinking in the face I'd feared I'd never see again, trying to ignore the similarities to the face I continued to try to forget.

Mrs. Fore set a plate in front of him. He ate like a famished man. I waited, wondering how to say all that needed to be said. After he'd emptied his plate, downed a glass of milk, and wiped his mouth, I beckoned him into the parlor, my heart pounding in anticipation. This was my opportunity, as with Lily Beth's eyes, to help a child get on the road to a better life, a better future.

"Mr. Comstock was here."

He hung his head in silence.

"He was very worried, you know."

Still no response.

I sighed. Perhaps we didn't need to discuss the Comstocks just yet. "Are you back to stay?"

A slight upward lift of his head. "I hope so." Quiet words, unlike his usual brashness. They seemed to say he recognized his foolishness.

I pressed my hand to his knee. "I hope so, too, Carter."

He looked up this time. I locked my gaze on his, forced it to stay steady. "But the board is very disconcerted by your current actions in light of your history."

His face screwed up, as if he were ready to spout justifications. I held up a hand to ward them off. His shoulders slumped as his head hung limp once again.

"I know you want to do what's right, Carter. And I'm going to help you. But you have to promise me—*promise me*—that you'll steer clear of any more trouble."

He nodded, then raised wide, innocent eyes. We could delve into the situation with the Comstocks later. For now, I needed to get him moved back into the Home before the board could object or Blaine could interfere.

"Hello?" Earl's voice carried into the kitchen a little while later.

I looked at Carter, not wanting to leave him for a moment, but desperately needing Earl's help.

Then Earl appeared in the kitchen, his gaze intent on mine, his arms opened wide, as if to hug me. The eager gleam in his sweet eyes drew me forward, seeking his comfort. Then heat flooded my face. I stilled my feet and sucked in a breath.

Carter was watching. And Mrs. Fore. And while I didn't believe Earl meant to imply more than friendliness, I didn't want others to come to the wrong conclusions. His arms dropped, though his grin never faltered.

He leaned closer. "You are quite charming when you blush."

Now my face burned. Would such acute embarrassment leave scorch marks?

Mrs. Fore sniffed. "I expect you'll take some coffee?"

Earl pulled out a chair and sat at the crude kitchen table. "Tea, if you have some."

Mrs. Fore's eyes narrowed, and her round cheeks filled with air.

I stepped between them. "I'll fix it." I smiled at Mrs. Fore, trying to forestall the gust of anger I knew waited behind her lips. "You've had quite a morning, too, Mrs. Fore. Why don't you sit down and take some tea yourself?"

She harrumphed, but sat. "Coffee will do for me, thank you."

I poured her coffee, then filled a kettle with water and set it to heat. Rummaging through the cabinet, I found a tea bag and set it in a cup.

When I turned, Carter and Earl were deep in conversation, Carter hanging on Earl's every word.

"I work for the Children's Aid Society of Pennsylvania, an organization that does the same kinds of things as the Raystown Home," Earl said.

"Oh." Carter's eyebrows drew together.

I laughed. "Not very exciting to you, I imagine, Carter. But it's quite important and fulfilling work to Mr. Glazier."

Mrs. Fore rolled her eyes. "Even if the rest of you have nothing better to do, I must work." She stood, pushed up her sleeves, and pulled out a knife and cutting board.

Earl continued to chat with Carter, and I noted a light dawning in the boy's wary eyes, a respect I rarely saw him show to anyone. His distrust of Earl from the evening at the Comstocks' had vanished. In the span of a few minutes, he'd become quite enamored of the man.

Perhaps if I brought Earl into our conversation about his behavior, Carter would listen. I could have a quick chat with Earl to that effect. Together, we could set Carter back on the right path.

"Carter, please take your things upstairs. We'll meet you in the parlor in a few minutes."

Tea in hand, I urged Earl toward the parlor, but as I was leaving the kitchen, the back door opened. I turned around.

Blaine. Eyes wild, body tense. He stepped forward, deep voice rumbling words too quiet for me to hear distinctly.

"He's back, but I think—" Mrs. Fore's mouth clamped shut as I dashed into the room. She abruptly returned to her work.

"He's back?" Blaine addressed me now.

I nodded.

"But you didn't tell me he was missing." A deep frown creased his face.

"No," I whispered, staring down at my hands.

One long stride and he stood in front of me. I didn't look up.

"Were you going to tell me?"

"Tell you what?" Earl's question from behind me.

My head jerked around. He leaned against the doorjamb with a natural grace. His immaculate suit fit his athletic body to perfection. My gaze moved back to Blaine, to his rumpled dungarees and faded plaid shirt.

I swallowed. Explain to Blaine or impress Earl? I shook away both options. Only Carter mattered at the moment. Blaine would rile the boy further. Earl might soothe him into submission.

"Blaine, I think—"

"I thought you said the parlor." Carter bounded into the kitchen like an eager puppy. Then he saw Blaine. He backed toward the wall, lowered his head, his eyebrows. "What's he doing here?"

I laid my hand on Carter's shoulder. "He came to make sure you were safe. Right, Blaine?"

Blaine nodded, though his jaw clenched as he darted a glance from Carter to Earl and on to me.

Curling my arm around Carter's, I tugged him toward Earl. "Now we're going to have our little talk. In the parlor." Just as I reached the doorway, I paused. "Thank you, Blaine, for your concern. We have everything under control now, as you can see."

As I joined Carter and Earl in the parlor, I prayed I could believe the words I'd just spoken.

Chapter 22

You have to learn to respect authority, son," Earl told Carter. "Not just now, when you live here or in another home, but later, when you have a job." Earl's intense expression held the boy captive.

I leaned forward, laid my hand on his knee. "We care about you, Carter. We want you to have a good future. But if you continue this way, the board will toss you out faster than curdled milk."

Carter nodded. "Yes, ma'am."

"And you'll have to apologize."

Carter's eyes cut to Earl. He nodded. Carter sighed.

Viola inched into the room. Carter's gaze crept in her direction before dashing back to Earl's and mine.

"I believe we are all in agreement." I rose and smoothed the wrinkles from the skirt of my green suit.

"Yes, Sadie." The meekness of Carter's statement made me nervous. Had Earl's presence helped that much? I clung to a thin thread of hope.

"Viola, did you finish that correspondence?"

"Yes, ma'am. All the letters are addressed and ready to mail."

"Good. Carter, I'd like you to take them to the post office for me. You can return to school tomorrow."

He nodded, eyes lingering on Viola.

I cleared my throat. "Viola, if you'll join me in the office, I'll get you started on something else. I need to telephone the Comstocks. Then Mr. Glazier and I will be off to visit with the Stratmores."

After Viola understood my directives for the day, I made a quick telephone call to the Comstocks and then the Stratmores. Fresh air dissipated the morning's tension when I finally left the Home. Tension fled altogether when Earl put my hand in the crook of his arm. Though I had wanted this job, this responsibility, it felt good to have someone help shoulder the burden. I glanced at my companion. He had been solemn during our meeting with Carter, but his jovial smile returned now. I squeezed his arm in silent gratitude.

"Less than two weeks until the big day," he said as we stopped on the corner to wait for the trolley.

"You mean Hazel's wedding?"

He nodded. "But I imagine you will be a vision of loveliness to rival even the bride."

Heat crawled up my throat. A gorgeous new dress—a gift from both Hazel and the professor—would hang in my room next week. I glanced down, pulled back the hem of my skirt, and stared at my feet. If only I had a new pair of shoes to match. But holding on to my personal money didn't come any easier than keeping up with the Home's finances.

"I hope you'll allow me to escort you to the ceremony and the reception, Sadie."

I almost blurted an immediate refusal, but then I thought better of it. Nothing restrained me from accepting such an invitation. Even if I couldn't marry and still keep this job, I could spend time in the company of eligible gentlemen, just as Hazel had with the professor. Besides, it might do Blaine some good to see that I, too, had moved on from our relationship.

I smiled at Earl, eager to step into this unknown territory. "That would be lovely. Thank you. But we still have some work to get done before we get to play, you know."

He turned serious. "Yes, but I'll be looking forward to the time with you, on our own." He winked.

The trolley clanged. I let out a long breath, thankful for the interruption. If he continued making pretty speeches and winking his golden-brown eyes, I'd have a hard time remembering I wanted to keep our relationship casual.

I stepped up, paid our money, then replayed his words in my head. *"Time with you, on our own."* Did he mean at the wedding? Likely we'd have little or no time to ourselves there. Perhaps I should warn him. But I wasn't eager to squelch his plans completely.

"The children are all invited to Hazel's reception, you know."

He chuckled without any apparent disappointment. "They'll bring plenty of life to the party."

I cringed. As long as they didn't bring too much!

Chapter 23

The Stratmores invited us in, served us tea and cake, and then told us they had decided not to take in a child.

I set down my refreshments. "I beg you not to make a hasty decision. A child may cause some hardships. I won't deny that. But you do understand that every situation is unique, don't you?"

They glanced at each other. Mrs. Stratmore's tiny lips drew together in her fleshy face. Mr. Stratmore cleared his throat, then stared down at his plate.

"We understand, Miss Sillsby. But we aren't willing to take that risk."

Pain seared across my chest, as if his words were the ax set to my heart, the tree. I looked to Earl, desperate for him to say something to make them change their minds. He didn't offer anything more than I had.

"We appreciate your coming to talk with us." Mr. Stratmore stood. We followed his lead. Our conversation had come to an end, but I wouldn't go without one last appeal.

"Mrs. Stratmore, didn't your own children ever make any mistakes?"

Open her heart to see it, Lord. These children aren't any different than her own. Not really.

The silence stretched. She squirmed, seeming to fight the urge to say no, her children didn't make mistakes, yet knowing well that they had.

With a hefty sigh, she relented. "Yes, Miss Sillsby, my children made mistakes. But never anything like—"

I grabbed her hand. "And did you stop loving them, stop trying to help them when they did?"

She shook her head as her mouth formed a no.

"Of course you didn't. All we're asking is that you give these children the same consideration. Don't judge all of them by one child's mistake. Carter hit a rough patch. We're hoping to right him again. Please reconsider your generous offer of a home to one of our other children. Please."

I would have dropped to my knees if I'd thought it could push her toward a favorable decision, but I imagined that would just look desperate. I stayed on my feet, staring into her face until she gave a nod of assent.

"We'll only consider it, mind you. I'm not committing to anything."

"I understand. Thank you, Mrs. Stratmore, Mr. Stratmore. I'll be praying the Lord's will for us all."

Earl tossed my cape over my shoulders. My shaking fingers fumbled with the button, finally securing it before we stepped into the bright day. I lifted my face to the warming sun, imagining it to be God's kiss of approval for a job well done.

"We have just over a month until the picnic. This is a list of ideas for the types of performances each child can give. We'll assign pieces to the younger ones. The older ones can choose their own."

Viola nodded. Her gaze swept over the paper I'd handed her, then lingered on the window facing the street. Her blue eyes widened and her lips curled in a slow smile. I didn't even have to look. Instead, I listened for the front door, the footsteps. Viola turned, and I spoke at the same time.

"Hello, Earl."

"Good afternoon, ladies." He performed a gallant bow. Viola's giggle melted into a dimpled smile. Would I have to send Earl away to capture the girl's attention again?

Better yet, I'd send her away.

"Viola, call the children down and sort out the picnic program, please. They'll need to begin work immediately."

Viola tripped off after a shy glance back. Earl watched her go before expounding on the few funding possibilities he'd explored on his trip to Philadelphia. The house filled with the din of gathering children. I tried to concentrate on Earl's words, but the racket grew loud. Unruly.

"Excuse me." I crossed the foyer to stand at the back of the parlor. Viola was trying to talk, but she couldn't be heard over the babble. Her lip quivered and tears stood in her eyes.

Movement on the opposite side of the room caught my eye. Lily Beth hovered at the edge of the gathering, near the wall, her eyes staring at her nose. If I went to her, perhaps my presence would calm the children into listening to Viola.

When I reached Lily Beth, I brushed her wispy hair from her forehead and looked into her elfin face. Something was missing. I leaned down, spoke close to her ear. "Where are your glasses, love bug?"

She shrugged, her thin shoulders remaining hunched around her ears, her chin meeting her chest. I lifted her into my arms, then turned to ask Viola about the glasses. But she finally had the attention of her charges.

The glasses would have to wait. Right now, Viola's confidence was more important than Lily Beth's obedience.

Mr. Riley decided to hold the April board meeting in our parlor. Dressed in my freshly laundered green suit, I haunted the foyer, waiting for the first gentleman to arrive. Miranda carried refreshments into the back parlor; the pocket doors would be closed when we'd gathered, to ensure privacy. Viola had copied out the report of the past month's income and expenditures.

Guilt niggled at the numbers I'd changed, but I couldn't believe it mattered much. The bank was right. As long as I started with their total, I'd be fine.

I hoped.

The rap at the door sent me flying to open it. "Earl!"

He sauntered inside, hung his hat in the usual place. "I ran into Mr. Brumbaugh at the hotel. He suggested I join you at the meeting tonight."

"Oh." Such an odd request, given that we'd determined to remain secretive about our fleece before the Lord concerning the Home's future. Even in all my strategizing with Earl, I'd never once let the board's decision escape. He had no idea that my frenzy to bring in money had everything to do with keeping the Home from closing.

"Come in, then. The others will be here soon." I led him into the parlor. Viola followed, eyes devouring Earl as if he were a chocolate from Gardiner's Confectionary instead of a man almost ten years her senior.

Earl sat. I feared Viola would join him on the sofa.

"Viola, I need you to get the children in bed. Yourself, as well. I'll lock up this evening."

Her expression soured, but she obeyed, albeit after a wistful glance at Earl. I shook my head. "I'm so sorry."

Earl crossed one leg over the other. "Don't worry. It's kind of flattering, actually."

The low hum of male voices alerted us to the arrival of the other board members. Earl greeted them as I did. Then we pulled the doors shut.

Mr. Riley took charge of the meeting. "First item of business—Carter Wellsmith."

I gave a short update on the situation. Mumbles of disapproval waved through the room.

"And how has he been this past week, Miss Sillsby?" Mr. Riley's pointed gaze froze me.

I licked moisture into my lips. I didn't want to lie, but I couldn't chance Carter being tossed out. He'd have nowhere to go. If only he and Blaine had been able to get along. But that experiment had ended much the same way it had with the Comstocks, and both had declared they wouldn't consider such an arrangement again.

"I haven't had any reason to fault him." I glanced back at Earl. "And Mr. Glazier has been a particularly good influence on him."

"Have you taken Carter to apologize to Mr. Comstock?" Mr. Philpot asked.

My head jerked up again. "No, I haven't. Not yet."

Mr. Philpot crossed his arms and frowned at me. "I suggest you attend to that immediately. We can't afford to have situations where generous families have been treated ungraciously. We're teetering on the edge of extinction even now."

"If I might speak?" Earl rose from his seat and took my place in the front. "As you know, I've talked with a few of you as to how you might improve your work here. You've done a fine job with the facilities and the care of the children in the Home who are waiting on their own parents or on another family to take them in. However, as the case of Carter Wellsmith illustrates, you have a great need to be in more constant contact with the families who have already taken in children. If you'll pardon my saying so, the matron is already overworked with the daily tasks of running the Home, finding prospective families, taking in children, sending out children, raising the money, and preparing the reports on all these things to present to you each month."

My face warmed. He had stated the matter correctly, but I hadn't complained. To him or anyone else.

"And we pay her well to do all that," Mr. Delp chimed in. The others nodded and muttered their approval.

My stomach clenched. Did Earl think he was helping? I could read only discontent in the majority of faces. I'd worked hard to deserve this position. Would he unwittingly wrench it from my grasp?

I rose. "Gentlemen, what I believe Mr. Glazier is saying—"

Earl laid his hand on my arm. "What I'm saying is that you

need an administrator whose sole job is to keep up with the children after they leave this place, to help arrest problems before they begin, to mediate between foster parents and children." His eyes cut in my direction.

Was that admiration I spied? My breath released. I could trust him to be my champion.

Heads nodded. Conversations ensued. Mr. Riley cleared his throat. The room quieted again.

"And how do you propose we pay the salary for this position? We already exceed the amount of money we take in each month." Mr. Philpot's face reddened. Would he disclose what we'd all agreed not to reveal?

Mr. Riley held up one hand. "It's an interesting proposition, Mr. Glazier, and a prudent observation, Mr. Philpot, but I think it is a discussion for another time."

The business moved on. Everyone expressed surprise and pleasure over the month's financial report. Then Mr. Riley closed the meeting in prayer. Most of the men gathered their things to leave. All but Mr. Philpot and Mr. Delp. They pulled Earl into a corner. I stepped nearer, but not so close as to intimate a desire to be included in the conversation.

"Would you, sir, be willing to consider such a post should we create it?" Mr. Delp asked. My heart thumped against my chest. Earl would never forfeit his position with the prestigious CAS to come here, would he? If he did, would our working relationship mature into a more personal connection?

"Of course, the terms would have to be agreeable, but yes, I'd consider it." When Earl's gaze met mine, his mouth curved into a grin that melted me from head to toe.

Chapter 24

I told Carter we would visit the Comstocks after school. He clearly didn't like the idea, but he didn't argue. Still, I waited by the door to take him in hand before he got distracted.

Henry and Carl raced into the house first. Lily Beth tripped along behind, but no wire-rimmed spectacles circled her eyes. I wanted to scold—both Lily Beth and Viola—but held my tongue. There would be time for that later.

Carter dragged himself inside last of all, so far behind the others I feared he'd run off to avoid his apology.

"Let's go." I hooked my arm around his and led him out the front door.

His shoulders sagged, along with his mouth.

I poked him in the side. "Cheer up. You aren't going to hang for it, you know."

"Feels like it," he mumbled.

I steered Carter downhill. "Let's walk to town. The fresh air will do you good." No sense stirring up gossip on a trolley ride.

He shrugged, followed my lead. It was a quiet walk to the

center of town, to the livery stable. "Good afternoon, Mr. Winklemeyer. Do you have a buggy ready for me?"

"Yes, ma'am." He tipped his hat, then helped me up. Carter sprang up into the seat beside me. Once we'd left town behind, Carter turned pensive. "Why didn't Earl come?"

"I told you, he had other business to take care of." I'd asked him to meet with a family in Cassville while I dealt with Carter and the Comstocks, but I couldn't seem to shake his recommendation to the board for a second administrator. I didn't like the board thinking I couldn't do my job. All of it.

"I really need you to cooperate today. Can you do that? For me?"

He shrugged. "I don't know why saying a few words I don't mean matters so much to everyone."

I flicked the reins, urging the horse faster. If we didn't get to the Comstocks soon, I might throttle the boy myself. I took a deep breath and tried to imagine what Hazel would say in this same situation, and how she would say it.

"It matters, Carter. Not just to me and to the board or even to Earl. It matters to the Home, to the other children there. But most of all, it matters to you. Don't you see? If you let this situation go unresolved, you will be the one who suffers. On the inside."

My own words resounded in my ears. Did I believe that? What about my unresolved situation with Blaine? My feelings over my mother? Could those things hurt me the same way that being unrepentant could sabotage Carter?

"I'll only suffer when I apologize," he grumbled.

"Trust me, you'll injure yourself in ways you can't yet imagine. And if you can't bring yourself to believe that, then do this for me. And for the others at the Home. Don't let your pride punish all of us."

He didn't seem any more amenable to the task, but at least his mouth set in a straight line instead of a frown. As Pastor Uland had said, even a small victory was a victory.

"See? That didn't hurt, did it?"

Carter scowled and looked away. At least I had the consolation of knowing he'd done as I'd asked. I could rest in regard to the situation with the Comstocks. Now I only had to keep Lily Beth in her glasses, inspire Cynthia beyond her fear of speaking, and accumulate forty-five hundred dollars, of which we'd collected very little.

Back at the livery stable, I asked Mr. Winklemeyer to bill us for use of the horse and buggy. He agreed. Reluctantly. Then Carter and I started back up the hill toward home. It took much longer than the trip into town, for now we stopped to talk with friends and neighbors.

"Carter!" A scruffy-looking boy—man, actually—pounded a greeting on Carter's back. His rakish grin included me for a moment, as well. I turned away, straightening my skirt, letting them think I wasn't listening to every word that passed between them. Although I was.

The young man's voice didn't carry well, so I strained to hear. "Gloria said it's your turn to treat the gang this weekend."

Treat whom? With what? I kept my eyes on the ground but wished I could turn my head and observe Carter's face.

"I'll get the money. Don't worry."

Get money? From where? I leaned over, as if to repair the strap of my shoe.

The other young man mumbled something I couldn't make out as the trolley ambled past. Then the street quieted and his garbled speech clarified. "You can't pilfer that much candy from the counter."

I held my breath. Pilfer? Carter wouldn't steal. But how else would he come by cash? I doubted the Comstocks had given him any money. And I knew I hadn't. Blaine never trusted him with it. Besides, Blaine didn't have extra anymore. He had to direct all his profits toward his mortgage payment on the farm.

I straightened. "Carter, we need to go."

The young man cackled. "Your nursemaid's calling, little baby." He shoved his hands into his pockets and continued on toward town, still hooting his amusement.

Carter's scowl deepened as he watched his friend round the corner, out of sight.

"Let's go." I pulled at his arm.

When he turned to me, the hatred in his face frightened me more than the thought of the Raystown Home closing its doors forever.

My pencil scratched against the paper time and time again, but even when I managed to confirm the totals for our expenses and our income, the two of them didn't add up to the number in our bank book. I pressed my thumbs into the middle of my pencil. It snapped beneath my fingers. I hid the halves in the drawer instead of the wastebasket.

Viola popped into the office. The third time in an hour. I pinched the bridge of my nose.

"Yes, Viola?"

"I just found Lily Beth's glasses in the box of notepaper in the desk. Where do you want me to put them?"

I shut my eyes, counted to ten, and then opened them again. "You didn't check to see if she was wearing them when she left for school?" I let the words drip like honey, though they tasted like licorice.

Her forehead crinkled as she set one finger alongside her pursed lips. "No, I guess I didn't."

"Leave them here on my desk."

She flounced forward, set them down. "Where's Mr. Glazier today?"

I stifled a moan, forced a smile to frame my words. "He had other work to do, as do you."

Her eyes grew large, her mouth forming a perfect O. She nodded and scampered away. I cradled my head in my hands.

A few minutes later, Viola poked her head around the corner. "Sadie?"

"Yes, Viola?" I couldn't keep the sigh from my voice.

She plopped into a chair, resting her elbows on the desktop and her chin in her upturned hands, eyes staring into the distance. "I was just thinking . . ."

About Earl, I imagined. Or Blaine. The girl didn't have enough to keep her busy. Had I ever roamed the house with nothing to do? No matter. I could remedy her boredom.

"Why don't you go meet the children at school and walk home with them."

She perked up a bit.

"Go wait at the lower school. If the older children want to walk home with you, they'll catch up." I picked up Lily Beth's spectacles and held them out to her. "Make sure Lily Beth puts these on and wears them the rest of the afternoon."

She took the glasses, her smile not as enthusiastic as before. At least I'd have a few minutes of peace before the children arrived. And Lily Beth would wear her glasses.

If only I could trust Viola to work on the program for the Decoration Day picnic with as much diligence as she daydreamed about unmarried men.

Chapter 25

"Knit one, purl two." I put my own knitting needles in motion as I spoke the instructions to the girls, most of whom had no desire to be outside, working in the dirt. As a special treat, I'd opened the pocket doors and taken them into the back parlor, the one usually reserved for guests. Through the windows, I could keep an eye on those working with Blaine in the garden out back.

The younger girls tried to follow my lead. Cynthia's tongue poked out of her mouth as she concentrated. Then her face brightened as she held up her work for my inspection.

"That's it!" I said. "You're doing so well."

On and on we went, each of us working to create a simple scarf that we could use or give away. All except Lily Beth. Viola and Mrs. Fore had fussed over her until she felt it a special honor to be chosen to help them in the kitchen instead. I simply couldn't bear watching the girl struggle with her stitches.

Sylvia and Nancy wielded their needles skillfully as they sat close together on the sofa and chatted. A buzz rose up among the younger girls as a few grew frustrated and bored with their task, but mostly they persisted with quiet calm.

Through the glass panes that faced the back of the house,

we heard a shout. A bout of laughter. The clank and thud of metal against hard earth.

I shook my head as I helped Janet find her rhythm, imagining clods of mud flying up into the air and raining down on clean clothes, scattering in clean hair. But it made me smile, for I knew that long winter days indoors equaled torture for active boys.

"Keep on, girls. Sylvia and Nancy can help if you get tangled. I'm going out to see if anything worthwhile is being accomplished in the garden." I set aside my half-finished scarf and headed for the back door.

Mrs. Fore sat near the window, Lily Beth at the table patting out a small round of pie dough, Viola nowhere in sight.

Mrs. Fore gave me a knowing look. "I expected you'd be along soon."

My cheeks heated as I stole out the door, determined to stay far away from Blaine, especially with Mrs. Fore watching.

I walked straight toward Carter instead. He was leaning on a shovel handle, his delicate features alive with excitement as a group of younger boys stood mesmerized by whatever story he was spinning. A good sign, I felt sure. As long as he wasn't planting ideas in their heads that would take me weeks to weed out. Since his apology to the Comstocks and his encounter on the street, he'd been a model child. My concerns for him must have been colored by my anxiety over so many other things.

A few boys stopped working as I made my way toward them. Others waved and continued on with more vigor. I couldn't help but relish the unspoken compliment.

I gripped the pickets of the short fence enclosing the garden and encouraged the boys with smiles. "Making progress, I see," I said to Carl.

"Yes, ma'am." He tried to rest his arm on the top of the shovel handle like Carter, but it was too high. Dirt streaked his face and his shirt. I motioned him closer and dusted him off as best I could.

From the corner of my eye, I spied Blaine. With a turn of my head, I blocked him from my vision completely. No doubt he was waiting for Viola to come and make a fuss over him. It was a wonder she hadn't beat me outside.

"Not sure much is getting done, but they needed to work off some of their energy." The deep voice near my ear twisted my heart into a hard knot.

"Thank you for making the time to help." I glanced at Carter and his audience instead of at Blaine. Sunlight glistened against a stubble of blond hair between Carter's nose and mouth. I swallowed down the truth. Blaine was right. He was closer to a man than a boy now.

I lowered my voice and nodded in Carter's direction. "How's he doing?"

Blaine shrugged. "All right, I guess. I've kept away from him, mostly. Didn't want to ruin the day for the other boys. He hasn't really done any work, though. Was that part of his problem with Mr. Comstock?"

I stared across the churned-up plot of ground. I didn't want to discuss this with Blaine. I could handle Carter without his interference. Besides, it hurt too much to fall into such familiar conversation.

"Sadie?" Viola stopped beside me. "Oh, hello," she said to Blaine.

He nodded but couldn't seem to remove his gaze from her face. My eyes narrowed. "Did you need me, Viola?"

Her eyes widened, blinked. "Mrs. Fore needs you," she said, almost breathless.

I started to drag her back to the house with me, then I shrugged and trudged away alone. Blaine had no reason not to be infatuated with a pretty girl who seemed to be infatuated with him. Who was I to interfere?

The telephone jangled as I reached the kitchen. I crossed the room and lifted the receiver. The smoothness of Earl's voice wrapped around my heart.

After I hung up, I turned to Mrs. Fore. "Mr. Glazier will be here for supper."

"Hmph." Mrs. Fore lifted a bulge of bread dough and pounded it to the counter again. Then her hands stilled. "Can't you find a way to patch things up between you?"

The quiet concern in Mrs. Fore's voice made me quiver. If I wasn't careful, I'd find myself in her arms, sobbing out all my troubles. But I couldn't do that now. My personal life was of little concern in light of the needs of the Home.

I needed to keep Mrs. Fore on a more professional footing. "Mr. Glazier and I get along just fine."

"Now, you know I didn't mean him."

I waited for her to say her piece, but for once, Mrs. Fore didn't expound. I fidgeted with my skirt. "Blaine and I are friends, as always."

"I've known you too long to believe that." Her eyes pleaded. "Can't you forgive him? He only gets cross because he cares so much."

The garden plot drew my gaze with unrelenting strength.

At least Viola was nowhere to be seen. My arms tightened across my chest. I could forgive him for the mortgage. For not wanting to wait. What I couldn't forgive was his charging ahead without a bit of warning. I wiped moisture from the corner of my eye.

Yet the truth hurt more than the lie I'd told myself all these weeks.

It wasn't all Blaine's fault.

We both bore blame.

I wanted to drop into a chair and weep, until I spied Lily Beth, the spectacles perched on her tiny nose, just as I'd commanded. My purpose. My calling. I had work to do. Important work. I had to save this place and these children.

I pushed open the office door. Someone pulled from the other side. I stumbled forward, face-to-face with Viola. She looked as startled as I felt. Why wasn't she with the girls in the parlor or Mrs. Fore in the kitchen? It took me a moment to regain my composure.

"Did you need something?" I asked.

"Oh! Yes. I was looking for you." Her focus darted back and forth. "Mother needs me at home for an hour or so and wondered if I could be spared."

Mrs. Fore, Miranda, and I could handle things, especially with Blaine here. "Go on. But be back by suppertime."

Her head bounced with nods as she scampered away. Alone behind the closed door, the thought of her out from underfoot thrilled me more than it ought.

By late afternoon, golden rays of sunlight angled through my office window, drawing a path on the floor. A path that led into its warmth.

I stretched my arms over my head, then rolled my shoulders. Too many hours of sitting, not enough moving. The waning day drew me outdoors. I savored the bits of green grass poking through brown. The hydrangeas flanking the steps still had no buds, but that would take a while longer. At least the spindly branches had leafed out.

But they'd been neglected. I fetched a bucket of water and dampened the earth beneath each flowerless plant. The soil around them seemed to have eroded a bit. Grabbing my empty bucket, I trotted around to the garden plot, scooped extra dirt into my bucket, and then scrambled back to the front of the house and dropped to my knees. I shook soil from the bucket, half for each plant, then spread it with my fingers.

"Turning into a gardener, I see." Blaine set a foot on the bottom step and rested his elbows on his elevated knee.

I jerked upright. "Just trying to pretty up the place."

"In more ways than one." Blaine smiled. Or was that a grimace?

I brushed the dirt from my hands, but they refused to come clean. I rocked back on my toes. Blaine reached out a helping hand. I hesitated a moment before laying my dirty fingers against his palm and rising to my feet.

He shrugged toward my hydrangeas. "Still no buds?"

I lifted my chin. "I expect them any day now. But of course they won't bloom until June."

His eyes squinted, but he didn't contradict me.

"Are you leaving?" I hoped my tone invited him to do so.

He shook his head, then pulled a paper from his pocket and unfolded it. He stretched it toward me.

My pulse throbbed. This felt too much like that awful night when he'd told me he'd purchased his land. "What is it?"

Blaine cleared his throat, studied the ground. "My bill," he mumbled.

My eyes slammed shut. Breathing in the fresh-turned earth, I steadied myself before looking at him again. "Thank you. I'll make sure you get paid within the week." I refolded the page and tucked it into the pocket of the apron covering my skirt.

A bird chirped nearby, accentuating the silence. No need to linger. He'd done nothing more than honor our agreement. "So *now* you're leaving?"

He tried to smile, but it didn't last. "After I make a last check of things. The boys tend to use the tools and forget to return them to the shed."

I gave him a curt nod. "We'll see you next week, then?"

His gaze bounced to my unadorned bushes, then back to me. "And the week after that. And the week after that."

Unbidden, my mind returned to that morning so many weeks ago, to the feel of his hands on my shoulders, his face hovering above mine. My heart ached to feel those things again.

Until I remembered the price of our food.

He'd made his choice already. As had I.

Chapter 26

Early Monday morning, a light knock sounded on my bedroom door. Nothing good could come of knocks on my door before dawn. I lifted a quick prayer as I tied my wrapper in place and opened the door. Mrs. Fore's ample chest heaved and she wheezed as if she'd come a long distance. I bade her to sit.

"Thank you, dear. From the cellar to here can be a long haul when I'm trying to move faster than usual."

"What's wrong?" I sat beside her, glad to see her breathing return to normal.

"Nothing a quick trip to the grocer's won't fix."

"Before breakfast?"

"No, but as soon as it's served. No one told me the flour bag was empty. I'd planned noodles with our supper, and there's bread to make."

No one would be Viola. I couldn't imagine Miranda not mentioning such a vital thing to Mrs. Fore. Unless she wanted me to think it was Viola's fault. Treachery or neglect? I didn't want to deal with either.

"I'll get you some money for the trolley." I hurried away, letting Mrs. Fore amble down at her own pace.

An old tin box sat beneath a pile of ledgers in the bottom drawer of an old filing cabinet in the corner of the office. The emergency cash. Enough for trolley fare when needed. Like now.

I opened the box. Nothing. Not one penny.

I didn't remember using it. Not since Earl and I had taken the trip out to see the Stratmores last week. There'd been at least six dollars in the box then.

So how could it be missing now? I rocked back on my heels and stared at the emptiness once more. Only Hazel and I knew the location of our stash.

And Viola.

A groan escaped. I'd shown Viola the cash box, just as Hazel had shown me.

Maybe one of the children needed something and Viola forgot to tell me. I had been out of the house quite often of late. That was it. That had to be it.

But what to do for Mrs. Fore in the meantime?

I reached for my pocketbook and took out a few coins. All I had left after the clothing I'd purchased. I'd get money from the bank later. And after Mrs. Fore left, Viola and I would have a talk.

I lingered in the kitchen after breakfast, observing Viola send the children off to school. She didn't have the closeness with them that I'd enjoyed, but then, that would come.

Confident that the children would be to school on time, I

returned to the office. A few minutes later, the house quieted. Then Mrs. Fore bustled in, a small hat askew on her head.

"I'm off to the grocer's," she said.

I waved her away. As soon as the front door clicked shut, I spied the open tin box.

I had to find Viola.

Not in the kitchen.

Or the parlor.

She'd have no reason to be upstairs, but I trudged up the steps anyway and rapped on her bedroom door.

"Yes?" came the reply from inside.

I pushed open the door. Viola sat on her bed, staring into the mirror, fixing her hair. Thick blond curls arranged just so. I smoothed back my straight hair, tied in a hasty knot at the nape of my neck. Then I pulled my hand down. We weren't here to look beautiful. We were here for the children.

"The money from the cash box is missing. Did you need it for something and forget to let me know?" *Like you did with the flour for Mrs. Fore?* I kept a smile pressed on my face as I watched her expression waver in the mirror.

Her lashes lowered. "No, ma'am."

My smile faltered. I pulled it back into place. "Then do you have any idea where it has gone? You and I are the only ones who know where that money is kept."

Her head shot up, tears pooling in her wide eyes. "I don't know." Her bottom lip quivered. "But—but I did see Miranda coming out of there. On Saturday evening, before she went home."

I couldn't move. Would Miranda do that? Stealing from the Home was the same as stealing from the children. For all our differences, I hadn't imagined Miranda capable of such a thing. And yet . . . had she meant to throw suspicion on Viola? On me? We each held a position she had desired. Was this her revenge?

"Hello?" called a cultured voice from below us.

Earl. He would help me sort this out. Before I could move in his direction, Viola swept past me, the eagerness on her face worrying me more than a few dollars gone missing.

The thud of something heavy hitting the floor. The clink of metal against metal. I quaked. Then the plop of water, the steady *scritch* of bristles against a wooden floor. Just Miranda.

I glanced after Viola. She'd be occupied with Earl. Perhaps now was the best time to ask Miranda about the money. Rounding the corner, I found her on her hands and knees, skirt damp around the hem.

"I need to ask you a question, Miranda." I worked hard to keep malice or accusation from my words. I truly wanted to ask what she knew about the money. I hadn't known Miranda to lie. I had known Viola to be . . . distracted.

She stopped her movements and nodded her head but didn't look up.

I folded my arms over my chest. "Do you know anything about the cash fund that's gone missing?"

Her whole body jerked as her head whipped in my direction, her mouth turned down. "There's money missing? From here?"

"From the office." I took a deep breath. "You were seen coming out of there on Saturday."

Her face crumpled in confusion. "Viola sent me in there. She said you wanted the trash emptied and the room tidied."

My head tipped to one side as I thought back. Tending the hydrangeas. Receiving Blaine's bill. Did my desk look more organized when I returned inside? I couldn't recall. I couldn't verify or deny Miranda's story.

"And what were you doing here so late on a Saturday evening?"

Her unflinching gaze met mine. "Pressing the creased dresses and collars so that they'd all look presentable for the wedding this weekend." No guile appeared in her expression. At least none that I could see as I scrutinized every blink of her eye, every twitch of her lips.

"Thank you, Miranda. I appreciate your honesty."

She went back to scrubbing, then stopped again. "I saw Viola and Carter outside when I left that evening. She'd given him something, but I couldn't tell what."

I rubbed my forehead to forestall the throbbing as I remembered Carter's conversation with the boy in the street about the need for cash. Who was I to believe, Viola or Miranda?

Chapter 27

Hazel and John's small wedding ceremony took place in the little stone church across from the college campus. After the vows, the entire wedding party crossed to the campus lawn for a reception with light refreshments.

A much larger crowd was expected here, including all the children, under Viola's watchful eye. At least, I hoped her eye would be watchful.

The sun shone high above us, lending unseasonable warmth to the late-April day. With one hand, I held my blush-pink skirt away from the ground. Rosettes of darker pink accented the skirt. An ecru lace overlay covered the bodice and short sleeves, extending down past my waist, ending in scallops near my knees. A brighter pink sash marked my waist while a wide-brimmed hat completed my ensemble.

The most elegant dress I'd ever owned. I almost felt as if it were my wedding day. Earl slowed his step until we fell behind the rest of the wedding party.

He pulled me closer. "You're beautiful, you know."

I imagined my cheeks matched my dress now. Maybe my hat would throw enough shadow over my face so no one would notice. "You said that before," I mumbled.

"Yes, but I want you to believe that it's true." He squeezed my hand, then let go as we reached the gathering of well-wishers.

The moment Carter spied us, he straightened his coat, his tie, brushed the errant hair from his face, and pulled back his shoulders. He sped to Earl's side, even matched Earl's stride.

I indulged a small laugh. For all his wayward behavior, at least he'd taken pains with his appearance and manners since he'd become fascinated with Earl. I couldn't think of anyone better for him to idolize at the moment.

Lily Beth bolted toward me. I held out my hands, stopping her before she crushed herself against my dress. She looked up at me and blinked.

"Where are your glasses, sweet pea?"

Her dazed expression turned hard. She shook her head until the bow in her hair drooped at an odd angle. I sighed. I'd specifically instructed Viola to make sure Lily Beth had them on. Dr. Lawson had emphasized the need for her to wear them every day. And I didn't want Hazel to think her trip to Philadelphia had been for naught.

"May I get you some punch?" Earl asked. I nodded, righting Lily Beth's bow, then capturing her hand in mine and leading her into the crowd. Carter trotted after Earl. He even picked up an extra cup of punch, then stood looking around, as if wondering who to give it to. Earl came back toward me; Carter darted off to his left. I followed his progress, wondering who had drawn his attention.

Viola accepted the cup from Carter's hand, her dimples deepening as she lowered her lashes. My eyes pinched into a squint. Blaine could look out for himself, but Carter was only a child.

Or was he? Only two years younger than Viola.

Carter's slender frame angled toward her, as if trying to keep anyone else out of their conversation. My hands turned cold beneath my gloves. His mouth continued to move while Viola stared over the rim of her cup, her gaze locked on someone else.

I followed her line of sight.

Earl.

Why, the little chit! Flirting with every man or boy who crossed her path.

A squeal and a shout caught my attention. Carl and Henry were chasing Janet and Cynthia through the clusters of guests, bumping and shaking everyone in their path. All while Viola cast cow eyes at Earl.

I lifted my skirt and stalked toward the offenders.

Then the commotion dissipated. I slowed my steps. Who had grabbed hold of the rambunctious children? Someone like Miss Pembrooke, who couldn't wait to share their sins with me? Or a more sympathetic soul?

I prayed for a man or woman of understanding to have them, both for Hazel's sake and for mine. But I wasn't prepared for the sight that greeted me.

Miranda, hands on her knees, was stooped in front of the four offending children, her face level with theirs. Each gave a solemn nod before retracing their steps and offering a polite "I'm sorry" to each of their victims.

My jaw dropped. I shut it again, shaking away my shock. Earl had apparently followed me. He handed me a glass of punch.

I let the cool drink soothe my parched throat. "I can't believe it."

"Can't believe what?" He surveyed the scene. I motioned toward Miranda.

He shrugged. "Nothing unusual."

"How can you say that?" I sputtered.

His expression turned more serious than usual. "Because I've watched her interact with the children." He sipped his punch, eyes sweeping the lawn until they landed on Carter and Viola's tryst near the trees. "I've watched Viola, too."

My stomach twisted and squeezed like laundry under Miranda's reddened hands.

Earl's attention returned to me. "That girl is a bit . . ."

"Young? Immature? Flighty?"

He chuckled. "I was going to say *determined*."

"Determined. That's an interesting choice of words. How so?"

"Let's just say I don't think her goals have anything to do with dependent children." His slow grin sent a flash of warmth into my cheeks.

Dreaminess washed over me as Earl and I walked from the trolley stop to the Home. Stars twinkled overhead, lending a final air of romance to the day. It had been perfect—except for my worry over Viola, Carter, Miranda, and the missing money. Not to mention Blaine, whose name always occupied the back of my mind.

All thought of romance faded. Why hadn't Blaine come to celebrate with Hazel and the professor?

Earl tugged me closer. "Penny for your thoughts?"

I blessed the night sky that kept my embarrassment from exposure. I sighed, thinking back on Hazel's bright face, the exuberant love shining from her eyes when she looked at her bridegroom. "They are so fortunate to have found one another."

"Yes." His arm curled around my waist. He pulled me closer. Not the polite gesture of a colleague, but the intimate movement of something more. I glanced over at him, but his open stare sent my gaze to my feet as my heart pumped at twice its normal speed. I could care for him, couldn't I? His handsome face and compassionate heart would soon make me forget that other visage that had been so dear.

We reached the front porch. He lingered near, his breath warm on my face. I reached for the door handle, gave it a gentle push. At that moment, his head lowered. My eyelids curtained the world from view, waiting for a soft touch on my lips, wanting my heart to respond.

"Sadie? Is that you?"

My breath caught, then clawed for release as Earl leapt back, tipped his hat, and jogged away. My lungs released air, allowed me to answer. "Yes, Mrs. Fore." I stepped into the foyer. She peeked from the hall, clutching her wrapper closed at the neck.

I secured the door and tiptoed to the staircase. "I'm off to bed," I whispered.

The first stair creaked as my foot hit it.

"Sadie?" Mrs. Fore sounded almost frightened. Had something else happened while I was gone?

Reversing direction, I stood in front of Mrs. Fore, intent on deciphering her expression. But I could see little in the dark.

"Be careful," she said. "You don't know what kind of man he is."

I stiffened. I knew enough. "At least he came today. And he doesn't even know Hazel and the professor. Others who do didn't bother to show up at all."

"And if you'd asked, you'd have known that *others* have taken on extra jobs, struggling to make ends meet, I guess."

Which he wouldn't have to do if he'd stuck to our plan and not purchased the land until he could do so outright. I couldn't muster up sympathy, though I knew all too well the pressure of meeting financial obligations.

I mounted the stairs without response, forcing myself to recall Earl's face as it leaned in close to mine, believing God had turned my path away from Blaine, toward Earl. If I let Him, He'd teach my heart to follow.

Chapter 28

I rubbed my eyes as I tried to make the numbers in the columns sit still. Thankfully, Mr. Riley had opened a second bank account in which to collect next year's budget money. That simplified matters. Now I had to deal only with our usual monthly debits and credits and watch the other account balance grow, albeit slowly.

The house swelled with noise as the children came in from school. A sinking feeling in my middle warned me to check on Viola, especially after what I'd witnessed at the wedding. But I had no time to stop work. I'd have to trust that Viola was doing her job, as I was doing mine.

The din abated, and then the volume grew louder again. I covered my ears, tried to concentrate. The commotion continued. Finally, I rose, determined to be the voice of reason that Hazel had always been. Calm, purposeful steps carried me to the parlor. Viola was standing in the midst of the older boys, a cloth tied over her eyes, hands outstretched. She giggled as George pulled out of her reach. Carter sidled closer, as if trying to be caught.

I set my hands on my hips. "May I ask if this is an assignment for school tomorrow?"

The boys sobered at once. Viola's smile wavered before she removed the impediment from her eyes and dropped her gaze.

"I'm sorry, Sadie. I—" Her eyes cut toward Carter. His head was bowed, but his shoulders shook with laughter.

My jaw tightened, barely releasing the clipped instructions. "Viola, help the younger children with their schoolwork, please."

"Yes, ma'am." She hurried away, but not without a backward glance at Carter, her bottom lip caught between her teeth.

I waited until her footsteps faded. Then I turned my fury on the boys. "Every one of you knows better. You have homework and chores. I expect to see the work done and done well. Go. Now."

Three of them slunk away. Carter turned to follow, but without the same remorse. I caught his collar.

"Oh, no you don't. You're the ringleader of this and I know it."

His wide eyes feigned innocence. "How can you say that?" He pressed a hand over his heart.

"I can say it because it's true." Though I'd have chastised anyone else who said anything against Carter. Especially Blaine. I grimaced at that revelation. "I expect more of you, Carter. Both because you and I have a long history of friendship and because you are the oldest one here. Can you understand that?"

The light in his eyes dimmed even though his mouth grinned. "Don't worry about me, Sadie." He sauntered away, as carefree as if he hadn't been found in mischief and scolded.

"But I do worry about you," I muttered to the empty room. "We all do."

And then I had another revelation. I could no longer leave Viola alone with Carter. Which meant one of them had to go.

Back in the office, I cradled my head in my hands. I didn't have time for more interviews. If Viola had to go, I needed someone to step into her place immediately—and function independently. Especially getting the children ready to perform at the picnic, just four weeks away.

Clunk. A heavy object hit the floor outside my door. The slosh of water. The slap of wet cloth against floor.

Miranda? I chewed my bottom lip. She'd wanted my job. I still didn't know for certain if she'd taken the money, though I really didn't believe she had. And her lack of formal education remained a problem. How would she help the children with their homework?

Yet Hazel had advocated for her the first time. Even Earl had mentioned her rapport with the children. She'd handled them well at the wedding reception, as well as several other times, if I were honest about it. She seemed to know what the children needed—and when. Which already set her far above Viola's pitiful attempts.

Could she do the job? *Would* she, after I'd passed her over the first time? Could she and I put aside our differences and work together for the sake of the children?

The position of housemaid would be much easier to fill. We wouldn't have a problem hiring her replacement.

"Sadie?" Viola's penitent voice. I looked up. "I helped Janet with her math and Henry with his spelling. George took Carl to help with the outside chores, and Nancy and Sylvia are trying to get Cynthia to say her piece to them." Her smile seemed to ask for forgiveness.

"That's fine. Thank you, Viola."

"You're welcome." She tiptoed from the room, guiding the door shut behind her.

By tomorrow morning, she'd be crestfallen, for I couldn't risk another day. Not for the sake of the children. Or the Raystown Home. Or even my own reputation.

Tomorrow, I'd send Viola on her way and Miranda would take her place—if she was willing.

Please, God, let her be willing.

I changed my mind several times throughout the night and into the next morning. Each time, I asked the Lord for His wisdom. And each time, I couldn't shake the feeling that Viola needed to be let go and Miranda needed to step in. It didn't make sense, after my original decision, but the more I thought about it, the more I imagined Earl would approve. Hazel too.

As the decision solidified, my confidence grew. I called Viola into my office before breakfast and explained that her services were no longer required.

"But—but—but—" Splotches of red dotted her face before the tears started to fall. "You don't understand. Mama is counting on me."

"What do you mean?"

She cried harder, shook her head.

"I'm sorry, Viola. Truly I am. But this isn't working. For either of us."

Shoulders shaking, she trudged upstairs to pack her things while I told Mrs. Fore what had transpired.

"You did exactly right, Sadie." She stirred the oatmeal as

she talked. "That one had other things on her mind instead of work. I'll help out with the children as I can. We'll make do."

"Oh, I already have someone in mind for the job." I hesitated. Although I trusted both Hazel and Earl, it still rankled a bit to take their advice about Miranda.

"Someone with experience, I hope."

"Yes." I stared at my hands, took in a steam-laden breath. "I'm going to offer the job to Miranda." I'd said it. Committed myself.

Mrs. Fore beamed with delight. "That's a fine idea. She'll make you proud, I'm sure of it."

Everyone seemed so sure of Miranda. Everyone except me.

Children ran through the kitchen, into the dining room. Viola lagged behind, eyes rimmed red, suitcase in hand.

"But why?" Carter asked, walking backward in front of her.

Viola glared in my direction. Carter turned to look at me, too. His face hardened. I didn't smile. Didn't frown. I'd done the right thing. For all of us.

It would be a good lesson for Carter, too. He needed to understand the consequences of not doing a job well.

Mrs. Fore led Viola to the small table and shooed Carter into the dining room. "Sit down and have some breakfast before you leave."

I knew I ought to join the children, both for oversight and to get out of Viola's way, but I couldn't make myself go. Then the back door opened. Miranda ambled inside. One look at Viola's face and Miranda stood still. "What's happened?"

Viola didn't speak, just kept emptying her bowl of oatmeal into her mouth between tiny hiccuped sobs. Mrs. Fore's eyebrows arched toward the ceiling.

I cleared my throat. "Viola will be leaving us today."

"Oh?" Miranda blinked at me, then at Viola. If Viola had driven me to distraction, I felt sure Miranda wouldn't mind bidding the girl good-bye, either.

I laced my fingers together and lifted my chin. I needed Miranda to take this position, but I had no intention of letting her lord my desperation over me. "We'll discuss the situation in more detail after we get the children off to school."

Viola hopped up from the table. "You needn't wait on me." She grabbed the handle of her suitcase and jerked it from the floor. "I'm leaving now. You can have my final pay sent to my *home*." She flung the word at me, burst into tears, and ran from the room. A few minutes later, the front door opened and shut. I let out a long breath. It wasn't pretty, but it was done. I needed a few minutes to recover before putting the rest of my plan into motion.

"Mrs. Fore, will you and Miranda supervise the children's breakfast, please?"

"Of course, dear." She patted my arm, then nodded Miranda to the dining room. I needed the sanctuary of my office to gather my thoughts.

I passed the parlor. Sniffles. Muffled voices. Hadn't Viola left? I glanced toward the kitchen and dining room. I'd made sure Carter hadn't followed her, though he'd looked as if he wanted to.

"Thank you." A sniffle. Definitely Viola.

Charging into the parlor, I prepared my tongue-lashing.

I jerked to a stop. Viola dabbed her eyes with a handkerchief while Earl patted her head to his chest. He turned. His arms fell from the girl.

"Sadie!" After a quick glance at Viola, he came to me and took my hands in his.

Viola yanked up her suitcase, tossed her curls, and stomped past me, a glint of victory in her bright blue eyes. I followed her into the foyer, making sure that when the door clicked this time, she'd taken her leave.

"A pity, to be sure. But the right decision." Hands cupped on my belted waist. Earl smiled. Though I tried to resist, I could almost taste the sweetness of warm maple syrup when his eyes held mine. "I ran into her as I arrived. She needed a shoulder to cry on."

Of course she did. But no amount of compassion disguised the fact that Viola still had a lot of growing up to do.

"What will you do for an assistant?" The freshness of his shaving soap filled my nose as his breath whispered warm against my cheek. My body wanted to melt into him, but could such feelings penetrate to my heart?

Without warning, he let go. I feared I'd collapse in a heap, but I managed to stand, to walk at his side as if nothing had sparked between us. I'd never felt quite this same fiery connection with Blaine. Blaine was more . . . comfortable. The roughness of his hand engulfing mine, the familiarity of his lips brushing against my cheek.

I wet my lips. "I'm offering the job to Miranda."

A grin covered his face. "I'm proud of you, Sadie. I never imagined you'd have the courage to do it."

My feet faltered. He didn't imagine I'd have the courage to do what was best for the children? Perhaps he didn't know me as well as he imagined.

Chapter 29

Miranda sat in front of my desk, her work-worn hands twisting in her lap.

"I let Viola go. She wasn't attending to her responsibilities."

Miranda's eyes narrowed. "I see."

Did she think I'd called her in to fire her, too? Best to set her mind at rest. "I'd like you to take her post."

Miranda sat as still as a cat stalking a bird. Then her nose twitched, as if trying to scent the air and see if she'd heard correctly. "You want . . . *me* to be your assistant?"

"I do." I forced myself to look into her bewildered face. "I made a mistake in not giving you the job in the first place. Forgive me."

She ran her tongue over her lips, then nodded once. "Starting today?"

"Yes. Today. Your salary will increase to ten dollars a month, plus room and board."

She sucked in a breath. I smiled, remembering what a fortune that had seemed to me until a few weeks ago.

"Go get your things and set up your new room while the children are at school." With a jolt, I realized I didn't know where she'd retrieve her possessions from. I'd never asked if she lived alone or with family, in a house or in a rented room.

She cocked her head. "But what about the cleaning?"

"I want you to oversee the hiring of someone this week—though if we can manage, I'd prefer the new housemaid work fewer hours than you did. We are attempting to economize yet again." Miranda had been around long enough to understand that without explanation.

She nodded, stood, and turned to leave. "Thank you, Sadie," she whispered, her back to me.

Before I could reply, she was gone.

I heaved out a breath. It was done. Now I had to make it work.

Of course, if the money didn't come in, I wouldn't have a job to worry about. Neither would Miranda. Or Mrs. Fore.

More than the futures of the children rested in my hands.

Ensconced in my old room, Miranda donned the role of overseeing the children that afternoon as if she'd been doing it all along. And perhaps she had. Once the children left for school the next morning, the real test would come. Just Miranda and me, working together. I wondered if Miranda's nerves quivered at the thought. Mine did.

The morning proceeded smoothly. At least until I handed Lily Beth her spectacles as she bounded through the kitchen on her way to school.

She blinked up at me, her mouth slack. Slowly, she took the glasses from my hand and set them on her face.

I smiled. "Much better." I bent to hug her, but she remained stiff. When I looked up, Miranda ducked her head and handed Janet a lunch pail.

"Go on, now." I gave Lily Beth a gentle nudge out the door, but she needed no impetus to leave. She took off after the others, hair billowing out around her head like a cloud in a stiff wind. She never even glanced back.

I shook my head. When Earl returned from his quick trip to Philadelphia I would ask his advice on dealing with Lily Beth's eyes. It was right for her to wear her glasses. I knew it was. But one niggling doubt lingered, as irritating as a cricket on a quiet night.

What if I fixed her eyes and lost her love?

I pressed my lips together, determined to quiet the chirping. "Come, Miranda. We have much to do."

I didn't wait for her reply, just proceeded into my office. I would ask her to work on the correspondence while I worked on the bills. Again. Maybe this time the numbers would come out right.

By that afternoon, I had no qualms about leaving Miranda in charge. Ready to leave for my appointments, I stopped in the kitchen.

"Do you need anything while I'm out?"

Mrs. Fore sighed from her chair at the worktable, peeling a mass of scrawny carrots. Carrots from Blaine's cellar, no doubt. At least come summer we'd have our own harvest. Assuming we were still operating.

"Blaine never did bring any meat."

My lips pressed together before letting out tight words. "We can't presuppose anyone's generosity, Mrs. Fore. Even those who have been faithful before."

She harrumphed but kept working.

"But the children do need some meat. I'll talk with Mr. Hartzler about it this afternoon, after I meet with Mr. Wylie. With all Mr. Wylie's money, surely he can spare a little for us."

Or a lot? Four weeks wasn't much time to gather more than three thousand dollars in donations.

After donning my shabby hat, I stood on the porch for a moment, breathing in the freshness of spring. It quickened my pace down the three steps, where I stopped to examine my hydrangeas. A flurry of new growth felt soft beneath my fingers, though I saw no buds as yet, in spite of the unseasonal warmth. But they would appear at the appropriate time. I felt more sure of it every day.

I waited behind several customers for my turn to speak to Mr. Hartzler, the butcher. After a disconcerting interview with Mr. Wylie, I wasn't in any hurry to grovel again. It seemed Mr. Wylie did not have a generous or community-minded heart. Would the results have been different if Earl had been with me? I couldn't help but wonder.

Mr. Wylie had done everything except pat my head and tell me to be a good little girl. I doubted he'd have been so condescending with Earl. Anger smoldered in my chest, but with a few kind words, Mr. Hartzler could douse the flame.

I stepped to the counter, trying to keep my eyes off his

blood-spattered apron. Putting on my best smile, I asked after his family.

"We're all fine, Miss Sillsby. 'Course, Opal's busy with the little ones, so she doesn't come into the shop much anymore." He shook his head. "Sure could use some help around here."

"Haven't you any apprentices?" The minute the words left my mouth, I wanted to draw them back in again. What he needed was a son. An almost-grown son. Before he could reply, I jumped in again. "I came to see if you had any cuts of meat you could sell cheaply. We are in desperate need of some."

I thought of my own lack of nutrition when I'd arrived, the rickets that had pained my legs, my belly. The good food that had righted my body's torment. Suddenly my request had nothing to do with money and everything to do with the good of our children. My children.

Mr. Hartzler scratched his head with one hand and tapped a pencil against a pad of paper with the other. "Well, now. I do recall a couple of chickens no one has spoken for."

"At a discount?" I held my breath, praying he would be more giving than Mr. Wylie.

He nodded, retrieved the chickens.

"One more thing, Mr. Hartzler?"

"Yes?" He wrapped the naked birds as he spoke.

"Have you ever considered not an apprentice, but a son? One of our children, perhaps? We have several boys of such an age that they could help you in the shop. Not only would you provide a family for them, you'd teach them a trade."

I held my breath. Waiting. Praying.

He handed me the chickens but refused to meet my gaze.

"I don't know, Miss Sillsby. I've never thought of such a thing before, but it does make some sense."

Excitement shot up from my toes and brightened the grin on my face. "Will you think about it now? Talk to your wife? I'd be happy to answer any questions."

He hesitated. The door opened. He greeted another customer, then nodded at me. "We'll consider it, Miss Sillsby."

I wanted to squeal with glee but remembered the need for dignity. "Thank you, Mr. Hartzler." I held up my package. "And thank you for these, as well. Bless you for your generosity."

Chapter 30

Supper's ready!" Cynthia stuck her head into the parlor where I sat helping George with his book report.

After washing my hands, I busied myself in the dining room as the children trickled in to take their seats. A deep voice rumbled from the kitchen. Blaine. What was he doing here?

Even with Mr. Hartzler's generosity, the chickens had not fit in my budget. I now placed that shortfall squarely on Blaine's shoulders. I listened for the kitchen door to open and shut and his voice to disappear. But it stayed.

He stayed.

I stormed into the kitchen. Ran right into Blaine's unmoving mass. His hands instinctively clasped around my arms, holding me steady. I blinked up at him.

He let go of my arms. "Mrs. Fore invited me to stay for supper."

My face burned. "You didn't say yes, did you?" I hissed. And hated myself the moment the words left my mouth.

All resolve to act with Christian charity crumbled beneath

the thought of sitting at the supper table with Blaine and the children as if nothing had changed between us.

His gaze remained steady. "I most certainly did. I wouldn't hurt Mrs. Fore's feelings for anything. Or anyone."

I averted my eyes, pushed up my sleeves. My head twisted first one way, then the other, looking for a way to escape. At least Earl wasn't at the table, as well, to further my discomfort.

Mrs. Fore stepped between us, one arm wrapped around each of us. "Time for supper, you two." She patted my back, nudging me forward. I had no choice but to do as she expected.

Bowls of beets, potatoes, and corn filled the table, all products of Blaine's labor, sold to us now, no longer given freely. Food rose to my mouth. I chewed, swallowed. Bite after bite, tasting nothing. I had no idea what to think, so I tried to think nothing, to immerse myself in the children instead of painful reminiscences.

Miranda encouraged Henry to eat his beets. Janet wiggled her new loose tooth. Blaine offered to pull it for her with some string and a door handle. She shook her head, eyes wide with fright.

The boys tried to outdo each other's stories of feats of daring or strength. Blaine wiggled his eyebrows, belted out deep laughter, and concocted outlandish stories of his own.

Just as I thought to dismiss his behavior as childish, I noticed him tap Carl's knife to encourage him to use it to cut his chicken, then watched him pick up a dropped napkin and return it to Henry's lap. And a dozen other things that encouraged the boys' table manners in such a way that they didn't even realize they'd been corrected. These boys needed Blaine, I suddenly realized. Keeping him from their lives destroyed something precious. Something vital.

And perhaps deep down I'd known this. For I hadn't asked him to stop visiting, had I?

A knot of worry tightened in my belly as I caught a glass of water as it threatened to tip, dipped another spoonful of corn onto Janet's empty plate, and wiped a dribble of gravy from Lily Beth's mouth.

She giggled at my touch. I smiled in spite of myself. And, yet her wandering eyes continued to break my heart. Where were the child's glasses?

After all the time and expense, she ought to wear her spectacles whenever possible. It was the only way her eyes would come back in line. I wanted Lily Beth to at least have the hope of that in her favor if her mother did happen to come back for her.

Mrs. Fore brought in a pound cake. I hid a grin, knowing it would have been a butterscotch pie had she had advance warning of Blaine's company. While the rare treat mesmerized the others, I leaned over to Lily Beth. "Where are your glasses, love bug?"

Her pink lips drooped, trembling at the corners. Tears magnified her imperfect eyes. I took her hand, stroked it. "You can tell me. I won't be mad."

Her head dipped. "I don't want to wear them."

"But sweet pea, they'll set your eyes right."

Her chin quivered, and fat tears rolled down her angelic face. I pushed the wispy hair back from her face. "Don't you want your eyes fixed?"

She shook her head, sobbing openly now. I lifted her from her seat and carried her away from the curious eyes of the other children. Oh, how I wanted to make things right in her life. I lowered her to the sofa in the parlor, knowing the others would finish their dessert before they left the table.

Frowning, I stroked her head and tried to quiet her tears. "What happened? Did someone tease you?"

She shook her head, hiccuped. "Mama won't know it's me. When she comes."

My heart shattered. I took her face between my hands and stared into the eyes that refused to focus on mine. "I promise your mama will know you, pumpkin. We'll make sure of it."

The words threatened to stick in my throat as I thought of Mrs. Ashworth and her shifty eyes, not even taking time to say good-bye to her own child. Lily Beth was too young to know her mother's character.

I lifted her chin, my voice kind but firm. "You will wear your glasses. Every day. Do you understand?"

Lily Beth scrambled to the far end of the sofa, away from my touch. "I won't! I won't!"

I reached for her, but movement caught the corner of my eye. Miranda stood behind us, her shoulders tense.

"May I speak with you, Sadie?"

Lily Beth's hysteria started to build. If I left the room for a few moments, she'd likely calm, so I followed Miranda into the foyer.

"I think you need to leave her alone about the glasses."

I stared, mouth gaping. Was she taking me to task after one day on the job?

"If she cared about looking like everyone else, we would

have to force the glasses from her face while she slept. But she doesn't care. She's worried that—"

"I know why she's worried," I hissed. "But that woman won't come back for her. I guarantee it."

Miranda's gaze sought the floor as her shoulder rose and fell. "Maybe not. But right now Lily Beth needs to believe her mama will come back for her. She'll grow up and have to face the truth soon enough. Leave her be for now."

"How dare you tell me how to care for these children!" My words stripped Miranda's face of the polite veneer. Her eyes narrowed and her lip curled. Her whole body stiffened, as if preparing for a physical blow. But she didn't back down.

"You can't force her to want what you want for her, Sadie. For heaven's sake, she needs someone to mother her, to love on her, not to order her around."

My fists clenched, as did my teeth. "That's what I'm trying to do."

Miranda shook her head. "No you're not. But you can't see. It's the same with Carter."

I threw my hands in the air. "What about Carter?"

"He needs consequences, not coddling."

"So I don't do anything right? Is that what you're saying?"

"No. I'm saying that each child deserves to be known—and loved and disciplined—for just who they are. Without our being concerned for what others think." She walked away, then turned back. "If you still want me to stay, I'll stay. And I will work under you. But only for the children. Only for them." She left me standing alone in the foyer.

I pulled back my shoulders, drew in a deep breath. All I'd ever wanted to do was help others, to extend the grace that had been extended to me. To Lily Beth. To Carter. To all the little ones who walked through the doors of this place and took up residence in my heart. It just seemed harder now that I also held other responsibilities in my hands.

Lily Beth's quiet crying floated from the parlor. The children's conversation punctuated with laughter drifted from the dining room. Each sound seemed to steal air from the room, from my body. Then anger flamed in my chest. I shook with rage at Miranda.

A strong hand gripped my elbow. Blaine looked down at me, his eyes soft with understanding. The look doused my fury, leaving ashes of self-doubt.

I let him gather me close to his chest, to the place where I'd once felt safe. And loved.

"I know you want good things for her, Sadie." He stroked my hair, then rested his chin on the top of my head.

Dizzied by Blaine's nearness, I wished I had the courage to take his face in my hands, force his lips to mine.

But that wouldn't help either of us. Or Lily Beth. I wiggled until his embrace loosened. Then I retreated into my office.

Chapter 31

How are the children coming with their pieces for the picnic?" I asked Miranda the following day. With the bank account growing, albeit slowly, I held high hopes that their presentations would bring us the donations needed to continue operation. The Lord wouldn't leave us with no provision. Not when this had been His work from the beginning.

"Just fine."

"Even Cynthia?"

Miranda nodded but didn't elaborate.

Whatever our differences, I knew she wouldn't lie. And even if she didn't know the full implications of our success—or failure—at the picnic, she'd been around long enough to understand its importance.

"Wonderful. I'd like to hear everyone recite next week."

Miranda nodded, stood. "May I go now? I have work to finish."

"Of course." Oh, how different she was from Viola. The thought almost softened my heart toward Miranda. She and I would never see things the same about Lily Beth and Carter, but at least we knew how to stay out of each other's way and get our jobs done.

The telephone shrilled from the kitchen, then stopped. Miranda must have answered, as she should. Then she appeared in the office again.

"It's for you. Mr. Delp, from the bank."

And the board.

"Overdrawn?" My voice rose higher than I'd intended. I glanced behind me. Mrs. Fore's eyebrows shot toward the ceiling. I kept my back to her as I moved closer to the mouthpiece. "But how can that be? We have several thousand—"

"In the other account, Miss Sillsby. The one I am referencing is your expense account. You have evidently paid out more than we have taken in."

My heart battered against my chest as I tried to draw to mind the last set of numbers in my ledger.

Mr. Delp continued to yammer in my ear, scathing words about my competence.

"I understand, Mr. Delp. Please move over some of next year's money."

"You can't count those funds toward next year, then."

"Yes, I understand. And don't worry. I'll find the mistake and it won't happen again."

I set the earpiece on top of the wall box.

"Trouble?" Mrs. Fore spoke only compassion, not condemnation. I shook my head, fighting back tears demanding release. Then Mrs. Fore's arms surrounded me. I laid my head on her shoulder and cried.

Staring down at the ledger, palms pressed to the sides of my head, I tried to find my mistake in the numbers.

Was it in the addition? The subtraction? My stomach soured. Or the numbers I'd changed to match those from the bank?

Whatever I'd done, I could never undo it. The financial future of the Raystown Home rested in my incompetent hands.

Help me, Lord. You gave me this position. I know You did. So I have to believe You will provide what I need to do it well. But I don't have any skill with numbers. What am I supposed to do?

Footsteps drew my attention. Miranda reached across the desk and set a cup of coffee near me. The comforting scent filled my nose.

"Thank you." I wrapped my hands around the cup, raised it to my lips. Miranda remained, unmoving. I noticed her attention fixed on the paper where I'd been adding the numbers, every answer different. The coffee burned down my throat. I set it aside.

Her finger touched one total I'd scribbled. "This one's correct."

"What do you mean?" I pulled the paper toward me and studied the place she'd indicated.

She nodded toward the page again. "That one's added up right."

"How do you know?" I scrutinized my work once more.

She shrugged. "Numbers come easy to me. Always have." She took a step back, as if she feared she'd said too much.

I swallowed down desperate words that threatened to kill my pride. I didn't want to say them. Didn't want to ask. But my lips opened, and the request jumped past my reticence. "Can you rework these figures?"

I pushed the ledger toward her, followed by a fresh sheet of paper and a pencil. Her lips pursed.

"It's $162.50."

My mouth dropped open. She hadn't touched the pencil or paper. Only her eyes had moved across the column of numbers. Could I confirm her answer? It would take me several tries. If she'd figured it correctly, I had no wish to display my weakness in front of her.

"Thank you." I wrote down the number, then picked up a stack of unopened mail. "If you could read and sort these for me, I'd greatly appreciate it."

"Of course," she said, her voice as quiet as a reprimanded child's. The whisper of her skirt told me she'd left. I breathed relief, then began the arduous task of copying and adding the column of numbers. Once. Twice. Three times. One of my answers was $162.50, but I needed more confirmation than that.

Four. Five. Six.

Sweat beaded on my forehead, dripped down the side of my face. Still no two answers the same. If only Earl were here to help. Or Blaine. When he'd learned carpentry from his foster father, he'd learned to work complicated figures in his head.

I bit my lip. Slowly, carefully, I added each number, totaled the column, carried and added again: $162.50.

The pencil rolled from my fingers. I pushed to my feet, stumbled into the parlor, and found Miranda sitting at the small desk, two piles of letters in front of her. She looked up, eyes wide in a face that had seen so many more years of life than mine had. Had I really imagined her to be ignorant?

My tongue felt large and dry, but I worked the words around it. "I wondered if you could help me."

"I told you before, I'll do whatever you need me to do. I meant it." Her chin lifted, as if in defiance.

I wished a hole would open up in the floor and swallow me, save me from having to admit my wrong. But my feet remained on solid ground. I gripped my hands behind my back. "The financial records. They're all . . ." I took a deep breath. "They're all wrong. I can't . . . I can't find the mistake. Could you redo them? Find the errors?"

She hesitated.

Would she refuse? Would she see me humiliated in front of the board so she could prove herself in possession of a skill I lacked? I deserved no loyalty or consideration from her. Not after the assumptions I'd made, the way I'd behaved.

"I'm sorry." I squirmed with the admission, wondering how I'd fallen into such haughty thinking. I'd wanted others to give me grace, yet I'd withheld that exact thing from Miranda.

I looked to the ceiling, wishing I could see through the building, into the sky and all the way to heaven. *Forgive me, Lord.*

Miranda's expression softened into a smile of acceptance.

"Thank you," I whispered.

In the office, I offered her my place behind the desk and watched as she scanned three pages of numbers.

She looked up, wrinkles creasing her forehead. "This will take a little while."

"Fine." The calm word belied my fear. "I'll be in the parlor, taking care of the correspondence."

An hour later, Miranda called my name. I ran to the office, praying she had good news. Or at least better news than I deserved.

She pushed the ledger book toward me, fresh pages written with new totals, right down to our current fix of being overdrawn. She'd accomplished in an afternoon what I'd muddled through for weeks.

"Do you want to check it?"

I shrank back. "No."

Her lips parted in a silent gasp of surprise.

"But could you do one more thing?"

She nodded.

"I need to write up a report for the board. Not just the totals, but percentages and things. And where we've gone over our budget. Can you do that, too?"

"Yes."

I put my hand on the doorpost but stopped before I passed into the hall. I couldn't turn around, couldn't look into her face. "And Miranda? Would you please accompany me to the board meeting to present the budget?"

"I'd be happy to come." No triumph cloaked her words.

"Thank you." I bowed my head and walked away.

Daylight held on longer now that we were several days into May, though the mountain that shadowed our borough still purpled the day sooner than we liked. As I sat on the front porch step, chin resting on my knees, I thought of Blaine's farmland, more in the center of the valley. Day lingered there, the warmth of the sun over new sprouts of green in loamy fields. Then I forced my mind to Earl, his work in Philadelphia. Were we still on his mind? Our needs? Would he return with news of funding I so desperately wanted to hear?

I waited for my heart to patter at the thought of his return, but the only swell of sentiment involved money for the children, for the Home. I sighed. Why wouldn't my heart follow my head? It seemed as stubborn as Cynthia's mouth, which refused to open so she could speak her piece in front of others.

The door creaked behind me. I didn't turn. A heavy tread. The swish of a long skirt. I stared at my flowerless hydrangeas, trying to convince myself I could, indeed, do something right.

"May I join you?" Miranda asked.

I scooted over, made room for her on the step. She sat beside me, her hands clasped below her knees. The open windows exposed the children's after-supper chatter, their bit of evening freedom.

A sparrow swooped from a nearby tree, his song mingling with the rise and fall of the voices from inside. Peace spread its net around me, around us, around the house, though I wondered what Miranda wanted.

She hugged her knees more tightly. "No one ever gave me a chance before."

Her words slammed into my stomach like a fist. I hadn't given her a chance, either. Not until I risked failure for myself. I sat up straight. Stiff. Wondering what direction the conversation would take.

The sparrow intensified his song. A burst of laughter trailed out the window behind us. She might say she didn't blame me, but until now, it seemed she had.

"It's been hard, not having the same schooling as everyone else, knowing they thought me stupid." Miranda looked at me now, her eyes bright and sad at the same time. "I didn't quit school because I couldn't do the work, you know. I quit because my pappy made me." She studied her short fingernails. "There were little ones to care for. I was the oldest girl. My brother Jim quit, too. Joined our pappy felling timber." Her words stopped as abruptly as they'd started.

I knew how much they had cost her. I had those kinds of words inside me, too. Words I hadn't trusted to anyone in a very long time. Even Hazel hadn't heard the story from my lips. She'd read it in the log books.

Sarah Sillsby, aged 4. Taken from her mother's cell in the county jail. Father: unknown.

Almost two decades of trying to live down the way my life began. Though I didn't want to admit it, Miranda understood more of me than Hazel ever could.

Taking a ragged breath, I denied the fear that threatened to choke out my story. I needed to say the words. To Miranda.

I focused on the bright green leaves of my hydrangeas as my heartbeat quickened. "I lived here, you know." My voice turned husky, almost unrecognizable. "My mother was a prostitute. She was arrested, eventually, for plying her trade in a local tavern." The revolting smells and sounds rushed back. I coughed, choked, pressed my hands to my mouth. As I drew in the fragrance of spring through my nose, the nausea receded.

"I had no one to care for me, so I sat in the corner of her

cell for weeks. Four years old, playing with the rats, relieving myself in a bucket." I shuddered with a phantom chill, then forced my mind back to my clean skirt, my full belly. "It affected my body with disease. Pain that made me cry until my mother screamed her annoyance."

I fingered a leaf. Green and firm. Living, growing. Rescued from certain death in the scorching summer sun and given the shade it needed to thrive. "Someone heard of my situation. Rescued me. Brought me here. I spent six years healing, believing my mother would come for me. She never did. Finally, the Ramseys took me into their home."

I glanced at Miranda. Chin tucked to her chest, she scratched the toe of her worn boot across the dirt. She didn't have to look up for me to know that she envied my home. The Ramseys had given me in those few years what her parents hadn't given her in a lifetime. An education. A future. And yet even then, the past continually whispered in my ear.

Miranda's hands balled in her lap. My hand covered the gripped fists. "I'm sorry, Miranda. Truly, I am." Inadequate to encompass so much wrong, but all I had to give.

Her fingers released, hands turning over to rest their palms against mine. This woman, nearly twenty years my senior, whom I'd treated as a drudge, now embraced me.

When she looked up, her eyes held no malice. A smile started, stopped, then stretched and stayed. "Thank you."

My fingers laced themselves through those of my new friend.

Chapter 32

My eyes peeked over the top of my book as I relaxed in the parlor on Sunday afternoon. My mind couldn't concentrate on the novel. Too many children had been with us for too long. They needed homes. Families. Something that resembled normal life. And they needed them soon. Would the Hartzlers come to see the good they could do with one of our boys? Would the Stratmores forgive Carter's faults and take in a child? I prayed so. Every day. Surely the Lord would see my hard work on their behalf and grant my requests.

Lily Beth smiled at me from across the room. At least I assumed it was at me. She sat snuggled beneath Nancy's arm, listening as the older girl read from one of our few picture books. No glasses bridged her nose.

My eyes roved over the other children. I breathed a prayer for their well-being. Then I realized one wasn't among us. I set my book aside. "Has anyone seen Carter?"

Heads shook before each returned to their quiet Sunday activity.

Perhaps he'd decided to nap. Upstairs, I found both bedrooms empty and undisturbed.

I plodded back down and wandered into the kitchen. Mrs. Fore's snore penetrated her closed door. The dining room remained empty, as well. Where had Carter gone? And Miranda, too?

Standing at the kitchen window, I scanned the backyard for movement. Nothing stirred.

Miranda might be asleep in her room, like Mrs. Fore. But that still left the mystery of Carter. Perhaps Miranda had sent him on some emergency errand. Mrs. Long, down the street, had been ill. Perhaps she'd sent Carter to check on her.

Yes, that had to be it.

I lifted the coffeepot from the warming shelf at the back of the stove and filled a cup. Leaning my back end against the counter, I let the first bitter taste coat my tongue.

The door creaked open. Carter backed into the room and closed the latch without a sound. Stopped. Relaxed.

I set my cup aside, crossed my arms. "And just where have you been?"

He jumped around. I searched for some telltale sign, but not one speck of dirt or unusual rumple marred his best suit of clothes.

He grinned. "Just needed a bit of fresh air is all."

"I see. And did you tell anyone you were leaving?"

"I, uh . . ." His eyes darted from one side of the room to the other. Then he shrugged. "No one was around."

My eyebrows lifted.

"Except you, of course. And I didn't want to disturb you."

"Next time, disturb me. Understand?"

"Yes, ma'am. But say, Sadie? When's Earl coming back?"

I dipped my head and lifted my cup to hide the warmth that sprang to my cheeks. "He is Mr. Glazier to you, young man."

Carter tossed back the swatch of hair that lurked in front of his eyes. "He said I could call him Earl."

I sighed. All the children did call me Miss Sadie. Could it hurt for Carter to address the man as Earl? I cleared my throat, met Carter's gaze. "He'll be here sometime tomorrow, I believe."

But in truth, he'd left his return plans vague. I still didn't know what to think of our relationship. My physical attraction to him was undeniable. But given what I'd observed from Viola and Miranda, that was true for every female within the scope of his smile. Except Mrs. Fore. She couldn't be swayed by a pretty face.

Though it seemed I could. I thought of Miranda's admonition about coddling Carter. Had his winsome appearance clouded my judgment, as well? I wanted to ask Carter about the man he'd talked to on the street, the mention of money, and our missing six dollars, but to do so would disturb our semblance of peace.

"May I go now?" Carter inched toward the front of the house. I waved him on and lifted my cup for a sip of coffee, but a sharp rap on the front door interrupted the motion. I set my cup aside. Visitors often arrived unannounced on Sundays. Sometimes donors. Sometimes board members and their wives. Sometimes a family bringing a gift for our larder.

I pulled open the front door. A man and woman I'd never seen before stared back at me. "May I help you?"

The man whisked a shabby bowler from his head as his

large mustache twitched. "I hope so. Our niece—my wife's sister's child—is said to be here. We've come for her."

"Well, Mr. . . . uh . . . ?"

"Lindstrom. And this is my missus."

"Mr. Lindstrom. I'm Miss Sillsby. I run the Raystown Home. Why don't you and your wife step into my office and we'll get things sorted out."

He stepped aside to let his wife through the door first. I noticed a frayed hem, a turned seam. It wouldn't be the first time someone had tried to take a child from us expecting some kind of gain for himself or herself. We didn't pay our foster families any type of stipend for the child's upkeep. It was a gift of charity on their behalf. But some came looking for free labor. I'd verify this couple's story before letting them leave with any of my children.

"If you'll excuse me for a moment, I need to ask my assistant to watch the children."

They nodded. I raced up the stairs, but Miranda's room stood empty. Back down I went, knocking at, then opening Mrs. Fore's bedroom door. I shook her shoulder. "Mrs. Fore?"

She snorted and shifted and opened her eyes. Then she sat up. "What? Is the house afire?"

"No, nothing like that."

She pressed her hand to her chest and breathed deep.

"I can't find Miranda and I need to meet with a couple who just arrived asking about a child. Could you . . . ?"

"Of course. Don't give it another thought. I'll take care of things."

"Thank you, Mrs. Fore. Oh, and if you see Miranda, would you send her to me in the office, please?"

"Certainly. Go on, now. Before they get impatient."

I hurried back. Mr. and Mrs. Lindstrom sat silent and unmoving before my desk. I put on a brightness I didn't feel. "Now, then. What is the name of the child you're inquiring about?"

Mrs. Lindstrom leaned forward. "Lily Beth Ashworth."

I dropped into my chair, trying to hold the smile on my face. "And you say you are Mrs. Ashworth's sister?"

The woman glanced at her husband, then nodded.

"You'll understand that I need to confirm this information. And talk with Mrs. Ashworth, of course."

The woman mumbled her agreement while frightened eyes darted in her husband's direction.

My insides quaked. If this woman's claims could be established and if we couldn't locate Mrs. Ashworth, they'd expect to take Lily Beth home with them. Would their home be better for the child than this one?

Miranda slipped in, stood against the wall behind the Lindstroms.

Mr. Lindstrom crossed one leg over the other. "You see, miss, my wife has been estranged from her sister for several years now. We only just learned of the child's existence. And that the huss—that Mrs. Ashworth left her here."

Mrs. Lindstrom turned her large eyes on me. "We'd like to raise the girl with our own. After all, she's family."

I shuffled papers on my desk. "Have you spoken with Mrs. Ashworth recently?"

"No." Mr. Lindstrom drew out the word, smoothed down his mustache. "But when we heard the child was here, we came right away."

"Please let us do this for her." Mrs. Lindstrom's voice broke.

Miranda cleared her throat, nodded. I shook my head. She nodded again. I frowned, let my eyes meet Mrs. Lindstrom's instead of Miranda's.

"You know about her . . . condition?"

"Squint, as I was told."

"More than that. Eyes severely crossed. Are you prepared to take such a child?"

Mrs. Lindstrom's thin fingers gripped the edge of the desk. "I'd do anything for my sister's girl since I can't seem to do anything for my sister."

I dipped my pen in the inkwell, let the excess drip off, and prayed my hand wouldn't shake and splatter the page. "I need your name, address, employment information, references, and any papers you have with you that might prove your relation to the child. You understand that we need to be thorough."

Mrs. Lindstrom looked at her husband. He nodded. I pulled out a sheet of paper and concentrated on my handwriting.

"Miss?"

I looked up.

"Could we . . . see her?" Mrs. Lindstrom's timid request pricked my heart, but I held fast.

"I don't think—"

"I'll go get her." Miranda darted out the door. I wanted to snatch her back, but the deed had been done. I supposed there would be no harm in them seeing the child. And those eyes might put them off anyway, as they apparently did her mother.

As I finished transcribing their information, Miranda

returned. She gently urged Lily Beth into the room. Mrs. Lindstrom fell to her knees in front of the girl.

"Oh, baby." Mrs. Lindstrom brushed at the pale hair that billowed around Lily Beth's face. "I'd have been here sooner if I had known."

Lily Beth took a step backward, feeling for Miranda's skirt. Miranda put her hands on the girl's shoulders and leaned down near her ear. "It's okay, sweetheart. This is your aunt—"

"Belinda. Aunt Belinda. Your mama's own sister."

Lily Beth's mouth stretched wide, her face alight. "Is Mama here?" She wrenched herself from Miranda's grasp, trying to spy a hiding place. I sucked in a sharp breath. Nothing could erase the look of rapture on Lily Beth's face or stop the tumble of Belinda Lindstrom's words.

"No, baby. Your mama's not here. But Uncle Steven and I would like to take you home with us to live. With our little girls and boy. Would you like that?"

I jumped up, placed Lily Beth between myself and Miranda. "Lily Beth, you may rejoin the others now."

Miranda turned Lily Beth's shoulders toward the door, but the child broke free and threw her arms around her stranger-aunt's neck. Mrs. Lindstrom tightened her hold on the girl. With gentleness, I maneuvered them apart and guided Lily Beth to Miranda, my teeth grinding into one another as Miranda escorted Lily Beth from the room.

I resumed my seat behind the desk, worked to keep my voice calm and kind. "If you will answer a few questions, I will do my best to have some information for you by the end of the week."

Miranda and I stood on the front porch as the Lindstroms departed.

Even with all the information they'd given me, I didn't know who they were, what kind of life they led.

I crossed my arms and watched them go. "We have no idea if those people are even telling the truth. And even if they are, what if they are as unsuitable to raise a child as Mrs. Ashworth?"

Miranda frowned, eyebrows drawing down toward her nose. "Nothing in their manner suggested such a thing. They seemed quite respectable. Poverty doesn't make parents unfit any more than wealth deems them appropriate."

I paced the porch, fearing I'd spew my anxiety over Lily Beth onto my newfound friendship with Miranda.

Her voice softened. "You don't know anything about them, Sadie. Not yet."

I stopped, my skirt swinging about my ankles. I raised my chin. "But it's my job to find out."

"Just make sure you keep Lily Beth's best interests in mind as you do."

I pressed my lips into a hard line. I wanted Lily Beth to have a family, but I wanted it to be one that could give her a better life than she'd known. I wasn't sure that would be the case with the Lindstroms. Only after every last question had been answered satisfactorily would I release that child from my care.

Chapter 33

Earl didn't arrive on Monday, but Tuesday morning, he popped in and asked me to have supper with him.

"Go on," Miranda urged. "I can take care of the children. Besides, we need to practice our program so we can run through it for you later."

"You're right. It's fine." I turned to Earl. "Of course. I'd love to go." Why had I even hesitated? I had no fear about Miranda's capabilities. And Earl had done nothing but prove himself my champion in every way. With the appearance of the Lindstroms, I needed his advice. He'd studied these types of situations. This would be the perfect time to discuss Lily Beth. A business dinner.

But the moment his eyes met mine, I knew he intended it to be so much more.

The hotel dining room was finer than I'd imagined. I smoothed down my green skirt, wishing I had put on my dress from Hazel's wedding instead. Electric lights shone bright from chandeliers above our heads. A waiter dressed in a fine suit took our order, brought our food.

Earl regaled me with stories of Philadelphia, each one more amusing than the last. And no matter how hard I tried, I couldn't gain the opening I sought to bring up Lily Beth and the Lindstroms.

He ordered us pie and coffee after our meal. Clinks of silver on china plates and the murmur of quiet conversations swirled around us. Finally, my chance to direct the conversation arrived.

"A couple showed up on Sunday. They want to take Lily Beth home with them."

"The little girl with the crossed eyes? That's wonderful."

"They claim to be relations."

"Even better." Earl drained his cup, then pushed it and his empty plate away.

"I don't know." I set down my fork, folded my hands. "You see, they have several other children at home, and it doesn't seem that they have many more resources than Lily Beth's mother did when she left the child with us. Besides, I asked her that day about relatives who could assist her and she claimed she had none."

"Have you heard from the child's mother?"

"No. Not a word."

Earl shrugged. "Then their claim to her is the least of your concern. They want her—isn't that enough?"

I dabbed my napkin to my lips. "She doesn't need just any family. She needs one that will make her wear her glasses and encourage her to look beyond her circumstances."

Earl's slow smile brightened his face, but it didn't flutter my belly. He leaned back, as if unconcerned. "She'll be what she is, Sadie. Success is never certain with children from such backgrounds."

My hands shook. I clamped them together and laid them in my lap.

He's talking about Lily Beth. Not me.

"Investigate them as you would any other prospective family. If they have the desire and ability to provide the girl a home, send her with them."

I nodded, but it wasn't that simple.

"Will you speak to the ladies at the Baptist church this week while I see what I can find out about the Lindstroms?"

"Of course." He picked up my hand and brought it to his lips while his gaze remained on my face. "And I'm available for anything else you need of me, dear lady."

"Thank you." I eased my hand from his grasp, noting that his touch hadn't stirred my heart.

Earl paid our bill, leaving a generous tip for the waiter. Looking at the money made me realize he'd never offered any contribution to the Home.

I stopped at the desk, asked for the hotel manager, and complimented the food and service in the dining room.

"Thank you, Miss Sillsby. We appreciate your patronage."

Not mine. Earl's. I couldn't afford a supper like this even once a year. Nor could most others I knew.

Wealthy people dined out. Dined here.

The long counter stretched empty. What if . . .

"May I presume to ask a favor of you, sir?"

The man inclined his head with the same elegance Earl displayed.

"Would it be possible to set up a . . . a jar or a box or something on your countertop to collect donations for the Raystown Home?" I held my breath, waiting.

Earl grinned, but it seemed to hide an embarrassment I hadn't noticed before. The hotel manager struggled for an answer. His eyes cut in Earl's direction. Earl smiled and nodded as if the answer were already yes.

The manager pulled at his collar. "I think that would be fine. If you'll make up a placard, I'll secure a container of some sort in keeping with our decor."

Before I realized what I was doing, my hands found his and squeezed. "Bless you, sir."

He fidgeted, excused himself. Earl pulled me toward the street. Then I remembered that one of his stated objectives for his trip back to Philadelphia was securing funding for the Home.

"Did you make any progress seeking donations for us?"

"Ah. I regret to inform you that I did not."

My small victory moments ago now seemed worthless. A few pennies here and there would not fill the account for next year. If only Earl realized the true import of the situation, but as far as I could tell, the board members had remained closemouthed, even with Earl.

"But don't worry, dear Sadie." He chucked me under the chin as if I were a petulant child. "I have my sights on a patron right here in town."

Though his cavalier attitude irritated me, I brightened. "Really? Who is it?"

His hands disappeared deep into his pockets as his gaze broke from mine. "I'd rather not say at the moment. Not until this person agrees to help."

In spite of my curiosity, I didn't prod. If holding my tongue meant money to save the Home, I would oblige. It was the question of the Lindstroms that goaded me now. That and my underlying concerns about Carter. Carter had anxiously watched for Earl's return, yet Earl hadn't even asked after the boy.

For the rest of the week, I scoured county records, asked questions, wrote letters, and even visited the Lindstroms' home. Small, but clean and in good repair. In between compiling a report of the success of our foster homes, I made telephone calls, confirmed the Lindstroms' references, and searched for Mrs. Ashworth.

No, not Mrs. Ashworth. *Miss* Ashworth. I'd discovered that much. She was indeed Belinda Lindstrom's younger sister, born and raised near Hesston. But try as I might, I could not find Miss Ashworth's current residence. At least not in any of the surrounding counties.

My stomach roiled with the final confirmation. What should I do when the Lindstroms returned?

"You have no choice." Earl talked as I paced the office, a telegram in my hand. "They are her family, and they want her. Legally, morally, and financially, it makes sense." Earl crossed one leg over the other.

My fists clenched. Sending her with her aunt and uncle didn't fit with what I'd envisioned for the girl. I wanted her in a home so wonderful it obliterated the stain of her mother's past.

Then again, even the Ramseys hadn't been able to fully do that for me.

George rushed into the office. "Miranda says please come now. Lily Beth's aunt and uncle are here."

Measured steps took me to the parlor, putting as much time as possible between this moment and the one I dreaded. The one when I'd have to let Lily Beth go.

With what I hoped was an air of both grace and authority, I swept into the room. "So sorry to keep you waiting." I brushed one stubborn lock of hair from my face and tucked it into the knot of hair at the back of my neck. Miranda stood near Mrs. Lindstrom, who held Lily Beth on her knees.

"Do you believe us now, miss?" Mrs. Lindstrom's face was pale.

I needed something sure and solid to hold me. Something that would anchor me to do what had to be done.

Blaine passed by the window. I held my breath. He didn't turn his head to peer inside, just kept a steady gait, intent, I guessed, on his task. But his presence was enough.

"Miranda, would you take Lily Beth to gather her things, please?"

Miranda and Lily Beth left the room. Blaine passed the window again, this time going in the opposite direction. He usually helped with the garden on Saturdays, but what would draw him to the front of the house?

I forced my attention back to the Lindstroms. Their eager faces dissipated some of my suspicion. "Yes, Mrs. Lindstrom, I know you are *Miss* Ashworth's sister." I sat in the chair across from the sofa. "I've also learned that Miss Ashworth no longer resides at the address she left with us. No one knows where she has gone, and there are no indications that she'll return. She appears to have abandoned her child."

Mrs. Lindstrom's shoulders slumped as she leaned toward her husband. "I don't know what got into that girl. We weren't raised like that, miss." Her head drifted back and forth, a disbelieving gesture. "It isn't right for a woman to leave her child. 'Tisn't natural. I don't know what's got into Emmy." She buried her face against her husband's broad shoulder. He drew her toward his chest as she quietly cried.

Lily Beth raced back into the room, straight to Mrs. Lindstrom. The woman pulled away from her husband and took the child into her lap. "Would you like to go home with us, Lily Beth? There are cousins to play with."

Lily Beth nodded before turning to me, her eyes pointing to opposite corners of the room. I wanted to grab her up, never let her go. Instead, I cupped Lily Beth's elfin chin as a lump lodged in my throat. "Do you want to go with them?"

It wasn't her choice, really. But I needed to know.

"Yes." She grasped Mrs. Lindstrom's hand. The woman beamed.

My vision blurred. All I wanted for this child was a home full of love, a place where she could thrive. *Lord, could You give me some sign that the Lindstroms will provide that?*

Miranda leaned against the wall, watching the same scene. But her face didn't hold the uncertainty I felt. She radiated satisfaction. One work-worn hand reached up and wiped her cheek.

Miranda loved Lily Beth, would miss her as much as I

would. Yet she seemed to know, without a doubt, that this was for the best.

Desperate to grasp control of myself, of the situation, I stood. "If you will follow me to the office to sign the register book, we'll let you folks be on your way."

Mr. Lindstrom signed for them both. They gathered Lily Beth and her small bundle and headed for the door. My heart crumbled. Then Lily Beth pulled back, ran to me. Her arms circled my neck. I held tight to her waist.

Then I let her go.

A shaft of afternoon sunlight glinted off something in my open desk drawer.

"Lily Beth!" I held up the spectacles. "Don't forget to wear your glasses."

Lily Beth giggled as Mrs. Lindstrom placed them in her handbag.

"Thank you, miss. May God bless all you've done to help our Lily Beth." Mrs. Lindstrom's words washed over me like clean water on soapy hair, rinsing me free from the need to hold on. I raised a hand in farewell as Mr. Lindstrom snapped the reins and his horses started down the street, pulling the wagon behind.

Miranda's tear-filled eyes found mine. Her head bobbed once before she returned indoors.

Chapter 34

I moped about the house that afternoon, finally wandering into the kitchen.

"How're those flowers of yours doing?" Mrs. Fore pressed the heels of her hands into a lump of bread dough.

I blinked. My flowers? An image of the faded daffodils dumped upside down flitted through my head. Why would she bring those up now? Then I remembered. "Oh! The hydrangeas? They're fine." Though I realized I hadn't checked on them in a few days. "They'll burst with color by summer, for sure."

"Hmm." She turned the dough, then slapped it back to the work table and pressed in again.

My forehead crinkled. What in the world did those plants have to do with anything at the moment? I shrugged. At least she'd reminded me that they needed to be tended.

I hurried outside with a full bucket of water and took a deep draw of springtime—new grass mixed with scents of blooming flowers. I forced myself to notice my surroundings, the world God had dressed fresh after a long winter.

An abundance of leaves clung to the branches of my hydrangeas now, strong and green. Like some kind of sign from the Lord that He would take discarded children and fill them with life. Like the hydrangeas, they would flower in their time. Constant worry wouldn't hurry them, but maybe prayer would help.

So I prayed. For Cynthia to grow bolder in speaking her piece with others watching. For Lily Beth to remain rapturous about her new home. For George and the Hartzlers to take to one another. The butcher and his wife had agreed to meet George at church on Sunday and maybe take him home for the afternoon and see if they could all get along.

And Carter. He troubled me, though he didn't seem to be making any mischief. Still, I couldn't shake the nagging feeling that something wasn't right with him.

With my petitions ascending to the Lord, I ladled water around the base of first one bush, then the other. Mashing down the damp soil, I watered more, until I felt sure the moisture had reached the roots.

Back inside the office, I opened the windows wide before settling at my desk, trying to concentrate on my work. My pen scratched over the surface of the papers.

Thank you for your kind gift.

Thank you for your inquiry.

I'd taken back the correspondence and left Miranda with the mountain of numbers. I signed my name to the letters, rubbed feeling back into my hand, and sipped my cold coffee.

Giggles and shouts drifted through the windows, curling around me, taking me captive. I wanted to be out there with them. Enjoying them. Loving them.

I chose this, I reminded myself. And yet if I didn't find the money for us to operate next year, I had chosen nothing at all.

I rubbed my eyes, picked up my empty coffee cup, and carried it into the kitchen. As I peeked out the open window, the blowing curtains tickled my face.

"Go on out there," Mrs. Fore said. "It'll put some color back in your cheeks. You've looked pale as a ghost these past few days."

"I still have work to do." I turned away, not letting myself dawdle over the inviting picture.

"Work will wait. Those children won't." She waved her wooden spoon in my direction as if I were one of the children sassing her.

Still, I hesitated. "I'm sure Miranda has things in hand. I don't want to intrude."

This time Mrs. Fore opened the door, put a hand in the middle of my back, and forced me outside.

An arm waved in my direction. I shaded my eyes with my hand. "What is it, Carl? Another game of baseball?"

His legs churned toward me. "Not today. We're playing Haley Over. Come on! You can be on our team." He grabbed my hand and pulled me toward a group of boys and girls standing near the storage shed.

"But I don't know—"

"It's easy. One team throws the ball over the shed. Whoever catches it runs around the building and throws the ball at one of them. Whoever gets hit by the ball has to come to our side."

"Oh." That didn't sound hard. Sure enough, a rubber ball came sailing over the roof of the storage building. Carl called for it, caught it. Then he took off running. Squeals and shouts carried from the other side. Finally, Carl came back with Janet in tow.

The silly grin on the girl's face made me suspect she hadn't tried too hard to get out of the path of the ball. Then it was our turn. Carl threw the ball over. Cheers erupted from the other side. I held my breath, ready to scramble away from whoever appeared to throw the ball at our team, hoping to take a "prisoner."

My heart pounded. My breath quickened. Faster and faster, my feet carried me away from the corner Carl had navigated, assuming the player from the other team would use the same path. Running one way, looking another.

Wham!

A solid mass. I toppled. My feet tangled. My back hit the ground. Then a weight landed atop me. I fought to gulp air as my vision blackened. The heaviness moved from my chest. I caught my breath, attempted to blink the world into focus.

A hand reached down, pulled me to sitting. The stars cleared from my vision. Blaine knelt beside me, chuckling.

"Did I hurt you?" He brushed dirt from my shoulder, his hand stopping just before it touched a place on my face.

I shook my head. A long swatch of hair drifted into my vision. His fingertips brushed it past my temple, over my ear. I held the breath I'd fought so hard to find, my heart bouncing in my chest as erratically as the rubber ball across the hard ground.

"Does that mean Miss Sadie's on our team now?" Cynthia asked.

My eyes found Blaine's. Amusement skittered silent between us, like it used to when the children said something funny. He assisted me to my feet and caught me around the waist, his strong right arm holding me steady.

"I think Sadie's had enough for now. You keep on playing. I'll help her back inside."

Grumbling commenced, but the teams divided and returned to their game as Blaine led me across the yard, his arm still secure around my back. At least this time Viola wasn't around to witness my humiliation—or to interfere. I leaned into him, wishing his nearness didn't make me angry and needy all at once.

If only we could be together, taking care of the children. But we'd made our decisions—and neither included the other.

I pressed closer, relishing the strength of him beside me. His arm stretched along my back, lengthening the distance between us, erasing my daydreams. I must have hit my head harder than I thought.

By the time we reached the back door, Miranda had come running from where she'd been sitting under a tree with some of the older girls. Mrs. Fore had the door open and a chair ready to receive me.

"It's nothing, really. Don't make such a fuss." My voice trembled. Blaine stared hard into my eyes. I looked away, lightheaded.

I vaguely heard Mrs. Fore order Miranda out the door to watch over the children before disappearing into her bedroom with a flimsy excuse. The room suddenly felt small, Blaine and I both searching for somewhere to look, anywhere but into each other's faces.

He shoved his hands into his pockets. "I'd better be off," he mumbled, shuffling toward the door.

Though I desperately wanted to make him stay, I couldn't do anything but watch him go.

Earl accompanied me to pick up George from the Hartzlers on Sunday afternoon. We rejected the trolley, choosing to indulge in the spring breeze and exercise. Once we reached downtown, we slowed, peering into the plate-glass windows of the closed shops, pointing out unusual items or things we liked. Several other couples were doing the same, luxuriating in a spring stroll instead of a drive.

"Oh, look!" I pointed to a large hat in Miss Prince's shop window. Feathers and lace dripped from the crown, around the brim. I touched my shabby headdress. If only I had the time to create something fresh. But my days didn't revolve around my wardrobe. Nor did my money. In fact, I'd saved but a few dollars from my pay, choosing instead to repay our account for my bookkeeping error.

"You'd look stunning in that." Earl pulled my hand into the crook of his arm and smiled. My face heated. I looked away, not wanting his amusement to embarrass me further.

But as I concentrated on the opposite side of the street, I paused. In front of the confectioner's window stood a familiar form. I almost called Blaine's name, but then a girl turned her head to smile up at him.

Viola.

I whipped around, hid myself between Earl and the millinery, as if I couldn't take my eyes off the fancy hats. Had she seen me? She hadn't given any indication. She'd been too intent on Blaine.

"What is it, Sadie?" Earl's breath teased my neck, his mouth near my ear. I turned slowly, peeked over his shoulder.

They faced us now, Viola pointing, Blaine's face scrunched in confusion. I ducked. Earl laughed, then turned.

"Why, if it isn't our friend, Miss Brown." He crossed the street. Alone on the sidewalk I felt naked. Exposed.

Trotting after him, I tried to decide who I'd rather face—Blaine or Viola.

Truthfully? Neither.

Earl and Viola chatted like old friends while Blaine's eyes refused to meet mine.

I pulled at Earl's arm. "We need to go. The Hartzlers are expecting us."

Blaine's bushy eyebrows rose.

"They . . . they have George. We have to get him."

Blaine's tension eased. For a moment. Then Earl cradled an arm about my waist to lead me away. I glanced back to see Viola curl her hand around Blaine's arm, her lips twisting in a smirk of conquest.

George chattered the entire way back through town. Mr. Hartzler this. Mrs. Hartzler that. And weren't their little ones cute?

By the time we arrived at the Home, Mr. Hartzler had called Miranda to confirm they desired to give George a home—and continue to provide our meat at a discount. Earl congratulated me with a kiss on the cheek.

Midweek, Henry led me into the parlor. "We're going to do our program the whole way through. Miss Miranda said so."

I sat on the sofa in the back parlor, the pocket doors hidden in the walls to give enough room for us all. One after another, the children sang, recited, dramatized. All well versed in their performance but still needing a bit of polish. With close to two weeks remaining, I knew they'd be perfect when the day arrived.

Only Cynthia remained to recite. Miranda herded us all

into the foyer with a finger to her lips. She raced up the stairs, then returned leading a blindfolded Cynthia.

"Should we keep waiting?" I whispered to Sylvia after Miranda and Cynthia passed into the parlor.

Sylvia shrugged.

Then Miranda reappeared and motioned us forward, again in silence. We crept back into the room. Cynthia stood facing the back windows.

"'How do you like to go up in a swing, up in the air so blue?'" Robert Louis Stevenson's words spilled easily from Cynthia's mouth. When she finished, we clapped and cheered.

Cynthia spun around, eyes wide above her upturned nose, mouth round beneath it. "Oh! Oh! Oh!" Her hands fluttered in front of her face. Her feet danced. "I did it! I did it!"

I wanted to laugh and cry. I covered my mouth, waited for her pudgy arms to encircle my waist. She flung herself into Miranda's arms instead.

My joy faltered, then stumbled headlong, falling into a deep pit. After all the time I'd spent helping her, drying her tears, encouraging her, she'd chosen Miranda over me.

I'd desired this with Viola—for the children to look to her instead of me. I just hadn't imagined it would be for their successes as well as their failures. And I hadn't imagined the wound would slice so deep.

When Cynthia finally pressed herself to my side, I couldn't stop the tears that drizzled down my cheeks. "You did great, sweet pea. I'm so proud of you." I looked up. Miranda was watching us, her mouth in a thin, serious line. "And I'm so thankful Miss Miranda found a way to help you."

Chapter 35

Miranda sat with Earl at the back of the room while I presented our financial information to the board of trustees the following evening. Miranda's smile encouraged me as copies of the report made their way around the room and I explained the figures. Mr. Delp's eyebrows drew together as he scrutinized our work. My heart thumped in my ears.

Finally, Mr. Riley stood. "You've done an excellent job, Miss Sillsby."

My stomach felt hollow. I couldn't take the credit. "Not me, Mr. Riley. Miranda Jennings, my assistant, did the work."

Earl shook his head as if he couldn't believe what he'd heard.

I pinned my attention on Miranda. "She's quite proficient with numbers and details."

Some of the men turned. Miranda's cheeks pinked as she held an awkward smile. I wondered how in the world we'd managed to avoid becoming friends before now.

Mr. Riley cleared his throat. "I'm sure there are those with questions."

"What further efforts have you taken to economize?"

"Have more children been placed in homes?"

"Do you foresee any further expenses for the upcoming year?"

"What other plans do you have to bring in needed funds?"

Each question was carefully crafted to conceal our fleece from Earl and Miranda. I answered the inquiries purposefully, patiently. But even as I did, my heart sank further toward the floor.

"We've economized all we know how."

"I don't foresee a significant drop in the number of children we feed and care for on a monthly basis."

"Some repairs need to be taken care of around the house, but I hope our garden harvest will curtail the rising expense of food."

With a deep breath, I plunged into the final question. "As you know, we've planned our annual fund-raising picnic for a week from Monday, to coincide with Decoration Day. This year, the children will present a program—recitations, singing, and the like." My eyes locked on Miranda's. She nodded. "I believe such entertainment will show that our children are not hoodlums or hopeless cases, but talented, charming, intelligent children who simply need a loving home and a bit of hope."

Mr. Wise rose to his feet. "While I appreciate your efforts, Miss Sillsby, I think such an undertaking will hardly result in a significant return of funds."

I refused to bow under his naysaying. I tilted my head in his direction. "And I beg to respectfully disagree, Mr. Wise. The children have worked hard on their program.

Miss Jennings, Mr. Glazier, and I will make sure as many people as possible receive a personal invitation to this event. And I believe the Lord can do exceedingly above what we think or imagine."

God had to make it happen or these men would vote to close our doors.

Mr. Wise turned to Earl. "I'd like to hear your assessment of the situation."

"I think this is worth a try. In any case, it can't hurt. Though like you, I doubt it will yield much increase from previous years. I believe you need to focus on securing large benefactors."

Mr. Wise nodded. "As I suspected."

I wanted to jump up and shake Mr. Wise. He knew about the fleece, the need to gather next year's budget by July. Earl, on the other hand, had no idea. He came to us with his big-city ideas, not understanding that we'd always received support from the community, not from one or two benefactors.

For the first time, I wondered what benefit Earl Glazier derived from putting so much effort into helping our small ministry. Would he or the CAS swoop in at the final hour and be the Home's savior? Did he desire to run the place himself?

Miranda's hand came around my shoulder, as if she knew my struggle to keep my lips sealed. At least God had given me one true ally in this battle, even if she didn't yet realize the intensity of the fight.

"Please?" Carl stood at the office door on Friday after supper, hands clasped under his dirt-smudged chin.

Henry peeked out from behind him, fingers pressed together as if in prayer. "If you can't play, the teams won't be even."

"I haven't time for baseball tonight, boys." With the longer days, the boys now had time to play ball after supper. "I'm sorry. Ask Miranda."

"She can't run like you do. She's—" George lowered his voice— "old."

I hid a smile behind my hand before correcting my expression. "Never comment on a lady's age, George."

"Yes, ma'am. But please? Won't you come?"

"I can't."

Their shoulders sagged as they trudged from the room. I rolled my pencil beneath my fingers, mouth drawn downward. I hated telling them no. I wanted to tousle heads and shout encouragement, dry tears and kiss skinned knees. Picking up the pencil again, I stared down at the bank book and wished the amount in the account for next year would grow like my hydrangeas. But then, it would still be a few weeks before I'd spy their colorful blooms. Perhaps it would be the same with the money, arriving at just the right moment.

I chewed my lip. If only Earl would get here with his news. He'd called earlier and said he would drop in and cheer me up. Maybe his mysterious donor had come through. Then I could rest, at least from financial strain. I stretched, rolled my shoulders, and listened for the crack of the bat against the ball. Instead, voices rose in heated disagreement.

I tossed my pencil to the desk. I might as well enjoy the evening. I hurried to the back of the house and waved to the gathered boys. "Here! I'm here!"

Carl's eyes widened. "You'll play? Really you will?"

I nodded. In a flash, the teams were sorted out. My team started in the field. I covered the stretch between second and third base. Knees bent, I readied for a hit. George hurled the ball toward home plate.

Crack! went the bat.

My chin angled toward the sky, searching for the small ball in the glare of the dying sun. I jogged backward, arms up, hands ready to receive it. Then the heel of my boot sank. I stumbled. The ball dropped to the ground beside me.

Carl raced forward, picked it up, and threw it to third base. A two-bagger for Henry. I returned to the shortstop position, determined to make up for my miss.

George walked the next batter. And the next. Bases loaded, with nine-year-old William at the plate, I crouched lower. Some of the girls stood cheering behind home plate. My team shouted encouragement to George. The other team yelled for William to bang the ball into the next county.

I held my breath. The ball spun toward the plate. William swung, connected. The ball flew over my head, toward Carl in the outfield. Runners advanced. I called for the ball. Carl threw it to me. I caught it and reached for William sliding into third. We collided before his foot reached the base. I held the ball in the air, triumphant.

"Hooray! Hooray, Miss Sadie!" My team gathered around me, jumping and shouting. My heart swelled with the joy of the moment, drinking in the praise. I helped William to his feet. He dusted off his pants. I shook out my skirt.

The raucous noise died away. I turned.

Earl's gaze, with none of its usual charm, traveled from

my untidy hair to my dingy boots. His slim eyebrows lifted just a bit. "I hope this isn't a bad time."

Then Mrs. McNeil appeared, head wagging, tongue *tsk*ing.

I took in Earl's immaculate tailored suit before noticing Mrs. McNeil's large hat above a stylish dress. She didn't say a word, but I felt chastised all the same. I shook more dirt from my skirt and smoothed errant strands of hair into their usual knot.

I swallowed hard. "I'll ask Mrs. Fore to serve tea in the parlor. Please allow me a few minutes to join you."

Earl nodded and stepped aside. My vision blurred as I attempted a stately walk to the back door, to get inside as fast as I could without appearing more hoydenish than I already had. When the door shut behind me, I dashed toward the stairs, calling instructions to Mrs. Fore as I passed.

I took the steps two at a time. In my bedroom, my hands shook as I poured water from the china pitcher into the bowl on the washstand. A bath would have been better, but I hadn't the time for more than a few splashes to loosen the grime and towel it away. Then I climbed into my green suit, buttoned it up, and rearranged my hair.

In this outfit, I'd always felt like I fit the part of the matron of the Home. But from the expressions I'd last seen on their faces, I wasn't sure anything would convince Earl and Mrs. McNeil of that now.

Chapter 36

Seated on the settee, pouring tea, I felt like a child caught cheating on a test. Earl shoved his hands into his pockets and paced in front of me a few times before sitting. Mrs. McNeil perched on the edge of a chair, glaring at me over the rim of her cup.

She didn't speak. Just looked.

Earl cleared his throat. "Mrs. McNeil and I came to talk about a sizable donation, although I'm not sure . . ." He looked down at his hands.

My gaze traveled back to the woman who held the Home's future in her hands. I had no idea if her "sizable donation" would eliminate our needs or only make them more manageable. Either way, the arrogance on the old woman's face didn't inspire confidence that it would happen now.

She set down her cup and pulled at the wrists of her gloves. "I expressed my reservations to Mr. Glazier before. Now I am justified in that thinking."

She rose. Earl and I hopped to our feet, as well.

The woman scrutinized me. "I told Cecilia Ramsey that

no good on her part would overcome your parentage. You're all gussied up on the outside, but I don't see that you're much different from your mother. Impropriety takes many forms, Miss Sillsby. I can't approve my late husband's legacy being tied to such a one as you." She inclined her head as if she'd just given me a compliment instead of a skewer to the heart. Then she lifted the short train of her skirt and swept from the room.

Earl raced after her while I dropped to the sofa and covered my face with my hands.

Perhaps she was right. I'd never be anything other than a prostitute's daughter. These children, this place, deserved more than that, no matter what Hazel and Mama Ramsey had tried to tell me.

I shut myself behind the office door, pulled out the old admittance ledger, and opened to the page I hadn't looked at in over a decade but which lived stamped on my mind. The ink had faded, but the words remained sharp. I ran my fingers over my mother's name: Eleanor Sillsby. I had no idea what happened to her after I'd been brought here and she'd been released from jail a few weeks later. I never saw her again.

After replacing the book, I knelt next to my chair and begged God not to let my shortcomings be the ruin of this place. I shouldn't have played with the children. I should have maintained an air of propriety at all times.

A light knock interrupted my pleadings.

"Sadie?" Earl stepped inside. I rose from my knees but didn't ask him to stay or tell him to leave. I couldn't even bring myself to look at him. When I sat again, he rested his hands on my shoulders, kneading his fingers into their tightness. The tension released. Until he spoke.

"What were you thinking, Sadie?"

I had no answer.

He turned my chair to face him, squeezed my hands between his. "You are the spokesman for this institution. You must be above reproach at all times."

I winced. Mrs. McNeil enjoyed spreading news of another's failings. I had no doubt she'd expounded to him on mine. And my mother's.

"I'm sure she told you everything," I whispered.

He nodded. "Though I don't think she meant to reveal her husband's infidelity."

"What?"

"Her, uh . . ." His face reddened. He stared at the floor, cleared his throat.

Infidelity. With my mother? No wonder the woman hated me. I swallowed hard, desperate for acceptance. But Earl's handsome face no longer regarded me with admiration or amusement. Had I lost his respect because of circumstances present or past? My mother's actions or my own?

My muscles contracted. I wasn't sure it mattered now. "Whatever my history, I can still do my job and do it well. In fact, I believe I am a walking testimony to the rightness of the ministry here."

"That's true, but with you as matron, we'll never receive Mrs. McNeil's generous support. Her gift would have greatly enhanced the Home's ability to operate."

I pressed my fingers against my temples, trying not to scream. "So we just bow to old biddies like Mrs. McNeil? What about the children?"

He shrugged. "What about them? They don't have the

means to support themselves, let alone this place. You need those 'old biddies'—and their money."

I crossed to the window on wooden legs, wishing I could tell Earl to go back to Philadelphia, but knowing I needed him to stay.

He cleared his throat. "I've some work to attend to this evening, but I'll be by early Monday morning. Perhaps we can find a way to appease Mrs. McNeil."

I wished I could tell him not to bother.

Thump. Thump. Thump.

I jolted upright from a deep sleep, eyes blinking, heart pounding. Had I been asleep minutes or hours? No light peeked around the window curtains.

Thump. Thump. Thump.

I threw back the covers, thrust my arms into my wrapper. As my feet flew down the stairs, I secured the tie around my waist.

Thump. Thump. Thump.

Yanking open the door, I gasped. Policeman Ezra Long stood with his hat in one hand and his other fist poised to thump the door once more.

He nodded. "Excuse me, Miss Sadie, but I—"

I clutched at his arm. "Not Lily Beth. Tell me it's not Lily Beth."

His face screwed up into a question mark. He edged backward, scratched his head. "No, ma'am. Don't know a Lily Beth. I've come about Carter Wellsmith."

My heart jumped into my throat. I glanced behind me.

Miranda and Mrs. Fore hovered like specters nearby, their faces almost as white as their nightdresses. I stepped out the door and pulled it shut behind me.

"Carter? I don't understand." A chill wafted over me. I rubbed my hands over my arms and waited for him to continue.

Ezra backed down to the middle step, as if he feared being too close when he related the news. "There was a robbery tonight." He stared at his hat between his hands. "Two, in fact."

The wind picked up. I licked moisture into my lips, telling myself to remain calm. "What does that have to do with Carter?"

"He was one of them involved."

My eyelids dropped like curtains, shutting the world from sight. Sorrow rested heavy on my shoulders until I felt I couldn't stand beneath the weight, for I didn't doubt Ezra's words. I reached for the porch rail and gripped it until the pain in my fingers brought me back to the moment.

My eyes opened. "Is he—?" The almost-full moon illuminated Ezra's panic, his Adam's apple bobbing.

"No, ma'am. Just . . ." He lifted one shoulder, let it fall again. "We've arrested him."

My head thunked against the post that held the porch roof over my head. One of my boys, incarcerated. Indistinct memories flickered, sparking a shiver. I groaned. Carter would never get another chance now. "What happened?"

"Well . . ." Ezra scratched his head. "Best we can tell, a group of men took two horses from the livery, then broke into Gardiner's Confectionary through the front window. When we caught up with them, they had the money in hand. To be honest, we don't think Carter actually stole anything."

My head and spirits lifted. Perhaps this wouldn't be as bad as it seemed. "Then why was he arrested?"

"He was holding the getaway horses—the ones stolen from the livery stable."

My knees threatened to give way. Then an arm circled my back, held me up.

Miranda.

"Where is he now?" she asked.

"At the jail."

"Can I see him?" I whispered.

"Yes, ma'am. In the morning. But I wanted you to know he was safe."

Safe. In jail.

Ezra rubbed his chin. "Will you— Do you want to tell Blaine? I can go out to his place now, if you'd prefer."

My head seemed to have ballooned, my neck too small to hold it upright, but I managed. "No, I'll tell him."

Hurt would color his voice, darken his eyes, but I couldn't bear for him to hear it from anyone but me.

By the time Ezra reached his automobile, Miranda and I had groped our way back inside. Mrs. Fore shut the door before Ezra's engine puttered to life. With me in the middle, we huddled on the settee. I felt eighty-three instead of twenty-three.

Mrs. Fore shook her head. "A tragedy. A real tragedy."

Hands covering my face, I sucked in a sharp breath and held it. This wasn't like losing Lily Beth. At least with the Lindstroms there was hope for a better future. Carter had no prospects now. Nothing except a blotch on his already smudged character. How would he ever overcome this?

Guilt pressed in around me as I remembered all the times I'd made excuses for him, just as Miranda had said.

Mrs. Fore guided my head to her ample bosom. "Cry it out, dear, so you can be strong on the morrow. We'll handle the rest of the children. You needn't worry about anything here."

But worry was already spinning the wheels in my mind. I'd have to contact Mr. Riley. Earl too. And telling Blaine couldn't wait—even for morning.

"You two go on back to bed. You can rest and pray, even if you won't sleep. I'll call Mr. Riley."

Mrs. Fore pulled me to my feet. I wobbled. Miranda's eyes met mine, compassion spilling over and strengthening my legs, for I had no doubt that she cared for Carter as much as I did.

Chapter 37

I telephoned Mr. Riley first. When I finished relating all the information, the line went quiet.

"Mr. Riley?"

"I'm here, Sadie. It's a hard situation, to be sure. But it's out of our hands now. He's almost an adult and he doesn't appear to want our help. I don't see that our influence is making much difference, anyway."

Though I'd prepared myself to hear those very words, my chest heaved. I reached for the wall. "You can't abandon him, Mr. Riley. Not now. This is when he needs us the most." Tears hovered on the edge, but if I fell apart, who would take care of Carter?

"I'll consult with the other board members in the morning, but I know these men. They'll agree with me." Another pause. "Have you told Blaine?"

I sucked in a deep breath. "No. I'd like to go out to his place and tell him in person."

"It should be done now. Perhaps the three of us should discuss it together."

My heart clenched. Part of me wanted to see Blaine alone,

to throw my arms around him and sob out the news about his brother, beg him to help the boy in spite of their past conflicts. But another part relished the thought of an intermediary, a barrier to keep me from falling into Blaine's embrace. That could only lead to more pain.

"I'd be grateful for your presence, Mr. Riley." I swallowed, told myself it was the best choice.

"Fine. I'll be by to pick you up in fifteen minutes."

"I'll be ready." But even as the words squeaked across the telephone wire, I knew it was a lie. I'd never be ready for a trip such as this one.

Mr. Riley and I chugged down the rutted lane with only the dim headlamps to guide our progress. Finally, the old farmhouse appeared in the shafts of light. It had stood on this land for decades and was nearly falling apart when Blaine took on the lease three years ago. He'd shored it up since then. Made it presentable.

More than presentable.

Adorable.

In the wash of moonlight, the white paint glistened beneath the gabled roof. It looked like . . . home. I could only imagine the pride of ownership that stirred in him now. And I despised the sudden lament that circumstances had torn this dream from me.

The motor silenced. The thrumming in my ears continued, drowning out the night sounds. We hadn't reached the porch before the front door swung open and Blaine tromped out, pushing his shirttail into his pants.

Hands low on his hips, his eyes darted between me and Mr. Riley. "What's happened?"

My fingers clamped tightly to each other; my throat grew stiff and tight. I opened my mouth but couldn't say the words, even though I'd determined I would.

"Carter's been arrested." Mr. Riley blurted the news without preamble.

Blaine's head dropped, hiding his expression from any beam of light. "I guess you'd better come inside."

In the mostly empty main room, he lit a lamp. His jaw ticked several times. Was he fighting back anger—or tears? I couldn't tell. But when he lifted his face, all emotion had vanished. "What'd he do?"

The weariness in those words made my arms ache to cradle his head to my shoulder, to soothe away the furrow of his brow. But for the sake of our . . . friendship, I had to do something much harder. I had to tell him.

"He was with some others who robbed Gardiner's Confectionary." I remembered the slouched shoulders and steely visage of the man Carter had conversed with on the street. No doubt he'd had a hand in this. Or had at least goaded Carter into participation. "After they'd stolen horses from the livery." My chin dropped to my chest.

He blew out a heavy breath. "I guess he's made his choice, then."

"We have to help him," I whispered, my eyes imploring both men.

Mr. Riley put his hand on my arm. "The Raystown Home can't do any more for him. I expect you know that."

Blaine nodded once, his jaw tightening to a steady bulge. "Go home, Sadie. I'll visit him tomorrow."

I pressed my hand to Blaine's arm. "I'm so sorry. I—"

What else was there to say? I'd failed Carter, just as my mother had failed me. My hands dropped to my side. "I'll see him tomorrow, too."

Stumbling my way to Mr. Riley's automobile, the earth quaked beneath me at the thought of Carter facing the consequences of his actions. I clutched at Mr. Riley's coat sleeve. "Please promise I can at least see Carter through this. I can't desert him now. He'll need me, no matter what happens." My voice broke. Tears shimmied down my cheeks. "Please."

Mr. Riley pulled at his collar, looked away. Then he cleared his throat, put the motorcar in gear, and started down the dusty road. He didn't say a word until he escorted me to the front door of the Home. "Offer him support and advice, but we cannot spend one penny on his defense. Nor can we offer him a home—either now or later."

My stomach clenched with the knowledge that it might not be only Carter who would lose his home. It might be all of us.

Before dawn, Miranda, Mrs. Fore, and I sat in the kitchen sipping coffee. Miranda's chair scraped the floor as she pushed away from the table.

"I'll wake the children." She shuffled from the room. I wondered if she felt as numb as I did.

I rubbed my forehead, trying to massage away the pain that thumped as loudly as Ezra Long in the middle of the night. Never before had one of our kids been locked in jail, accused of a crime. We'd had runaways and school dropouts and even those who needed a strong hand to keep them in line. But not this. Never this.

Not until the responsibility had rested on my shoulders.

I stumbled to the office, cradled my head in my arms on the desk. Blaine had said he would see Carter today, and I planned to, as well. But I didn't want to cross paths with him. I raised my head, pressed my palms together, and set my fingers in front of my lips.

Earl strolled in, more serious than usual. Still mourning yesterday's loss of Mrs. McNeil's money, I imagined. I no longer cared about that.

Hands limp in my lap, I wondered if he noted my puffy eyes and uncombed hair. Did I now resemble the friendless child I'd always been? His handsome face blurred.

"What is it, Sadie?" Compassion again softened his tone.

I wanted to wail out my distress, but he wasn't just Earl. He was Mr. Glazier, an agent of the Children's Aid Society of Pennsylvania. Could he separate the professional from the personal? I found I could not. I had to prove to him—to all of them—that I wouldn't crumble beneath the pressure, no matter how great.

Swallowing down my tears, I drew in a bracing breath. "There was a robbery in town last night. Two, actually. Carter Wellsmith was caught leaving the scene. He's in jail." Flat words, void of all the emotion that stole feeling from my limbs.

Sadness dawned in his eyes, the regret over a child who couldn't be saved from his past, from himself. He pushed back a mass of my tangled hair, tenderness radiating from his face. Did he see me the same way I saw Carter? As one to be pitied? "I feared something like this."

I stiffened. Blaine had made that same dire prophecy dozens of times, but coming from Earl's mouth, the words felt different. Carter worshiped Earl. If Carter had offered that same devotion to Blaine, would things have turned out better? Earl had been kind to Carter, but nothing more.

Conversations from the past few weeks skittered through my mind. Earl had spoken little of individual children, unless a situation warranted a decision of policy or procedure. Never emotion. Never a love that went beyond the idea of helping children in need.

Pulling my shoulders back, I let a calm I didn't feel compose my face. "If you'll excuse me, I have to make a visit to the jail."

Even if I couldn't help Carter out of this scrape, I refused to discard him as a lost case. No, the Lord had called me as a missionary to orphan and friendless children, even if those children resided in prison.

Hadn't that been where someone found me?

Earl insisted on escorting me to see Carter, though I curtly informed him I didn't require his assistance.

At the jail, they directed us to the courthouse, saying they'd hoped the judge would meet with him. Earl ushered me up the tall stone steps and through the heavy door. Stale air churned the black coffee in my stomach. I chided myself for not forcing down at least a piece of toast.

Ezra Long met us at the bottom of the stairs. "You both want to see him?"

I turned to Earl. "I think it's best if you stay here."

He nodded, seated himself on a bench against the wall.

I followed Ezra up the staircase and down a long hallway lined with doors. Heat filled my belly as we stopped outside the last one. Low voices rumbled from inside the room. Surely a trial didn't commence this quickly. I gulped in air, trying to keep down the rising bile.

Ezra sifted through a ring of keys. "Guess they're still at it in there."

"Who?" The minute the question left my mouth I regretted it. The judge. Maybe the others who were involved. They'd be here, too. Wouldn't they?

"Blaine's in there," Ezra said through my musings. "He's been here since the break of day."

A voice rose from downstairs. "Where's Ezra?"

"I'd better see who it is." Ezra motioned to a bench along the opposite wall. "When Blaine comes out, you can go in." His footsteps echoed down the corridor, then the stairs.

Blaine's deep voice resonated, but I couldn't make out individual words. I tiptoed closer. The last thing I desired was an awkward confrontation, but I needed to hear what Blaine had to say to his brother. I pressed my ear against the door. Voices clarified.

"But aren't you even going to get me a lawyer?" Carter's baritone.

"Do I need to? You're guilty, aren't you?" Blaine's voice, strong but overlaid with kindness. "Wouldn't it be better to tell the judge you're sorry and take your punishment like a man?"

I held my breath, straining to hear Carter's mumble.

"I want this to turn out good for you, Carter, but that means paying for your mistake. It isn't for the rest of your life, thank the Lord, though it could have been if anyone had died. Don't you see? This is your chance to own up to your choices, to change your direction."

"You've never cared before. Don't act like you care now." Carter spat the words. They stung like a slap in the face. If Blaine didn't care, he wouldn't be there, and he wouldn't speak with such kindness. Couldn't Carter see that?

I rattled the door handle. The voices fell silent. A scrape. A step. The door opened. I charged through. Carter tensed behind the bare table.

"He's right, you know." I kept my eyes on Carter's face. "You have been given a great grace."

Carter snorted. "I got caught. How's that a great grace?"

"Because now you have the opportunity to face your sin, to admit your wrong and go in the opposite direction." I reached for Carter. He flinched, retreated to the opposite wall, and folded his arms across his chest.

"So you aren't getting me a lawyer, either?" The sarcasm dripped thicker than molasses on a winter's day.

I looked down at my hands, my heart threatening to burst from my chest. "No," I whispered. "You're on your own in this."

In spite of all his bravado, Carter's hand shook as he raked it through his golden hair. Shadows purpled the pale skin beneath his eyes. My heart ached, but I was powerless to help. Even if I wanted to secure him representation, I had no money to offer as payment.

I glanced around. Only the three of us occupied the room. "Where are the others?"

"What others?" Carter scowled as he plopped down on a low stool.

"The other boys. The ones who were with you."

Carter stared at the floor.

Blaine cleared his throat. "The other *men* are being held at the jailhouse. They brought him here, hoping the judge could talk to him today. He's still a juvenile. That might be in his favor."

Men. I wet my lips, remembering Carter's face when the scruffy-looking young man had called him a baby. He'd been trying to prove himself. Like Blaine with his land. Like me at the Home.

The thought skewered—all three of us needing some sort of outward approval to make us feel valued. Mama Ramsey hadn't raised me that way. She'd told me I needed only Jesus' approval, nothing more.

If only I could believe that.

If only *we* could believe that.

The enormity of the thought overwhelmed me. I had to come back to something I could understand. Something in this moment. "What will happen now?"

"A trial. It would be better if he'd confess his guilt." Blaine shrugged his broad shoulders. "Either way, given his age and the offense, it likely means time in the reformatory, but not prison."

I let out a long breath. I knew about the reformatory. An imposing structure that sat just outside of town. Kids who'd been in trouble were given schooling and taught skills, then released to be productive members of society. Perhaps they could do what we couldn't. I clutched at the slender thread of hope even as Carter turned his back to us.

Blaine grasped my elbow. "Let's go, Sadie."

New lines had appeared around his mouth since last night. His full lips pulled downward, as if they had weights on their edges, attesting to the toll Carter had taken on him.

I hated that he had to bear more pain. He'd had too much of that already in his young life, as I'd had in mine. In spite of all that had gone wrong between us, my greatest desire in that moment was to soothe away the sorrow etched deep into his face.

Blaine called down for Ezra to return and secure the room. An awkward silence hovered between us while we waited. Then Ezra appeared, sending us back to the main floor. As we descended the stairs, Earl leapt from his seat.

"How is Carter?" He took my arm and led me to the place he'd vacated.

"He's . . ." I looked into Earl's liquid brown eyes. They held me—then repelled me. Like a pie with too much sweetness. All the pressure of the past few weeks rested on my chest. I struggled to draw breath.

My lips quivered as my gaze moved past him, to Blaine. The one I loved. The one who had loved me. Were those feelings still there? Was there any hope we could find each other again?

Ezra loped back downstairs. I approached, hands wringing with worry. "What will happen now?"

He scratched his head. "We'll hold him until Judge Bascom can hear his case. Might be a week. Maybe less. If you post a bond . . ."

I shook my head. Money I didn't have. Money Blaine didn't have. I glanced at Earl, but he hadn't been paying attention to the conversation.

Blaine cleared his throat. "I'll be back this afternoon to visit him."

Ezra nodded. "You're welcome anytime, Blaine. Sure hate to see him go wrong so early in life."

Blaine opened his mouth as if to speak. Then his chin dropped toward his chest and he plodded away, shoulders slumped in defeat.

The numbness in my body spread to my heart, and I wondered if I'd ever feel anything again.

Chapter 38

I vaguely noticed the dry goods store, the bank, and the funeral home as Earl and I walked from the courthouse. Miranda and Mrs. Fore would be anxious, waiting to hear from me. Mr. Riley, as well, in spite of his insistence that Carter had chosen to put himself outside of our sphere of influence. I wanted to move faster, but my legs wouldn't obey.

"These things happen, Sadie. There isn't much you can do but cut ties. Of course, once the news gets out, especially in a place as small as this, you'll have a few lean months."

He didn't understand. This wasn't about money. Carter held a piece of my heart that I would never surrender, no matter what choices he made. I shook Earl's words from my head. I needed to be at the Home, with the children. With those who cared what happened to Carter.

Strength surged into my legs, and suddenly I was running. I ran past the livery, where they'd stolen the horse. Past the confectionary, with its boarded-up window. Past houses and shops and churches.

"Sadie! Sadie, wait!" Shoes slapped the ground behind

me. I lifted my skirts and ran as if I'd hit a long fly ball and home plate was in sight.

The pattering stopped. My name faded.

As I ran uphill, my legs churned, my heart hammered.

If I'd accepted Blaine instead of the matron job, would I have been able to save Carter? Blaine and I could have taken him in after that first conflict with the Comstocks; I would have made sure of it.

Was this job really what the Lord intended for me? Yes or no, I'd chosen it. And now I had to see it through or risk being the reason the Raystown Home could no longer help children in need. But I had no idea what to do next.

A block and a half before I reached the Home, I turned left. A few minutes later, I stood on the Stapletons' porch. The minute Hazel answered the door, I fell into her arms and poured out the whole sorry tale.

Later, with Hazel's prayers ringing in my ears, I dashed toward the Home. My home. The place that held my heart.

Or at least the pieces of it.

The next morning, I couldn't shake my lethargy. After Mrs. Fore and Miranda both looked at me with sad eyes, I sent them into town to invite businessmen to the picnic next Monday. Then I wandered the house, memories playing like a phonograph record in my head. Carter as a small child, coming to me with a splinter in his finger or a busted lip. Young Blaine's soulful eyes watching me from across the room. Mama Ramsey toting me along when she came to volunteer in the kitchen or the office, doing whatever needed to be done. Hazel taking interest in a shy teenager, encouraging me to apply for the position as her assistant after I'd finished high school.

I covered my ears, closed my eyes. If the money didn't come in, the Home would close. If it did come in, would the board choose to hire someone else—maybe someone like Earl—to oversee the work? The thought curdled the breakfast in my stomach. While he saw the need and the solutions, he didn't have the same love for each individual child that I had. That even Miranda had.

If a man like Earl took over, what would happen to Miranda? Mrs. Fore? The new part-time housemaid? Would they be dismissed in favor of more qualified staff? As if our hearts didn't qualify us most.

I strolled out the front door and looked for the first hydrangea bud, one that promised it would soon burst into a globe of color. But no matter how hard I searched, I found only leaves.

Where had I gone wrong? Was it only a few months ago that I'd been almost engaged to Blaine? And happily so? I drifted to the backyard. The clean smell of fresh-turned soil drew me toward the garden plot, green sprouts and sprigs and stalks covering the area.

Leaning over the short fence, I studied the plants, identifying some, wondering about others. Birds sang overhead. A horse clopped down the street, a wagon creaking along behind. In the distance, I heard the trolley bell and a motorcar. I breathed in the peace and willed it to still the upheaval inside me.

"You thinking of taking over my garden?"

I spun around, gripping the top of the small pickets behind me. "What are you doing here?"

Blaine opened the gate and walked into the garden. He bent and pulled a few weeds, then straightened. "I went to visit Carter and thought I'd check on things here before heading back to my place."

"How is he?"

"Stubborn as ever. The judge got called out of town at the last minute, but they've set the court date for June 15. I guess that's a good thing. More time to talk him into pleading guilty."

My teeth clenched, and my fingers balled into the palms of my hands. "You were right all along."

"Right about what?" He moved closer, the heat of his body radiating though the short fence between us. His breath caressed my neck. If only he'd step away. Then I could think. Then again, I didn't want to think. Not about Carter.

I pressed my fists into my eyes. "He'll never change."

"If he pleads guilty, it'll go better for him. But he still doesn't see that." His strong hands held my shoulders. "I won't give up, Sadie. I. Won't. Give. Up."

I shook a little with the intensity of his words. My forehead touched his chest now. "Why can't we help him?" A sob escaped before I could swallow it down.

"We are helping him. Can't you see?"

My head moved back and forth. I longed for his strong arms to circle and hold me. Instead, they fell limp to his sides. I looked up at the man whose gentle strength had held me captive for so many years.

He stepped away, turned his back to me. His large fingers

raked through the thick hair at the top of his head. "Ever since Carter was born, I've prayed that he wouldn't turn out like his father. Why my mother married that man, I'll never know."

Blaine's shoulders slumped. I wanted to rest my head between those shoulders, but I didn't dare. "The land was mine. Did I ever tell you that? My inheritance from my father. I guess Carter's father thought the land was my mother's, that it would be his when they married."

He blew out a long breath. "You'd have liked my mother."

My chest contracted. I doubted he would have liked mine.

"She was sweet and soft. Always a kind word. She had a deep faith, always helped those in need." His voice trailed away.

The silence stretched. I fidgeted with my skirt, plucked a dandelion from the ground and squeezed the milk from its stalk.

"She died giving birth to Carter." His voice grew hard, each word like a brick falling to the ground. "She had argued with Carter's father. He pushed her. She tumbled off the wagon. Carter came too soon." His voice broke. He steadied it. "She left me alone with him and my baby brother."

"Oh, Blaine." I reached for him, then pulled back, closed my eyes, and begged God to spare him more pain. But I feared He wouldn't answer as I wanted.

Carter's name—and his association with the Raystown Home—splashed across the newspaper during the next few days. Phone calls came in from board members, longtime donors, and folks who just wanted to know more. By Saturday my nerves had frayed. I started giving orders—to Miranda, Mrs. Fore, the children. If anything went wrong at the picnic on Monday, we might as well close our doors that night instead of waiting another month.

"Have you written out your remarks?" Earl followed as I flitted from office to kitchen to parlor and back again. I appreciated that he hadn't abandoned us, but his directives chafed.

"No, but I will. Miranda?" I left him behind and hurried into the parlor, where she had the children gathered to practice their pieces for the program. "Did you remember to—"

"Yes, the ledger books are ready to record donations. Yes, Mrs. Fore has all she needs to prepare the food we will take for the children's meal. Yes, the invitations were posted three days ago to all foster and adoptive families from the past ten years. Anything else?"

I shut my mouth. I hadn't thought to do any of those things. Yet remembering the smallest detail came as easily to Miranda as adding a column of figures. Names, dates, amounts. Bits of information she'd seen or heard sat filed in her head, ready for recall.

Then I noticed the children behind her. So much more orderly than when I'd had charge of them. And yet they loved her, in spite of the way she forced them to do as they ought.

Or perhaps because of it.

"Go on." I crossed my arms, tapped my toe. "Keep practicing."

"Continue please, Cynthia." Miranda's quiet, authoritative tone.

Cynthia's bottom lip quivered, and tears flooded her eyes.

Her gaze shifted from Miranda to me and then back again. "I . . . I can't."

"Yes you can. Just like we practiced." Miranda sounded so much like Hazel now. Calm, but firm.

Cynthia squeezed her eyes shut as tears poured down her cheeks. She shook her head, then rushed from the room, wailing.

Miranda scratched her forehead, her lips pressed into a straight line. "Henry, why don't you practice your recitation next."

Henry hopped up. "'Listen my children and you shall hear of the midnight ride of Paul Revere. . . .'"

At least someone knew what to do and was ready to do it.

Angry all of a sudden—at Cynthia for not pushing through the shyness, at Miranda for doing my job better than I had, at Carter for not taking the many chances he'd been given, at the unfairness of the Home's predicament—I stomped back to my office and nearly slammed the door. Earl's laughter startled me. Disarmed me.

His hand found the curve of my chin. "I do love your passion, Sadie. It's one of your finest qualities." His touch turned the heat of my rancor to desire. If I responded to him, would he take me away from this place, allow me to leave behind all my failures? The warmth in my face betrayed me. He closed the gap between us. I held my breath, braced for the moment his lips found mine.

Then my head jerked. His lips grazed my cheek.

I would not be my mother. I would not forfeit my virtue, not even for the future of this place.

Footsteps drew near. I distanced myself from Earl, wet my lips, ready to greet whomever sought me.

Blaine filled the doorway. My smile froze.

His gaze swept past me, to Earl.

"Mr. Glazier was just leaving," I said, turning to Earl. "Weren't you?"

Earl's placid face splotched red, nostrils flaring above his gaping mouth, making him look like a fish on a hook. I held the door open until he stumbled across the threshold.

A decisive click confirmed Blaine and I were alone. An ache pushed at my chest, then burst into a sob.

Blaine pulled me close. "Please don't cry, Sadie."

For the first time in many months, I wrapped my arms around his solidness and clung.

Chapter 39

Gray clouds chased each other across the sky the morning of the picnic.

Please, Lord. Not bad weather on top of everything else.

Blaine arrived and piled the children and Mrs. Fore's food into the back of his wagon. He and I nodded to each other but refrained from conversation. But then, I'd hardly spoken to anyone that morning; I seemed to be saving my words for our would-be patrons.

His sturdy horses plodded off toward Mr. Wise's farm as Hazel and Professor Stapleton arrived to drive the rest of us. Earl squeezed into the front seat beside Hazel while Mrs. Fore, Miranda, and I situated ourselves in the back.

My stomach reeled. So much depended on today. So much that I couldn't make happen—just like I couldn't make Lily Beth wear her eyeglasses or Cynthia overcome her fears or Carter choose to do right. So much was out of my hands. I had to trust it all to the Lord.

We jostled over bricked streets, then dirt roads. Fields

stretched wide in every direction, broken only by an occasional canopy of leafy green fruit trees or a small homestead. The mountain loomed in the near distance, dark with foliage, as if flaunting its coolness to those of us under the bright sun. Professor Stapleton parked on the span of land in front of Mr. Wise's house, opposite Blaine's wagon. A few other buggies and automobiles had arrived before us. Board members, I assumed. Were they as nervous over the fate of the Home as I was?

Over the next hour, more families arrived. The scent of warm horseflesh and gasoline mingled in the early summer freshness. Bouts of laughter spilled amid conversations and squeals of playing children. But I sensed unease hovering over the gathering, as well. The yard around the house didn't fill completely. I chewed my lip, knowing Carter's arrest had kept some away.

I lifted my chin and strode through the crowd, talking with parents and children, with donors and foster families and those considering either role. No matter that others chose to judge us on the basis of one child's behavior. I would concentrate on those with open hearts for our work, our children.

Another group rounded the corner of the house. I turned to greet them. My eyes brightened.

"Lily Beth!" I swept her up in my arms, spun her around. Her giggle warmed my heart. Mr. and Mrs. Lindstrom stood behind her. Three young towheaded children peeked out from behind their mother's skirts.

"Thank you for coming." I shook Mrs. Lindstrom's hand,

giving her a genuine smile. "It's such a lovely surprise. And I've missed this little one." I tweaked Lily Beth's cheek and noticed the glint of brass that crossed the bridge of her nose. My fingers grazed the rims, but I didn't trust myself to speak. The girl's head turned. Her eyes widened. She ran, hair flying out behind her, and leapt into Miranda's arms.

Miranda's face softened—no tightness around her mouth, no wariness in her eyes. Even our friendship hadn't done that for her. But this child had.

Miranda led Lily Beth back to us. She talked with Mrs. Lindstrom, asking questions I hadn't yet thought to ask. My face warmed. I'd missed Lily Beth, yet I didn't seem as attuned to her real needs as Miranda.

A light touch grazed my elbow. I turned. Earl nodded toward another family making their way across the grass. I needed to go to them, but I longed for more time with Lily Beth, to put her before the work that tugged at me.

But that wasn't my place. Not anymore. I'd been charged with raising funds and running the Home, with providing direction and making business decisions for the good of all instead of the needs of one. And while there remained a certain satisfaction in those tasks, I found myself throwing wistful glances over my shoulder toward Miranda, Lily Beth, and the Lindstroms as I walked away.

Families spread out blankets and settled down to eat the picnic dinners they'd brought with them. My face ached from smiling. My head pounded with fatigue. But I'd secured a few promises of donations.

Roaming among the seated groups, bits of conversations reached my ears, but I didn't latch on to any of the words until I heard Lily Beth's name drop from Mrs. Lawson's lips.

"Such a precious child. I'm so grateful she has those glasses. Not that my dear doctor wouldn't have found a way to get them for her, of course."

"Didn't Dr. Lawson pay for them? I'd heard he did," the other woman replied.

"Oh no. Blaine beat him to it. Said he wanted to make sure the girl had what she needed, whatever the cost."

I froze. *Blaine* had paid for Lily Beth's glasses? Up to fifty dollars, Dr. Lawson had told me. A small fortune—and right when he had so little cash to give away. Was that why he'd been working other jobs and charging us for produce?

My mind returned to the day of Hazel's good-bye party, Blaine whisking Dr. Lawson to the porch for a private conversation. I rubbed my head. Why hadn't he just told me?

I searched the crowd for my friend's face, needing to thank him silently, if nothing else. I finally spotted him, sitting with his back against a tree, his gaze intent on the person speaking to him.

The girl speaking to him.

Viola.

I whirled away and rushed in the opposite direction. This wasn't a random Sunday stroll, where they could have met on the street. This was Blaine taking a meal with her—and her mother. In a public gathering.

I swallowed down tears. It was over. Really over. Though I'd told myself that several times in the past few months, I'd still felt a pull between us. Thought perhaps he felt it, too.

Evidently not. His contact with me proved nothing more than his heart of compassion for the Home, its inmates, and his brother. The sooner I accepted that fact, the better.

A touch on my arm. Blaine held out a cup of lemonade. "You look famished. Have you eaten at all?"

My heart thumped with the desire to confront him with all I'd just heard and seen, but I feared my emotions would spiral out of control. I couldn't risk that. Best keep to the subject at hand. "I've nibbled a bit here and there."

Our fingers brushed as he passed the cup to me. I wished I could curl my hand around his arm and lay my head against his shoulder. What would Blaine think if I told him I craved such a moment here in front of everyone?

"Miss Sillsby? Are your children ready?" Mr. Riley's voice pulled me back to the tasks of the day. I nodded, wishing I felt more composed. But it didn't matter. I stood in the place of leadership, and I would not let them down. Any of them. Hazel. The children. The board members. Miranda might be able to run figures and keep all manner of information in her head, but I could make the most passionate plea to save the Home.

Mr. Riley quieted the crowd and introduced me. I climbed the porch steps. A smattering of applause filled the silence.

Looking out over so many who had been our faithful friends, my grin came naturally. "Today we have quite a treat planned for you. The children of the Raystown Home have prepared a sampling of their efforts at school this past year." I introduced Henry and stood out of the way as he leapt up onto the porch and launched into his Paul Revere poem. Then Nancy sang "Good Evening, Caroline" in her clear soprano voice.

When Miranda urged Cynthia up to the porch, the girl shook her head. I motioned for William and Sylvia instead. They recited a scene from *Romeo and Juliet*. When they finished, Miranda pushed Cynthia forward again. Others encouraged the girl. I gnawed at my lower lip. Then Janet took Cynthia's hand, led her up the three steps, and stood with her.

Cynthia started her recitation, her voice quivering and quiet, but steady. One stanza down, one to go. Laughter burst from the back of the crowd. Cynthia stiffened. Then she bolted from the porch.

Chapter 40

ynthia!" I raced after her, my skirts whipping around my feet. "Stop, Cynthia!"

I plunged into the cool shade of a stand of trees, calling her name, listening for a response. The brush of leaves. The snap of twigs. The beating of my heart and the distant murmur of someone speaking.

How had she disappeared so quickly?

I plunged forward, praying, shouting. "Cynthia! Miss Sadie needs you."

Fighting underbrush and branches, I forged on. Finally, I leaned over, hands on my knees. A small squeak sounded from my right.

Slower now, I made my way toward the noise, stopping and starting, hardly daring to breathe.

"Cynthia?" I whispered. Leaves rustled as a soft wind found its way down through the trees. "Please, honey. I just want to talk to you."

A bit of red caught my eye. I inched closer.

"It's all right, sweetheart. I'm not mad."

She shot out from behind the tree, almost knocking me to the ground. My arms closed around her, holding her still. "I'm so sorry, honey. Truly, I am." I stroked her curls as she cried. When she quieted a bit, she stuttered out her fears, thinking the laughter had been for her.

"Oh, sweet pea, no. It wasn't you at all." I forced her eyes to meet mine. "I'm so proud of you. You stood up there and tried."

After a few more tears, she felt ready to join the group again. I picked her up, but almost immediately I regretted it. I stumbled, praying I wouldn't send both of us tumbling among the underbrush.

Then a tanned face framed by dark hair appeared. Blaine lifted the girl from my arms. She clung to his neck. His eyes fixed on mine. My knees weakened. If only he would quit appearing when I needed him most. Then perhaps I could make my heart forget.

Blaine strode into the yard, with me trotting along behind. The crowd had dispersed, only a few tarrying to the very end. He set Cynthia down beside me, then moved away to speak with someone else. What had I missed? Had Mr. Riley made the plea for funds? Had he been successful?

"We had a wonderful time, Sadie." Mrs. Lawson pressed her cheek to mine. When she pulled away, tears stood in her eyes. "Lily Beth is doing well."

"Yes. She is." I scanned the crowd for the Lindstroms. Was that Blaine crouched before Lily Beth, making her laugh, his finger stroking the frames around her eyes? I quickly searched the opposite side of the yard and startled at a disconcerting sight. Viola, arm curled around Earl's, batted her lashes as she smiled and blushed beneath his jovial grin and intent gaze.

The way he'd once looked at me.

I forced my attention to Mrs. Lawson, her face beaming with compassion as Cynthia clung to her. Mrs. Lawson wiped the girl's tear-streaked face, then sent her to the others with gentle words.

Had anyone ever *asked* the Lawsons to consider taking a child?

"You and Dr. Lawson have been such good friends of the Home for so many years."

She looked at me with a wistful smile.

I took a deep breath, plunged ahead. "Would you consider opening your home and your hearts to one of the kids?"

She ducked her head, but not before her cheeks bloomed red. "We've talked about it for years but never followed through." Her gaze fixed on Cynthia again. "But I think perhaps it's time." She squeezed my hand. "I'll be in touch."

The deep timbre of Blaine's voice drew my attention past the end of the porch. He lifted the little girls over the side of the wagon. They giggled and shrieked, clearly enjoying their flight through the air. He hadn't even noticed Viola's treachery.

Our eyes met for an instant. Then he climbed up on the wagon seat, checked his cargo of children, and urged the horses forward.

I walked the length of the porch, following his progress through the yard, noticing no one else, until a hand on my arm held me back.

"Sadie, we need to talk." Typically placid Earl sounded almost . . . guilty.

A buzz started in my ears. I didn't want to hear what he had to say, but I feared I had no choice.

His chest swelled as he pulled in a deep breath. "I'm leaving."

My forehead crinkled. "We're all leaving."

"No, I mean I'm leaving for good." He studied the hat between his hands. "I admit, I lobbied to be assigned to this place because you intrigued me. Then I stayed to see if I could survive a few years in such a small town."

Survive? Did he see Raystown as a wilderness? I couldn't try to read meaning into that word, so I latched on to the next ones. "A few years?" I bit my lip, more confused than before.

"A stepping-stone." He waved his hat as if shooing flies. "It doesn't matter. I've been offered a position in Washington, helping draft laws and make policy for the care of dependent children." A small smile, a shadow of his usual broad grin. "Don't worry. The CAS will continue its association with you. I just won't be their emissary."

"So this is good-bye?" But my heart knew the answer before my mouth spoke the question.

In spite of all the disappointments, my heart lifted the following week as I skipped down the street with one of Cynthia's hands in mine, the other in her older sister Nancy's.

"And we're going to stay here always?" Cynthia asked.

I glanced at Nancy. The fourteen-year-old's mouth remained in a grim line. It wasn't that she didn't want to come. Her eyes had lit brighter than a full moon when I mentioned that the Lawsons wanted her and Cynthia to live with them. Keeping the sisters together had been my greatest wish. Theirs too. But Nancy remembered the last time, how they'd been sent back from a family they loved when the family ran into desperate times.

"I hope you will, Cynthia, though we never know what changes life will bring." Oh, had I learned the truth of that! According to Miranda's ledger, we'd taken in less than five hundred dollars at the picnic. Well behind previous years. Well short of our goals.

Cynthia darted up the stone steps in front of us. I smiled at Nancy, urged her forward. Mrs. Lawson welcomed us all inside, fussing over both girls as if she hadn't just decided two days ago to take them in.

"Let me show you to your rooms." Mrs. Lawson mounted the wide staircase.

Nancy's eyes grew round. "Rooms?"

Mrs. Lawson nodded. "You each have your own." Then her face crinkled. "If you want. Or you can stay together."

Nancy laughed. Cynthia giggled and raced ahead. I feared I'd drown in a puddle of my own happy tears.

Two fewer children to worry over after the board closed our doors in four short weeks.

Dr. Lawson stepped into the room, shook my hand. He seemed younger. Lighter. As if a burden of sorrow had lifted from his shoulders. "I haven't seen Gwen this eager about anything in years." His laughter echoed through the room. "Or myself, either."

"I'm so glad. Nancy and Cynthia are such good girls. They just want someone to love them."

Dr. Lawson nodded. "We have an abundance of love, and we're happy to share."

"I know. I just wish others felt that way. About sharing, I mean."

"Yes. Your Miss Jennings made quite a plea that we all do just that."

Miranda? Had *she* taken on my role when I'd gone after Cynthia? No one had mentioned it. My head felt light, and my vision narrowed. I swayed. Dr. Lawson caught my elbow.

"Are you ill, Sadie?"

I gulped in air. Why should I doubt? Miranda had excelled in every task she'd undertaken. Numbers. Discipline. Fundraising. She knew how the house should be kept and how the children should be nurtured. Honestly, she'd left nothing at all for me to do.

Cynthia burst into the room, arms outstretched, headed straight for me. I gripped the back of a chair, braced for impact.

"I'll miss you, Miss Sadie." She buried her head in my middle.

"I know." I stroked her corkscrew curls. "I'll miss you, too. But I'm not far away. Nancy's with you, and I know you'll love the Lawsons."

A brilliant smile creased her impish face. She let go of me and threw her arms around the doctor's wife. Mrs. Lawson pulled Nancy in to complete the embrace.

Chapter 41

Miranda accompanied me to the courthouse for Carter's hearing the next week. Carter sat at a front table, an expression of disgust on the face that had once displayed such exuberant charm and inspired such devotion from me. I bowed my head and prayed he'd receive mercy.

"Thy will be done," Miranda whispered beside me.

"What?"

"Thy will be done. It's the only prayer we can pray now."

Guilt barbed my heart. I didn't care about God's will at the moment. I cared about mine. I wanted this over with. And I didn't want Carter's actions to hurt our chances of raising the last thousand dollars.

I bowed my head again. I wanted so many things. But had I prayed for God's will over my own or had I prayed expecting God to conform to my will? I laced my fingers and pressed a thumb into my palm.

Miranda's elbow poked my side. She nodded toward the front row. Blaine was leaning across the railing, talking with his brother. I saw past Carter's scowl to the paleness of his skin, the fear that kept his gaze from settling on anyone, anything. Blaine continued to speak. Carter nodded every few moments. Then Blaine turned and walked out the door.

I frowned. He wasn't staying? I understood his not paying for Carter's defense, but to abandon him altogether was quite another thing.

Miranda grabbed my elbow and lifted me to my feet as the judge entered. The gavel banged. We sat. But I continued to puzzle over Blaine's behavior.

Then the back door opened. A man in a suit hurried up the aisle. "Your honor, may I approach the bench?"

The judge granted permission. The district attorney joined them. I strained my ears but couldn't hear a thing.

The men retreated to their tables. The gavel banged again. "We'll begin in a half hour, after Mr. Shedd has a chance to confer with his client."

His client? I almost lunged out of my seat. Miranda held me back. I twisted, searching for Blaine as a buzz of conversation hovered over the room. Miranda and I squeezed hands while the clock ticked away the allotted time.

Blaine slipped into an empty seat just before the judge entered again and asked for Carter's plea. Mr. Shedd rose. "Guilty, your honor."

My mouth dropped open. Miranda let go of my hand. No, no, no. Even though I understood the need for him to admit his wrong, now that it was done, I couldn't shake the feeling that this would be the final death knell for the Raystown Home for Orphan and Friendless Children. In trying to save the one, had I sacrificed the many?

The judge conferred with both attorneys for what seemed like hours. Then they returned to their places while the judge ordered Carter to rise. The boy's Adam's apple bobbed in his slender throat. He looked so alone.

"Son, you understand what you did was wrong. Correct?"

Carter bowed his head, gave a slight nod.

"Even though it does not appear that you were involved in the actual theft of property, you aided those caught in the act." The judge peered over a pair of spectacles. "You didn't choose your friends wisely. I guess you know that now."

Carter's chin dropped to his chest.

"But just because you've done wrong doesn't mean there is no hope for you. In your sentencing, I'm providing an opportunity. If you take advantage of it, I believe you will come out on the other side as a man who has something to offer to society."

I held my breath. Maybe the Lord would have mercy on us all through this judge.

"Carter Wellsmith, I sentence you to six months in the Reformatory of the State of Pennsylvania." The judge's gavel banged. He stood and left the courtroom.

Miranda urged me from my seat. At the end of the aisle, I turned for one last glimpse of Carter. He stood at the railing, crooking a finger in my direction. Ezra Long stood at the boy's elbow, ready to lead him away.

Back down the aisle I went, bumping into others trying to leave, fighting my way to the child who needed me.

Hands on the railing, I leaned close. Ezra tightened his grip on Carter's elbow.

Carter's narrow chest swelled as he pushed back that unruly swatch of hair that insisted on dangling in his eyes. Eyes similar to Blaine's in shape and depth, if not in color. Eyes now as skittish as a caged animal.

"Can't you get me out of this, Sadie?" He wet his lips. "I don't want to go."

"Oh, Carter." I clasped his icy hand in my warm one. "I can't do anything to help now."

"Will you come? To visit?" He glanced at Ezra Long, as if looking for affirmation that such a thing would be allowed.

"Gladly." My throat thickened as the familiar words from Scripture whispered through my mind. *I was in prison, and ye came unto me.* Carter wasn't exactly in prison, and yet he was. And maintaining my relationship with him, tenuous as it seemed, held greater significance than wooing any patron to our work. For if I worked to raise the money but lost a child's heart in the process, what had I gained in the end?

"I am sorry, Sadie. You know that, right?"

A lump worked its way up my throat. I nodded, blinking back tears.

"Truly I am. I never meant to hurt you. I just . . . I just . . ." He gulped down what sounded like a sob.

"I know," I whispered. "But you made some bad choices, and now you must accept the consequences."

The slightest forward movement of his head told me he'd heard.

I took a deep breath. "I'm sorry, too, Carter."

His head tilted, wary of my words, waiting to see what they meant.

I let go of his hand and fumbled with my purse. "I was so caught up in my new position I failed to see how much trouble you were in." My hand stilled. "Will you forgive me?"

His eyes glistened for a moment before he gave a curt nod.

"I can't have you back at the Home. I imagine you realize that. But I promise you this—if ever I have a home of my own, you will always have a place with me."

His head jerked up and he peered at me as if trying to judge if I spoke truth. I held sincerity on my face, though I already wondered if I'd made too rash a promise. But I wouldn't fail Carter twice. Not if he desired my help.

"I mean it, Carter. Truly, I do."

He glanced at Ezra, lowered his voice. "So am I forgiven?"

I thought of my mother's sins, how they'd landed her and her child in a prison cell. And I thought of those who'd brought me out, given me hope for a different future, a different life. In spite of Carter's actions, I could do no less for him now.

I set my arm across his shoulders. "Always forgiven, Carter. For love covers a multitude of sins."

I leaned over the rail and kissed his cheek. Tears magnified his eyes. I pressed a hand to my mouth, turned to go, then remained motionless.

Blaine shook hands with the lawyer.

As Ezra led Carter away, I reached for a chair to hold me upright. But Blaine appeared, his arm supporting me instead.

"It's for the best, Sadie. Really it is. He needs new voices talking to him. We've said all we can say."

"It's all my fault. I couldn't save him. I tried. And now the Home will close and—"

"Close?" Blaine raised my head, his thumbs swiping the moisture from beneath my eyes. "Why would Carter's conviction close the Home?"

I focused on his shirt button. I'd said too much.

"What do you mean the Home will close?"

My voice fell to a whisper. "The money. There hasn't been enough. The board will close the Home if we don't raise the entire budget for next year by July first."

Though I shouldn't have said the words, the release felt sweet.

"I still don't see—"

I couldn't stop myself. "Donations have been down already." I turned away. "When this hits the newspaper again tomorrow, I feel sure all our prospects for donors will be as dead as my daffodils." I tried to choke out a laugh. It came out as a sob.

"Why haven't you told anyone? If they know, they'll give. No one wants to see the Raystown Home close."

I pulled from his grasp, hugged myself. "I can't tell. *You* can't tell. The board wants to test the validity of the ministry. They said if the Lord wants it to continue, He will provide. But He hasn't."

Blaine's grimness frightened me. He'd had so many disappointments, from his mother's dying to his stepfather's cruelty to Carter's antagonism toward him. I'd broken his heart, too. Possibly Viola had, as well.

The back door opened. Miranda's head appeared.

I blew out a long breath. "Forget I said anything, Blaine. Please."

Before he could answer, I turned and walked away.

Chapter 42

As I sat at my desk, willing the sum in our bank account to grow before my very eyes, I heard a knock at the front door. Miranda's quiet voice answered, and then she appeared at my door. "Viola's here. Will you see her?"

Of all the people I didn't want to talk to, she topped the list. I still suspected she and Carter had something to do with the disappearance of our spending money.

But I rose, determined to take the high road. "Send her in."

Standing before me, Viola looked more pale than usual. She shifted from one foot to the other, all her brash confidence gone.

"How may I help you, Viola?"

Her lower lip trembled. She bit it still. Took a few deep breaths. Then stricken eyes met mine. "Do you know where he went?"

"He?"

"Mr. Glazier. Earl." Her shoulders shook. She pressed a hand over her nose and mouth.

I dropped into my chair. She was this upset over a flirtation? "He's gone. To Washington D.C."

"When . . . when will he be back?"

"He won't. He's taken a job there."

She reached for the desk. "I was counting on him."

"Viola, I don't think—"

Her big blue eyes met mine, some new desperation hardening the former innocence. "Don't you see? Without this job, Mama and I have nothing. Nothing. And there is no one else. No one else Mama says is worthy. Carter is still a boy. And now . . ." She shrugged. "And Blaine can't see anyone but you."

My heart seemed to quit beating. When it started again, I reminded myself that Viola didn't know all that had happened between Blaine and me.

"But Earl. He could have provided for us." She clutched at me. "What will we do now?"

Nausea waved over me as understanding dawned. She'd wanted his attention. He'd given it, used his words to flatter and cajole his pretty plaything. And she'd completely misunderstood his intentions.

"Oh, Viola." I pulled her into my embrace, just as I would have any of my children, and let her leak her sorrow on my shoulder. "He's not coming back. He has bigger plans than a place like Raystown. You are a smart girl. Find a job. Work hard at it. Wait for marriage to be about love, not financial security."

Suddenly I saw my mother, and for the first time, I wondered if her degradation had begun with an innocent flirtation instead of outright defiance, as I'd always suspected. What dire circumstances might have made her choose as she did? What if I'd misjudged her all along?

I put on my old sky-blue church dress the next Sunday, for I had no one to look sophisticated for and I wanted to disappear into the crowd. The old Sadie. The one with no ambition beyond marrying her best friend and living on a farm of her own.

Two boys in knickers rushed past me on the stairs.

"Not so fast. Remember, we're indoors."

"Yes, ma'am." They shuffled to the first floor and rounded the corner toward the kitchen. Then their shoes slapped the floor at the speed of a run.

I shook my head and smiled. Someday they'd slow down. After all, I'd never seen a grown man dash madly about the house.

The children gathered in the foyer, ready for our walk. I opened the door and led our procession onto the porch.

Globes of brilliant pink flowers covered the bushes that flanked the steps. Full blossoms from budless branches.

I couldn't move, couldn't speak.

"Oooh, look!" Janet skipped down the steps and pressed her nose to the flowers. "Aren't they pretty?"

My mouth curved into a smile. I wanted to clap my hands, dance a jig. I'd done it. The hydrangeas had burst into color, brightening our world in spite of everything.

A miracle.

A small one, to be sure, but perhaps it portended bigger things.

On Tuesday morning, I entered the kitchen just as the back door thudded shut. A box of food sat on the table.

"Blaine's been here?" I shoved aside the disappointment that I'd missed him.

"Yes. I'm so glad we're getting some fresh-picked things now, though our own garden helps." Mrs. Fore continued washing dishes as I pulled onions and tomatoes from the box. Then I unfolded the bill nestled beneath them.

I frowned. The total didn't look right. But then, I didn't trust myself to remember.

I left the unpacking to Mrs. Fore and went to my office to find the ledger book. I opened to last month's page. My finger traced the line between Blaine's name and the amount. I looked at the paper again. I was right; it wasn't the same. This bill was higher. Much higher. And not even in Blaine's handwriting.

I stormed back to the kitchen. "He's charged us double!" I rattled the paper in Mrs. Fore's face.

She threw her hands in the air. "Heavens! Now I'm supposed to keep up with food prices, too? Isn't that your job?"

How dare he! And after I'd divulged our circumstances, too! Was he behind on his payments? Likely. But no one had asked him to pay for Lily Beth's glasses. Or Carter's attorney. No one had asked him to take on a mortgage for a farm he couldn't afford. We couldn't be expected to bear the burden of his financial decisions, yet he'd apparently overcharged us to compensate for those things, even after Miranda and I had trimmed everything possible from our budget.

I planted my fists on my hips. "We simply cannot afford to pay these prices for our food. I know the garden helps, but not enough."

"He must have had a good reason."

"He did it to spite me, that's his reason." He evidently had plans to ensure my complete downfall. Did he think after this I'd come running back to him? Beg him to take me to his beloved land?

Mrs. Fore shook her wooden spoon in my direction. "Blaine Wellsmith couldn't spite anyone, even if he had a mind to."

Oh, but he had.

With a huff, I swept my palms over each other as if dusting dirt from my hands. Mrs. Fore glanced out the window before pulling off her apron. Heavy footsteps clomped up the stoop. "He's back. Now you can find out what's happened."

Mrs. Fore opened the door. Blaine stepped inside.

My teeth ground together, trying to keep my voice from shaking with anger. "May I see you for a moment, Blaine? Alone." I didn't wait for him to follow.

He entered my office and stood before me in his dirt-smudged overalls.

"I'll get right to the point."

His eyes narrowed, as if he was trying to read what that point might be before I spoke it. "Please do."

I inhaled, wishing for courage-tinged air. But it held only the scent of summer, of flowers. I held out the invoice. "I cannot in good conscience pay these prices for our food."

His fingers captured the page, drew it before his eyes. After one nod, he pushed it back in my direction.

I expected explanations, a defense. Something. His silence unnerved me.

"I can't believe you would do this to us, all because of your impatience to own a farm you can't afford."

I waited again. In vain.

"Well? Aren't you going to say anything?"

He stared at me for a moment with a sad smile, walked away, and then turned back.

"Do you even understand what that land means to me?" His deep, dark eyes pinned me in place. "He stole my land, Sadie. My inheritance from my father. He forced me to sign my name so he could take it away—I was only eleven years old." He shook his head. "As if that wasn't bad enough, he knocked Carter from the hay wagon, just because he wouldn't stop talking. He was three. Three! That's when I took Carter and left. I even used my father's name for both of us. I didn't want him to kill Carter like he had our mother. And I didn't want my little brother to become like that man."

I sucked in a breath. He'd never told me that part of his history with his stepfather. I didn't want Carter to become that man, either. And yet it wasn't Carter's fate that held me captive at that moment. I stared at Blaine's hands. Large. Callused. Dirt stained.

He needed his farm in a way I'd never understood before. He needed his name on the paper, needed it to be his own. The knowledge of it both hurt and helped.

Hands low on his hips, his whole person seemed to sag. "I'll try to stay out of your way from now on."

If I hadn't known it before, this time I was sure: I had lost my best friend.

Long after Blaine's wagon creaked away, I returned to the kitchen and stumbled into the chair opposite Mrs. Fore. She seemed tired, her eyes and mouth drooping slightly as she rubbed the knuckles of her right hand with her left.

"Did you talk with Blaine?" she asked.

"Yes, if by 'talking' you mean I told him we couldn't afford to keep him in business."

"And what did he say to that?"

"Nothing, really." My mouth pulled down. I couldn't reveal his history, and he'd still given me no reason for the rise in prices. I dug my fingers into the roots of my hair. "I don't know what to do anymore. Everything that seems right is wrong, and everything that seems wrong is right. I need—" I stopped, sighed. "I have no idea what I need."

More silence. I could find silence all on my own. I pushed away from the table. Mrs. Fore reached for my hand.

"I know the two of you don't see things squarely at the moment, but you know he cares about this place as much as you do. He wouldn't do anything toward its harm. Ask him again to lower the prices."

I shook my head. "I can't ask him to do anything."

"Psh." Mrs. Fore got up. "He's not one to forget his friends so easily. You know what kind of man he is."

No, I guessed I didn't, though I'd thought I did. Would I ever learn to judge others rightly?

Mrs. Fore set a plate in front of me. "Eat something. You'll feel better."

I pick up the fork, glanced down. A wedge of butterscotch pie.

I laid the fork on the table and left the room.

Chapter 43

Sadie, will you help me with my homework like you used to?" Janet looked at me with pleading eyes. I knew she missed Cynthia, though they still saw each other at school and church.

I let her pull me toward the dining room. She chattered without seeming to draw breath, heedless of the pain building within my chest. The doors of our Home would close next week. I felt more sure of it every moment—especially now that even Blaine had abandoned us. What would happen to Janet? Who would listen without shushing her? Who would understand that she had no need of help on her homework, but she needed the companionship, the affirmation? Where would she seek the attention she craved?

I glanced back toward the office. Though I couldn't see it from there, I knew that a small stack of bills was waiting to be paid, including the one for the most recent delivery of food. But then, did any of those things matter more than this little girl? If I'd learned anything over the past few months, hadn't I learned that?

All of my efforts, no matter how extraordinary, had yielded no miracle that would save the orphanage. Only the Lord could do that. Just as only He could save these children from their pasts. Only He could help me overcome mine.

My hand dropped Janet's as I pondered the new thought. Had I ever really believed God could love me the same way He loved others? Did I believe it now?

I let one of the chairs at the kitchen table catch me as my legs gave way.

What if I believed Jesus loved me the way the Bible said He did, the way Mama Ramsey had told me He did? A life lived with that kind of assurance would be a worthwhile life, regardless of how it appeared to the outside world. Such a life would change people, not places. And didn't Jesus come for people? For people like my mother? Like me?

"C'mon, Miss Sadie."

And for children like Janet.

A longing to hold her close, to speak tender words, welled inside me. I pressed my arms across my chest, holding my ache in place. If I believed God truly loved me, I could share that love with others, and it would make a difference. An eternal difference. Because of the work the Lord had done in me, not because of the work I'd done for Him.

When the Home closed, I would have nothing but my relationships. With Jesus, these children, Mrs. Fore, Miranda, Carter. And Blaine, if he'd let me. Those were the treasures I'd find stored up in heaven. My heart wanted to weep with the revelation.

I brought Janet's hand to my lips. "Let's get your homework done." My step felt lighter than it had in days.

Miranda sat at the far end of the long dining table. Sylvia's delicate features turned bright as she pressed her eraser to the page. "I understand it now!" the girl cried. "I do! I really do!"

Miranda's arm rounded the thin shoulders. She squeezed, then let go, checking over Henry's work, as well. Henry's features twisted in concentration as Miranda's quiet voice rose and fell. Not as exuberant as Sylvia, he finally nodded, scribbled, then slapped his pencil to the table.

"Don't you think, Miss Sadie? Miss Sadie?" Carl patted my leg.

"What? Oh, I'm sorry." I stroked his nut-brown hair, noting that it needed washing.

"I said, I wish you could still say our prayers with us at night."

I peered into the wistful face, remembering the day he'd arrived. A summer day. He'd worn tattered knickers and no shoes. His father, half drunk before noon, had walked away before I could gather any information at all.

What a treasure he'd discarded! A child full of life and love and wanting to share both with all he met.

I pulled him close. "I'll make time tonight. I promise. Now, are you all done with your work?"

He nodded and scampered away. I couldn't wait until bedtime.

"Would you mind if I joined you to put the children to bed tonight?" I asked Miranda as the mantel clock struck nine.

"Not at all." We mounted the stairs. A knock sounded at the front door.

"Who in the world could it be at this hour?" I motioned her to go on up. I'd join her as soon as I sent our visitor on their way, in time to hear prayers.

Opening the door, I blinked into the graying night. A woman in a shabby black dress pushed forward a little boy in dark clothing.

"We buried my husband today. I have no way to care for Oliver." Her voice broke as her reddened work-worn hand caressed the child's black locks.

I glanced over my shoulder, but of course I remained alone. "Can you come back in the morning? We're just closing up for the night."

The woman shook her head, her eyes filling with tears. "I have to catch the last train, to Pittsburgh. I've heard there's a hotel there that might hire me."

Unlike Lily Beth's mother, this woman's desperation inspired my compassion. But did the difference come from the circumstances or my heart? Yet the numbers in the ledger book chastised me. We had little money to feed and clothe the children that rested under our roof this night, let alone one more. And likely all these children would be parceled out to other orphanages in other counties when we shut our doors in less than a week. No, it wouldn't be right to take him now.

Eyes large in a thin face, the boy blinked up at me. No smile. No frown. Not a tear or a twitch. My heart twisted. "Can't you take him with you?"

"When I have no idea what I'll find when I arrive? When I've already spent every last dime on the train ticket for myself? Please, ma'am. Have mercy on my child. Have mercy on me."

Tears coursed down the woman's sallow cheeks, weakening my resolve. *Please, God. Please. What do I do?*

Bible verses about heeding the cry of the poor and ministering to the children sprang to mind, countered by the stern expressions of the board members at our last meeting.

"Economy, Miss Sillsby. That's what's needed."

"Please, ma'am. You're my last hope." The woman swayed a bit, as if she might faint. Had she eaten at all on this day of sorrow?

In spite of board members' cautionary words ringing in my ears, I drew the woman and her child inside. I knelt before the boy, took his hand.

"Would you like to stay here for a while? There are several other boys upstairs, some about your age."

Oliver turned big liquid eyes on his mother. The woman nodded. Oliver turned to me and nodded, as well.

I stood, noticing again the woman's unsteadiness. I put my arm around her and led her to the kitchen. "Let's get you both something to eat, and then we'll fill out some paperwork."

By the time the clock struck ten, Oliver's mother had left to catch the last train out of town. But at least she had a full belly, a few provisions for the journey, the coins from my own meager savings, and the promise that she would return to claim her child when she felt she could support them both.

As I led Oliver up the stairs to the boys' room, I realized I'd missed bedtime prayers once again.

I kissed Janet's cheek. Her eyelids fluttered, but she didn't wake. I checked once more on Oliver. His even breathing let me know he was finally sleeping. I groped my way through the dark to my bedroom.

My hand sought the cover of my Bible, the one given to me by Mama Ramsey when I graduated from high school. I thought of the verse I'd read that morning from the gospel of Luke, Jesus' words about welcoming a child in His name.

Was it true? Really true? That by welcoming these children discarded by those who ought to care for them, I'd welcomed Jesus? Welcomed the Father?

I wanted it to be so. I wanted to go back to that place of welcoming children, of pouring my heart into them.

Hazel had loved the children, but it hadn't impeded what she knew to be her calling—the administration of the Home. Miranda, too, seemed able to separate her work from the children, without sacrificing either.

I, on the other hand, could not.

I needed to play ball in the backyard, teach them to knit before the fire, kiss their hurts, cheer for their successes, and pray with them before their eyes closed in sleep at night.

Not sit at a desk and add columns of numbers. Beg people to help us. Not days filled with endless reports and meetings, details and crises. Every moment behind my office door or out of the house was a moment missed in a child's life.

Someone needed to do those things, yes. But I no longer believed it had to be me.

Chapter 44

In May, the board had agreed to forgo the regular third Thursday meeting and instead convene on June 30. But Mr. Riley telephoned three days before that to tell me he'd called an emergency board meeting. I donned my green suit after making Miranda cinch my corset tighter than normal. This night would be the demise of the Raystown Home for Orphan and Friendless Children, I feared, but I intended to go out looking the part of matron.

Setting a made-over wide-brimmed hat atop my head, I studied my reflection. Round face. Brown eyes. Nondescript features. I blinked. Nothing had changed since my days as Hazel's assistant—nothing except a few new clothes. But all they'd done was dress up plain old Sadie.

I thought of Viola and her mother, their desperate need for security. Had I been any different, seeking to make up for my mother's sins? I couldn't remember her. Perhaps that was the Lord's mercy, I didn't know. I only wished I hadn't spent years taking her burdens on my shoulders, where they were never meant to reside. My security rested in Jesus, not in obliterating my past.

Something within me melted into peace at the thought. I no longer needed the board's approval or affirmation. I no longer needed a title or a position. I hadn't been able to save anything on my own. Not the Home, nor its children. The Lord had always sustained this place. If He chose for it to continue, He could use anyone He desired to administer this work. I only needed to love those the Lord brought across my path with the same generosity that He loved me.

Of course, now I'd have to find a new job. And a new place to live. But I'd think about that later. After Mr. Riley delivered the news that would break my heart. After Miranda and I consoled each other over the fate of the children.

We met in the stone church that evening. Stained-glass scenes from Jesus' life towered in a line down the side walls of the sanctuary, sparkling under the electric lights. I considered each one, but my eyes returned again and again to the scene of Jesus with the children. Holding them. Loving them. Caring about what happened to them.

Soberness hung in the air, as tangible as a morning fog. I prayed the Lord would comfort all of us, but the children especially. That He'd consider them as tenderly as depicted in the picture on the window.

Mr. Riley climbed to the platform before us. "I know we have all been in close conversation over the state of things these past few days. And I realize that we have all lamented the lack of funding for us to continue this ministry that was borne out of revival so many years ago. But each of us committed our decision to be tied to the amount of funds we were able to raise before the beginning of our new fiscal year."

Shoes shuffled against the floor. A pew creaked under shifting weight.

Mr. Riley cleared his throat. "It seems quite fitting to me, then, to be able to stand in this place of worship and announce to you that due to an anonymous donation I received this morning, we have enough money to commit to another year of operation."

My head jerked up, hands flying up to cover my open mouth. Had I heard correctly? Or had I heard what I wished to hear? Applause erupted. Someone patted me on the back.

Mr. Riley's grin stretched across his face. "Forgive me for waiting to tell you. I wanted you all to hear the good news at once. I'm overjoyed at the goodness and faithfulness of God to continue His work in this way."

Someone in the back laughed before shouting, "Praise the Lord!"

It didn't feel real. I wouldn't have to inform Miranda and Mrs. Fore they needed to find other employment, wouldn't have to ready the children to be uprooted and sent to another location to wait for a family.

Mr. Riley nodded in my direction. "We thank you, Miss Sillsby, for your tireless efforts on behalf of the Home, and look forward to your continued leadership."

I thought of the many petitions I'd put before the Lord in the past months. Of them all, this was the one thing I desired most. For the ministry of the Raystown Home to continue. For us to help more children in need. Joy frothed and surged, rising like soap bubbles from the tub on washday. Building. Mounding. Floating off until they—

Burst.

I fell back to earth as fast as one of those fragile bubbles. I didn't want to wade knee-deep in the muddy waters of details and finances, meetings and fund-raising. Not if doing that meant neglecting people. And for me, it apparently did.

Pushing to my feet, I fought the shouts that assailed me, the ones that said I would turn out like my mother if I gave away this post with nowhere else to go, nothing to do. But to let go would be the best thing. For me. For the children.

For Miranda.

Suddenly it didn't matter if I took the least position—or any position—as long as I obeyed what the Lord whispered to my heart.

"I believe Miss Sillsby has something to say." Mr. Riley stepped aside. I took his place facing the men who'd sacrificed time, energy, and even their own financial resources to continue the work of our Home. I gazed at each one, wondering who had come forward at the eleventh hour to meet our shortfall. But I didn't detect any special twinkle of an eye or twitch of a grin.

Pulling in as much air as possible, I sent a heavenward plea that they would honor my final request.

"When I accepted the position as matron in March, I had no idea all it would entail. I thought I did, having served alongside Hazel for nearly five years. But I guess I saw the prestige of the position over my ability to carry out its responsibilities. And I found I missed my interaction with the children. I spent so much time working *for* them that I missed out on the children themselves."

I gulped in a fortifying breath as the men blinked in bewilderment. "I'm standing before you now to tender my resignation."

Mr. Riley rubbed at the creases that lined his forehead. "I think I speak for all of us when I say this is very distressing news. Are you certain?"

"Very certain. But I do have a final request, one I hope you will honor as a parting gift."

I noted the nods throughout the room, but they did little to still the nervous tumble of my stomach.

"Ask what you will, Miss Sillsby." A wry grin softened Mr. Riley's face. "Up to half our kingdom."

I smiled. Salome might have asked for John the Baptist's head, but I feared my request would be no less shocking. *Please, Lord, let them hear me out. Let them understand.*

"I would like you to give my place to Miranda Jennings."

Whispers skittered through the room. I raised my voice. "Miranda wanted to apply for the position when Hazel left. She has been serving as my assistant for the past two months, and during that time, I have come to value the unique talents which suit her for this position."

Mr. Riley's mouth turned down. "We all know she can speak well. We heard her at the picnic. But does Miss Jennings meet the requirements of the post? I seem to remember she has little formal education."

"It is true that she has less formal education than you stipulate, but she has a head for numbers, writes a decent hand, can hold every manner of detail in her head at one time, and is amiable with both adults and children. She is able to balance the work and the relationships. I believe her to be an invaluable asset to the administration of the Home at this moment. She could carry it into better years to come."

I held myself tall and met the eye of every man in the room before I continued. "I do not make this recommendation lightly, gentlemen. It comes at great personal cost and sacrifice. But I believe it is right. For all of us."

On the front pew once more, I trembled. Would they heed my request or would they remain fixated on a piece of paper Miranda didn't possess?

"Miss Sillsby, would you grant us a private session in which to discuss this unexpected turn of events?"

"Of course." My footsteps echoed in the near-empty room. When I shut the sanctuary doors behind me, I leaned against them in relief. Instead of angst or regret, peace stilled the waters that sloshed in my stomach. I didn't care what they thought of me now. I only wanted them to want Miranda.

After what seemed an eternity, the doors opened. The entire board followed Mr. Riley into the vestibule. I clasped my hands behind my back and steeled myself for their decision.

"You asked a hard thing of us, Miss Sillsby. But the more we talked it through, the more we realized that you have been in a unique position to evaluate her as a candidate for the position. So yes, we will offer Miss Jennings the post—this very evening if I may accompany you back to the Home."

My smile stretched so wide I feared my face couldn't contain it. I flung my arms around Mr. Riley's neck. "Thank you. Thank you so much."

Mr. Riley cleared his throat. I pulled away, noting his bright red face as he toed the carpet.

"You have done quite an extraordinary thing this evening, Miss Sillsby," Mr. Delp said from the back of the gathering.

"No, sir." I shook my head as a hint of sadness, light as dandelion seeds, descended on my heart. I tried to brush it away, but it clung with fervor. "I've only done what the Lord asked of me."

Chapter 45

Mr. Riley and I arrived to a quiet house, one light glowing through the parlor curtains, into the street. We found Miranda on the sofa, mending a pair of little-boy britches. She set her work in the sewing basket at her feet.

"I'm so glad you're awake." I hugged her but felt uncertainty in her stiffness. "Mr. Riley has something he'd like to ask you."

Her eyes turned fearful, almost pleading, as if she desired me to defend her. I hoped my smile reassured her, but the anxiety in her expression didn't abate.

Mr. Riley stepped forward. "Miss Jennings, we had quite an unusual meeting this evening." He glanced at me, then continued. "First, we are happy to report that the needed funds have appeared and we will continue to operate the Home as usual."

Miranda's quizzical gaze met mine. I blurted out the events of the past four months while her expression turned from curiosity to horror.

"I'm sorry I couldn't confide in you," I finished.

She swallowed. "I'm almost glad you couldn't. I'm not sure I could have endured."

Mr. Riley cleared his throat. Miranda's expression closed. She appeared to be the Miranda of old, before our friendship. I wanted to reach out and take her hand, assure her good news was coming. But I sat silent. It wasn't my news to tell.

"In other business, we discovered that we had an unexpected opening for matron of the Raystown Home."

I waited for her head to whip toward me, but only her eyes slashed in my direction, full of questions. I wished Mr. Riley would spit out all his words before the poor girl fainted.

"By unanimous decision, the Board of Trustees of the Raystown Home would like to offer you that position—at the express recommendation of Miss Sillsby."

Miranda's mouth gaped. She pressed her hand to her mouth as tears flowed over her cheeks.

I sat next to her, my own emotions close to the surface, and held her hand. "You deserve this. It just took me—and the board—a while to see it."

She blubbered incomprehensible words as I withdrew a handkerchief from my handbag and handed it to her. Within moments, it lay limp in her hands. She took a deep breath, swallowed hard.

"Truly?" she asked, addressing Mr. Riley.

"Truly, Miss Jennings. Now, if you ladies will excuse me, my wife will be expecting me home."

"Of course." I hopped up and accompanied him to the door while Miranda composed herself. When I returned to the parlor, she stared at me, dry-eyed.

"Why, Sadie? Why did you do it?"

I sat beside my enemy-turned-friend. "Because you are so much more fitted for this position than I am, Miranda. It isn't that I can't do it; I just hate doing it. It consumes me in a way it doesn't seem to do for you. I ended up sacrificing my relationships, with the children, with . . . everyone." I ducked my head as warmth crept into my cheeks. "Can you forgive me for lording over you as I did?"

"Oh, Sadie." She pressed her hand against mine. "You were the first person who ever saw me as something other than an uneducated maidservant."

"I'm thankful you'll be in charge. You'll do a great job."

"But what about you? What will you do?"

I shrugged. I wasn't sure yet. I knew I wanted to devote time to Carter. He wouldn't remain at the reformatory forever, and I had no intention of abandoning him. I'd need a job and a new place to live. Whatever employment the Lord brought, I knew that in some way I would remain a missionary to children, for they constituted my passion and my call.

"I don't know yet, I just know I won't be here. I want to leave you free to do your job, just as Hazel left me free to do mine. And I'll be fine knowing that the children and this place are in loving, capable hands."

Miranda shook her head, still disbelieving. "Whatever will Mrs. Fore say in the morning?"

I laughed aloud. If I knew Mrs. Fore, she'd have plenty to say. And she wouldn't stop until we'd heard it all.

While Mrs. Fore mourned my departure with true tears of affection, she also nearly danced a jig at Miranda's turn of fortune. The children would be told soon enough. And while I hoped they'd miss me a little bit, I surmised they wouldn't notice much in their excitement over being out of school for the summer.

Miranda darted out the door to supervise the children, her face alive with new joy, new purpose. I envied her the emotion, but not the position.

"And have you told Blaine of your change of fortune?" Mrs. Fore's voice remained low, as if not to be overhead, though no one remained in the house with us.

I swallowed hard. "I imagine he'll hear soon enough."

"Oughtn't he to hear it from you?"

I shook my head, even though she was working at the stove and couldn't see me. "After our last . . . altercation—over the food bill—I think it best if I just . . ."

Mrs. Fore turned. "It isn't his, if I hear rightly."

My body went rigid. "What do you mean?" But already my mind had latched on to the only thing that had been his: the land.

"I went to the sewing circle on my afternoon off. His farm's been sold. Seems he let go of it quick as he bought it." She shook her head. "Now, what would make him do such a thing, him so proud of owning that piece of ground?"

"He's leaving." The words came out before I even thought them, sinking my heart quick as a rock in a pond. It was the only explanation. He assumed the doors of the Raystown Home would close. After that, he'd have no ties here. Only a woman who'd spurned him and a brother who despised him. Who could blame him for wanting to go?

If only we could have talked. I might have made him see

this wasn't the answer, wasn't the way. Carter needed him. The Home needed him.

I needed him.

It didn't matter about his farm; he could find other work, buy other land. All that mattered was that he stayed.

A jumble of images and ideas rained down on me. The bill written in an unusual hand. The new harvest from the sold plot of ground.

"The prices. If he doesn't own the farm, he wasn't the one who raised the prices." I pressed a hand to my mouth to suppress a cry.

Blaine had done nothing but sacrifice for this place. How could I have accused him of doing the opposite?

Chapter 46

I grabbed my handbag and stumbled out the door with an incoherent explanation. Though Blaine might not forgive me, I needed to try to make things right with him before he walked out of my life forever.

I rode the trolley to the edge of town. Then I walked the long, dusty road to Blaine's farm—or what used to be his farm—praying Mrs. Fore hadn't heard correctly. Yet in my heart, I knew she had.

But why? Perhaps he hadn't made his payments and it had been taken from him. I still found it difficult to believe he'd choose to abandon the brother he had so tenderly cared for in their youth, but then, people changed.

I had changed.

As my feet trod the grassless path to the front door of the farmhouse, it occurred to me that a stranger might answer. Blaine had delivered the produce a few days ago, but did that mean he remained here if it wasn't his any longer?

I tiptoed onto the wooden porch and knocked at the attractive green front door. No one came. I walked around to the back of the house, to the kitchen. That door opened easily beneath my hand. "Hello? Is anyone home?"

Silence. I walked inside, admiring the finely carved cabinetry lining the kitchen walls. Blaine's handiwork. I knew it from gifts he'd given me when we were children, after he'd learned carpentry from his foster father.

But when had he done this? He worked from dawn till dark as it was. I ran my hand over an intricate vine and leaf design across the face of a drawer. More than functional, they were a work of art.

Had he meant this for me? My knees grew weak. Not only had I shunned his gift, but I'd given him reason to leave, the same as Carter had. If only I could take it back, do it over. I viewed life, viewed myself so differently than I had only a few months ago. I lowered into a sturdy chair by the round table.

Footsteps echoed across the porch. My heart crawled into my throat and lodged there. What had I been thinking, letting myself into a stranger's home?

The door pushed open. Blaine stopped, lips parted in surprise.

My heart dropped back into its normal place as I produced a weak smile. "I'm sorry I came unannounced."

"I'm sorry I wasn't here to welcome you." His gaze roamed the room, as if weighing what I'd seen.

"The cabinetry is beautiful."

His jaw bulged with tightness.

I looked down at the smooth pine floor, waiting for him to speak. But the silence held until my nerves jiggled like a taut fishing line. Best to get this over with. "I heard you sold the farm."

He shrugged. "It was necessary." Gruff words, like he used to speak to Carter, not to me.

My mouth pulled downward. "We're all sorry you're leaving."

"Leaving?" He cocked his head, eyebrows angling toward his nose. Not a perfectly sculpted nose, like Earl's, but one with strength and character.

My throat tightened. I force myself to stand. "I know you must have your reasons for selling, but do you really think deserting your brother is the best thing? After all you've done for him? To just give up now?"

"Sadie—"

"And it isn't just Carter you are letting down. Did you think of that? The children will miss you. Henry and Carl and Timmy. Even the girls. Mrs. Fore will miss you. I'll—" The words stumbled over a ball of tears that climbed up my throat.

His hands rested on my shoulders. "You'll what, Sadie?"

I shook my head, forced a tight-lipped smile. "You'll not have heard our good news. The Home—"

"Will stay open. I know."

"You do? Did Mr. Riley call you?"

He turned away and ran a hand through his unruly dark hair. "Because I gave them the money, Sadie."

"The money? You?" I tried to pin the words in place, but they insisted on racing circles in my head. He *owed* money on this place. He didn't have cash to give. Especially not a thousand dollars or more. I found the chair I'd abandoned and let it hold me once more.

"Mr. Sorrel agreed to sell me the farm when he decided to

move to Pittsburgh to live with his daughter because he didn't want Mr. Yoder, who owns the next parcel of ground, to have it. But with Mr. Sorrel gone, Mr. Yoder started pestering me with offers to buy. I didn't even entertain such a notion at first. I wanted the land. I thought I needed it more than anything. Not just to marry you. To complete me."

Blaine paced, expelled a long breath. "Mr. Yoder upped the price he was willing to pay. When you told me the Home was in danger of closing, I knew the extra might contribute to keeping it open. I hoped after I paid what I owed, the remainder would help the Home. I guess it did."

His head dipped in embarrassment. "I knew it would have broken your heart to see the Raystown Home close. I felt selfish holding on to my dream while watching you lose yours."

I fought for breath. He sold his land for me? Tears spilled out of my eyes, though I battled to hold them in.

He knelt in front of me, held my hands. "I tried to forget you, Sadie. To believe that our paths would never be the same. But I couldn't. You're part of my heart. You are my home."

I cupped my hands around his face. "But . . . oh, Blaine! The land!" I shook my head. "I didn't understand what it meant. I'm so sorry."

He tried to smile, but it wouldn't stay put. "I'm sorry I bought it without talking to you in the first place. I shouldn't have done that."

My hands fell back to my lap. "But what will you do now?" I wasn't sure I wanted to hear his answer.

"Mr. Yoder is letting me lease the house and work for him. So you see? You still have the Home, and in a sense, I still have my farm. We'll let the Lord figure it out from there."

My fingers and toes tingled. How could I tell him that the Home remained, but I didn't? I covered my face, unable to look at him when the words came out. And out they must come. I inhaled the sweet fragrance of new-mown grass that wafted in through the open window. "Miranda is matron, not me."

"Miranda?" he whispered. I could picture the confusion on his face, hoped it wouldn't melt into disdain. He cleared his throat, spoke normally. "I don't understand."

I sighed. "I love those children, that place, but I couldn't be the matron. It wasn't right. I . . . I gave up too much that was really important to me." Grasping his hands, I peered into those dark eyes. "Will you forgive me, Blaine? I never meant to hurt you. I never meant—"

I couldn't put my feelings into words. At least not after all the heartache I'd caused him. And myself. I sucked in a deep breath, asked the one question I couldn't avoid. "Can we ever go back to the way we were?"

He pulled me to my feet, led me outside. Two hydrangea bushes nestled against the back of the house. Full of leaves, but without flowers.

I gasped. "Did you—?"

A crooked smile appeared on his lips. "I'd do anything to make you happy. Even plant hydrangeas in the middle of the night."

My chest threatened to burst. He'd never quit caring for me. Never quit taking care of me, while I'd been selfish and fickle, sought out station and accolades to make me forget that little girl they brought out of her mother's prison cell. Could he truly forgive that?

He brushed a thumb over the dampness beneath my left eye. "You asked if we could go back. No, Sadie. I don't think we can."

My smile faltered. He ran a finger down the side of my face, stopping to caress the corner of my mouth. "But like your flowers, I think we can start again with something fresh. Something new, full of color and life."

His arms circled my waist, pulled me close. "I love you, Sadie. I've loved you since the moment Carter and I walked into that warm kitchen. Ten years old with ancient eyes, you understood suffering the way I did."

"So there's hope for us? For all our plans?"

One side of his mouth quirked upward. Like Carter's when he planned mischief. "Are you hinting for an engagement ring, Miss Sillsby?"

Heat blazed in my cheeks. Even with Blaine, I'd never been so forthright about my feelings. "No, I—" I wriggled away. "I may not be employed at the Home, but I know the Lord has some task for me to do with children. Especially Carter."

"Of course He does. It's what you were made for. I can't give up on my brother any more than you can." Clasping my hand in his, he led me back into the house. "Look at this kitchen. What do you see?"

I turned a circle. "It's . . . big."

"Yes. And I converted the attic to another bedroom, too. I never imagined we'd be happy without a horde of children overrunning the place. We'll have a few of our own, of course, but we'll take in as many others as can fit."

I stared up at him. "You . . . planned this all along?"

"It was in my mind."

"Mine too," I whispered. "I guess if we'd have talked things out, we might have saved each other a lot of trouble."

"Maybe. But perhaps the Lord was even in our shortcomings. You kept the Home afloat and discovered Miranda's gifts. And if I hadn't bought this place, even on credit, I wouldn't have been able to sell at a profit and meet the financial need to keep the Home in existence. We both did what God asked us to do. Whatever else happens, we can always hold to that."

I closed my eyes, realizing the rightness of his words. We'd both traveled the path the Lord set before us, not realizing it would wind back around to each other.

"But we can learn from our mistakes, too. I want you to understand that if you still aren't sure this is what you want, I'll wait until you are certain. I won't leave you. Ever."

"Like you won't leave Carter."

"Not exactly like Carter, no." He grinned, and his hands circled my waist, pulled me close. His head lowered. My mouth curved as my eyes fixed on his lips. I pushed up on my toes. He threw back his head in laughter. "I guess that means you like my idea."

I ducked my head, glanced up at him through my lashes.

He captured my face between his hands. "I love you, Sadie Sillsby. And I always will."

My arms circled his neck as his lips pressed into mine. My heart had found its home.

A Note From the Author

This story began to take shape after I read the history of the Huntingdon Home for Orphan and Friendless Children, which operated in Huntingdon, Pennsylvania (my husband's hometown), from 1881 to the late 1930s or early 1940s, when it merged into the State Agency for Children and Youth Services. I chose to meld many stories and situations documented in the Home's history and to use a fictional town in order to have the freedom to move events and places to serve the story without convoluting the true history of a real town.

I'm completely indebted to the Huntingdon County Historical Society for use of their research facilities, but most of all to executive director Kelley Kroecker for offering to call Nancy Shedd and see if she could meet with me. Nancy is the author of two books (at least!) on Huntingdon's history and has long been interested in the orphans' home, since her grandmother was the first matron.

In the course of two days, Nancy tracked down documents about the Home that she had thought completely lost. I will always remember the joy of that weekend researching with her. It was like discovering buried treasure! Thank you, Nancy, for your gracious help and support.

The actual writing of this book has been one of the hardest things I have ever done—from elusive research to an unwieldy story to characters who didn't give up their secrets until I'd rewritten the book multiple times. But God has been faithful. It has truly been His strength and my weakness that has accomplished what you have just read. I am grateful, and more in love with my Savior than ever before.

Special thanks to my patient editor, Charlene, who was always encouraging; my critique group, Mary DeMuth and Leslie Wilson (Life Sentence), who read multiple drafts, listened, and encouraged; and Lori Freeland, who spent an afternoon helping me brainstorm through one of the final revisions.

As always, my prayer team is invaluable! I am indebted to Jeff, Robin, Mary, Leslie, Becky, Becky, Cheryl, Cherryl, Andrea, Jill, Ann, Don, Debra, Kirby, Dan, Jennifer, Dawn, Billy, and Jana. Y'all are such a huge blessing to me!

Thank you, Jeff, for your continued encouragement and love. Celebrating twenty-five years married to you while writing this book will be one of my most cherished memories.

As I wrote of Sadie's love for the children in her care, I remembered again my great love for my three—Elizabeth, Aaron, and Nathan. You are gifts that I do not deserve, and everything good in you is due solely to the grace of God. Always remember that!

And finally, I want to thank my Pennsylvania family for giving me another place besides Texas to call home. I appreciate y'all taking me into your hearts so many years ago. I love you very much.

Anne Mateer has a passion for history and historical fiction, and she can often be found researching her next novel during family vacations in different parts of the country. She is the author of two previous historical novels, *Wings of a Dream* and *At Every Turn*. Anne and her husband, Jeff, live near Dallas, Texas, and are the parents of three young adults. Learn more at Anne's website and blog: www.annemateer.com.

More Heartwarming Historical Fiction From Anne Mateer

To learn more about Anne and her books, visit annemateer.com.

Driven to fulfill an unbreakable promise, Alyce finds help in an unlikely ally. But when her plan spirals out of control, will she have to choose between keeping her promise and the man who holds a piece of her heart?

At Every Turn